RESTLESS SPIRIT

Also by S.D. Tooley

When the Dead Speak
Nothing Else Matters

Written as Lee Driver

The Good Die Twice
Full Moon-Bloody Moon

RESTLESS SPIRIT

S.D. Tooley

Full Moon Publishing LLC

Published by
Full Moon Publishing LLC
P.O. Box 408
Schererville, IN 46375
1-888-922-1203

www.fullmoonpub.com

Library of Congress Control Number 2002108604
ISBN 0-9666021-6-1

First Edition: October 2002

10 9 8 7 6 5 4 3 2 1

Printed in the United States of America

ACKNOWLEDGMENTS

Although fiction to writers means, "make it up as you go along," there are some facts that require verification and advice from experts. Their vast knowledge and enthusiastic response has made my life a lot easier.

Dan Gunnell
Firearms Training Coordinator
Illinois State Police Forensic Science Center
Chicago, Illinois

Pamela Jean Owens, Ph.D.
Professor of Native American Studies and Religion
University of Nebraska at Omaha

Thomas J. Sanders
Assistant Prosecuting Attorney
Elkhart County, Indiana

William Sherlock
User Agency Coordinator
Illinois State Police Forensic Science Center
Chicago, Illinois

Garnett Watson
Chief of Police
Gary, Indiana

A special thanks to: Ellen Larson, Catherine Mambretti, and Shirley Robinson for sharing their talents with a writer who knows her limitations.

To Mom

Who always knew fact

from fiction

RESTLESS SPIRIT

1

The forest rarely gives up its dead without a fight. Fierce winds bury the disturbed ground with leaves. Heavy snows easily hide trails and footprints. And sometimes hungry creatures feast on exposed flesh and bone.

Along the path cutting through Briar Woods, a woman clad in a dark green warm-up suit moved cautiously, stopping every few seconds to peer between leafless trees and thorny bushes. Overhead a hawk carved graceful circles as it glided over the treetops in search of prey. Trees were skeletal remains, exposing the forest like an open wound, baring its blemishes and flaws. The woman watched the hawk for several seconds until she was certain it had nothing to tell her. To the casual observer, she looked as though she were hunting something or someone. In a way, that wasn't too far from the truth.

Stepping off the trail, Sam Casey studied the ground and stopped again to watch for signs. Her mother, Abby Two Eagles, believed it was Nature that spoke to Sam and showed her where the bodies were buried. Branches would bend as though pointing their fingers. Animals would scurry then stop, sniff, gaze up. It wasn't as if the bodies moved, shifting the surface of the earth or uprooting bushes. And the voices weren't loud, carried on a roll of thunder.

The signs were more subtle. Usually a cold would slice through Sam's body, the hair on her arms would bristle, and voices would lead her to within a few feet of a shallow grave.

Abby often said that whenever someone died an unnatural death, the spirit was unsettled, crying out to be discovered and released to its final resting place. But today the voices were silent. Sam could only assume that the rapists, deviates, and syndicate hit men were choosing more isolated woods in which to hide their sins.

She followed the path to a clearing where six brick homes were in various degrees of completion. Workers swarmed the construction site pounding wooden decks into form and installing windows. A flatbed truck carrying a load of decking pulled up to the curb and a segment of the swarm moved toward the street.

Peering through one of the windows of a gray brick bi-level Sam noticed a stone fireplace. The jean-clad workman struggled with a marble mantel, finally hefting it in place and wiping his forehead. He nodded for Sam to enter but she shook her head.

A wrap-around porch led to the front of the house where her attention was drawn to a stained glass elliptical window above the door. It captured the sun in a kaleidoscope of color.

"Anything I can help you with?"

Sam turned to find the jean-clad workman. "Sorry, just being nosy," Sam replied. A soft breeze played with her feathered earring and she gently untangled it from her hair. "I live on the other side of the forest." Offering him her hand she said, "I'm Sam Casey."

"No law against admiring. Cooper. I'm the foreman." He stuck out a mitt-sized hand dusted with grit and cement. She grimaced and quickly pulled back her arm. "Sorry. Kinda hard to stay clean on a day like today," Cooper said, a sheepish grin cutting across his face. "Can't beat this weather, though. Four weeks before Christmas and it's sixty-eight degrees."

Sam stepped over a two-by-four and almost lost her footing.

Cooper quickly grabbed her arm. "Careful there. Bet you have a hard time seeing your feet." He nodded toward her wide girth and laughed at the annoyed look she flashed in response.

"We have friends who are building a house in this area," she explained. "I just thought I'd see if I could tell which one."

An engine fired up behind them and Cooper maneuvered her from the path of a construction bobcat. Sunlight reflected off of the elliptical window and Sam shielded her eyes from the glare. As she stepped back, light glittered and danced around an object unearthed by the plow. She knelt down for a closer inspection. The letters *MB* were stamped in the center of what looked like a brass button. She dug the object from its grave and held it in her hand.

A familiar cold swept over her body and the hairs on her arms stiffened. She wrapped her fingers tightly around the button. As though Nature herself flipped a switch, sunlight was sucked from the sky, and the moon appeared over the treetops as if pulled by an invisible marionette string. The construction site had disappeared, replaced by a barren wasteland overrun with dandelions and littered with hints of private parties. The air was hot and muggy, filled with the scent of dewy grass. Sam slowly stood and willed her feet to move, but they refused.

A haze hovered close to the ground, curling around her feet. Suspecting she had nothing to offer, the haze quickly spread, seeping across the clearing toward the woods. Sam saw movement in the distance, a dark shadow that stumbled out of the woods and through the haze. The humid air pressed close but did little to ward off the chill racing through her body. She wanted to draw her arms closer but they felt like anchors.

As the figure drew nearer, Sam could tell it was a young girl, naked, eyes blinking in confusion. Heavy breasts swayed with each jerky movement.

"Who's there?" the girl called out. She giggled as she tried to keep her balance and Sam wondered if the girl had been drinking.

Another figure crept from the shadows to Sam's right, suddenly lurching toward the naked girl.

"Who are you?" the girl cried out again. But the stranger remained silent. The attacker raised something shiny and quickly struck down. Sam tried unsuccessfully to move, to cry out a warning, but all efforts proved futile.

The knife was raised again, bringing with it a stream of blood. The second stab felled the girl. Then the figure knelt and plunged the knife repeatedly. The attacker grabbed a handful of hair and jerked. When the knife was pressed to the girl's neck, Sam closed her eyes to what she knew would come next. Screams ripped the darkness.

A large hand shook Sam's shoulder. Her arms flailed in defense and Cooper had to fend off her blows. Several of the workers ran to her aid and Sam had to cover her mouth to choke back the screams. It was then she heard a name, drifting in the breeze, swirling around her head. A name only she could hear.

2

"I was so embarrassed. The guys thought Cooper had assaulted me." Sam opened another cabinet and peered at the contents. "It just seemed so real. Usually I pick up bits and pieces. But this was different, Mom. It was like watching a movie." She searched through drawers and then the canisters on the counter. "Didn't you go grocery shopping yesterday?"

"Yes, dear. But if you are looking for cookies, you know Jacob gave strict instructions not to buy any sweets unless we are having company."

Sam glared at her mother, then pulled open the refrigerator. "If I see one more carrot or celery stick I'm going to vomit. Didn't you explain cravings to him?"

Abby measured out the flour and dumped it into a mixing bowl. "You know your husband—the doctor of discipline and self-control." She whipped the ingredients together with a wooden spoon then used a spatula to scrape the sides of the bowl.

Sam noticed the way her mother's eyes lit up whenever she talked about Jake. It was a kind face, slow to anger. As a child Sam remembered her mother's face as the first thing she would see upon waking every morning. Cher had nothing on this woman's cheekbones. And, Sam had to admit, her mother had good taste.

"Discipline...right," Sam said. "This from a man who can't quit smoking." She pulled a bowl of fruit from the refrigerator and set it on the counter next to a bacon sandwich and a glass of orange juice.

"You have been doing so well, Samantha. I'm proud of you."

"Between you and me I would plow through a crowd of pre-schoolers about now just to snatch up their Oreo cookies."

Abby laughed and wiped her hands on the Mrs. Claus face appliquéd on the front of her bib apron. The kitchen was Abby's favorite room. It was light and airy with plenty of cabinets and counter space, a quarry tiled floor and a window box containing a variety of plants starving for the sun's attention. The house always emitted tempting aromas, especially around the holidays.

Sam peered into the bowl and inhaled. "Peanut butter? You've made how many batches of cookies already and nothing chocolate."

Abby covered the bowl with plastic wrap and placed it in the refrigerator. "Some are for the Christmas bazaar. The rest Jacob will take to the office. I didn't want to tempt you by making anything with chocolate."

"But the peanut butter cookies have large chocolate kisses on them, right?" Sam moved the flour and sugar canisters in search of the recipe.

Abby pulled the recipe card from her daughter's hands. After returning the containers to the cabinets and wiping off the counter-top, she grabbed her tea and joined Sam at the island counter. "Now tell me about the button." Abby tucked errant strands of dark hair into the thick knot at the nape of her neck, then picked up the brass button.

Sam repeated everything that had happened at the construction site. "There were times I thought I might be losing my touch because I haven't been involved in any cases lately."

"Your powers could be getting stronger, Samantha. Or this young woman died such a violent death, her spirit will never know rest."

A shiver ran through Sam's body. "She was so young. What a terrible way to die." She watched Abby clasp her fingers around the button. "Are you picking up anything?"

Abby shook her head. But that wasn't unusual. Neither one could pick or choose what was revealed to her. Besides, Abby's powers were with the living, Sam's were with the dead.

"Where do I go from here?"

Abby handed the button back to her daughter. "Do you really need to ask?"

"If it isn't the little mother." The desk sergeant stood and stretched a hand toward Sam.

She despised the term *little mother,* mainly because she didn't feel little. Her equilibrium was off, she longed to fit into a pair of leggings without looking like a stuffed sausage, and all she felt like doing was eating.

"Jake around?"

Sergeant Scofield handed her a visitor's badge. "He's in *The Box* interrogating a subject but you can wait in his office. You know the way." The room used for interviewing suspects and witnesses was as square and nondescript as a box with little more than a table and three chairs.

She turned to see several heads quickly bow. Her fingers made a sudden grab for her medicine bundle, force of habit when she found herself in uncomfortable surroundings.

Turning back to Scofield, she said, "Okay if I get a cup of tea?"

"Sure, sure." He waved a hand at her without looking up from his paperwork.

The break room was down the hall and around the corner. All she had to do was follow the worn tiled floor and the sound of laughter, which quickly died down when she appeared. After setting her tote bag on a chair, she fumbled for change and dropped it into an empty coffee can. Whispers and murmurs funneled their way through the silence and she stole a glance at her observers through the mirror. *Not a good idea,* she thought. She should have just picked up the phone and called Jake rather than make an unscheduled visit.

She gazed at her reflection. What she wouldn't give for smooth, manageable hair. When dry, hers looked like a burlap rug. When wet, it looked like a wet burlap rug. That was one feature of her father's she would just as soon not have inherited. His eyes, though, were the best Casey trait. They weren't a pale blue, the type people use *kind* or *soft* to describe. Sam's were more vibrant and could be termed *electric* or *ice* depending on her mood or who was pissing her off.

She tossed the tea bag into the garbage can and looked up to see people vacating the room as if she had brought a plague. Her gaze drifted to the vending machine but the candy bars didn't entice her. They wouldn't do much to quell her craving.

She made a detour back to Scofield's desk. "How long have you been a cop?"

He peered over his bifocals at her as though assessing the seriousness of her question. "Is there a right or wrong answer?"

"Only if it makes me happy."

"Twelve years in St. Louis, ten in Chasen Heights. Do I win a prize?"

"Maybe. Do you recall any homicides near the new Briar Woods development in which a young girl was stabbed to death?"

The sergeant pulled his glasses off and stared at the ceiling. "Stabbing," he repeated and slowly shook his head. "Don't think so. I haven't always been in Homicide, but news of any young girl being murdered would have run through every department in Chasen Heights." He slipped his glasses back on his nose and studied her for a few moments. "Why?"

Sam shrugged. "I volunteer for the Historical Society once a week." She turned and walked away.

"My ass," Scofield yelled out.

Sam stepped into Jake's office and closed the door. Folders were stacked neatly on the corner of the desk. Another stack was teetering in the OUT box. One lone folder lay in the middle of the desk.

A faint tapping on the window drew her attention to the two mourning doves. She grabbed a handful of sunflower seeds from the can on the sill and opened the window.

"How are you doing, boys?" The two birds backed away as she tossed the seeds to them. For all she knew they could be two girls, but it hadn't stopped her from naming them Tonto and Cochise.

Touching the leaves of the poinsettia plant sitting on the sill, Sam whispered, "See how long you last now that I touched you." The plant was lush and full of blossoms.

She stood for a while and peered out at the city. It was a typical growing community, racially and economically mixed. Some of the older sections butted against new developments. Even the original brick buildings downtown were getting a face lift in an effort to keep up with the modern strip malls and a bustling shopping center.

Sam turned away from the window and tossed her sweater coat on a chair. Through the glass partition she saw several people staring. She turned the wand on the blinds to shut them out.

She wasn't sure why she hadn't noticed before but Jake had a new desk of dark mahogany wood protected with a glass top. The city was obviously using up its funds before the end of the budget year.

The cushioned chair rocked when she sat down. Except for a coffee cup with the FBI logo, Jake's desk was void of all personal effects. No awards or plaques on the walls. As usual, Jake was unpretentious. It didn't bother her that he didn't have a framed picture of her on his desk. It was just as well since someone would eventually use her photo to practice graffiti.

Her finger nudged the lone folder lying in the middle of the desk and it yawned open. The right-hand corner read, *ANTON MOORE - Case 01207* in neatly typed letters. She remembered this case all too well. The airwaves had been filled with news about the three-year-old boy who had been set on fire by his mother's boyfriend four weeks ago. Jake had an uncanny ability to ferret out the abusers, to see what others couldn't see in their eyes. Sam assumed it was because Jake had grown up looking into similar eyes. What Jake saw in the eyes of men like Mo Williams was pure enjoyment. They took pleasure in the power they wielded over others.

From Jake's notes she discovered that the only thing holding up Mo's hearing was Keesha Moore's testimony. The six-year-old girl had been the only witness. Two weeks of her stay in the hospital was for treatment of second-degree burns. The third week was for counseling. The judge in the case wanted to meet privately with Keesha in his chambers. That meeting was scheduled for tomorrow.

She leafed through prior reports of abuse when Mo had allegedly beaten Felicia Moore. Sam wasn't surprised to read that Felicia would habitually drop charges against her boyfriend as quickly as she picked up the phone to report the incidents. A co-dependent. Those were the dangerous ones. Cops would show up to pull the husband off the wife only to have her pick up something and start pounding on the cops for hurting her boyfriend/husband/significant other. It happened too many times.

In Anton Moore's case, Felicia believed Mo's story…that Anton was playing with matches while Mo was in the shower and Felicia was at the store. The fire hadn't done much damage to the couch. Anton's clothing had caught fire and his sister had tried to put it out.

Sam studied the picture of Mo Williams. She had expected a three-hundred-pound bully built like a prize fighter. Instead, she was staring at a lean pretty boy wearing an Army camouflage shirt. His long Afro was pulled back and wrapped in fabric, like a horse's tail. There was a deep scar under his left eye, and another one on his chin. He had a cocky look on his face and eyes that dared you to challenge him.

There were pictures of Felicia following a variety of 911 calls. Bruises, abrasions, fractured arm, a laundry list of injuries. During the heat of the moment, in each of the instances, she had pointed a finger at Mo. But the next morning when her bruises didn't seem to hurt as much and her heart filled with eternal love and devotion to the night time security guard, she would drop those charges and the two lovebirds would walk out of the precinct hand in hand.

"Stupid girl." Sam closed the folder and turned toward the monitor. She tapped the mouse and the screen lit up. "Good." Jake was already signed on to the system. There was a time she knew the password to access records but it was changed after her suspension.

The query form was the same. She clicked on HOMICIDE and typed in STABBING. Under VICTIM she typed F and under AGE she typed in a range of 14-20. Sam guessed the victim to be high school age but with the mature shape of her body she could be wrong. She clicked on SEARCH and drummed her fingers on the desk.

"Let's not take too long." She stole a quick glance toward the door and hoped Jake would be delayed a little longer. Twelve names appeared on the screen. Two victims were female, both were stabbed once, and one victim was African American. Two of the homicides were domestic disputes. The rest were gang-related.

Sam heard the door click shut.

"Hope that's a love letter you're typing," a familiar voice said.

Sam winced. "Of course. How do you spell *Dear John?*"

Strong hands wrapped around the armrests and pulled the chair away from the computer. Then the chair was spun around until Sam was staring at a face that was more drill sergeant than scout leader.

"As usual, I'm sure you have a good explanation."

His look was stern, eyes expressionless. It had taken Sam awhile to get used to Jake's serious nature. On rare occasions she would catch a gleam in his eyes whenever he looked at her, like now.

Sam smiled sweetly. "Of course."

His finger made a circle in the air then pointed toward the chair in front of the desk. "Park it."

"Nice to see you, too, sweetheart. How is your day going?" She stood up slowly, stepping closer to him, catching a whiff of his aftershave while her fingers played with his tie. "Did you have a meeting today?" Jake detested wearing ties unless absolutely necessary. He took a step back. "Nervous? Afraid someone will walk in on us?"

Jake pulled away, slipped out of his tweed sportscoat, and hung it on the hook behind the door. His badge was clamped to the left side of his belt, his Sig Sauer in a belt holster on the right.

"You're supposed to bribe me with fry bread before breaking into my computer." He stole a quick glance to make sure the blinds were closed, then planted a kiss on her forehead. "What are you up to?" Jake sat down and studied the names on the screen. He pushed his chair back and propped his right ankle over his left knee.

Sam settled into the seat opposite him and filled him in on the construction site. He listened intently, hands clasped over his stomach, a worry line slowly etching across his forehead.

"What movie did you watch last night?"

"When?"

"In the middle of the night, Sam. I rolled over around three in the morning and you weren't there."

It wasn't unusual for her to have trouble sleeping nights. Some days she napped so much that her sleep patterns were screwed up. But leave it up to Jake to think otherwise.

"I'm not having nightmares, if that's what you're thinking. And I watched the tape of *Sleepless in Seattle,* so I wasn't influenced by any blood and guts movie."

Jake shoved a fist under his chin and regarded her thoughtfully. He cocked his head toward the computer and studied the screen again.

"Jake." Sam studied her hands and tried to stifle comments about how over-protective he was and that she had no control over when *it* happens. She pulled the brass button from her pocket and set it on the desk in front of him. "I heard the name Wy-chin-sky repeated in my head. It could be either the killer's or the victim's name. I was trying to see if the database had a list of homicides with multiple stab wounds."

Jake held the button between his fingers. "Did you think perhaps the button fell off of a hitchhiker and the killing happened in another state?"

"No."

"Or perhaps it belonged to one of the construction workers who might have committed a crime somewhere else?"

She leaned back with a sigh. "Well, you sure know how to let your logic put a damper on things."

"That's me. Mr. Logic." He placed the button on the desk, flipped it around so the initials were facing him.

"Have I ever told you how absolutely irritating that is?" She saw a hint of a smile in his eyes and had to admit it was one of the qualities she admired about him, sometimes. "It would take forever to go state by state and not every police department has its records computerized, Jake."

He glanced back at the monitor. "Did you search for a Wy-chin-sky in the computer?"

"Didn't know how to spell it."

"We only have ten years worth of records input into our system so far, Sam. Besides, you've lived here all your life. You don't remember such a murder?"

Sam shook her head. "Abby and I were probably visiting the reservation. We usually did during the summers and the murder definitely happened during a hot summer." She studied the button closely. It looked like something off of a college blazer. "When the scene unfolded it was *that* forest preserve and *that* clearing. My gut tells me the murder took place right here in Chasen Heights."

Jake grew pensive, steepling his fingers and tapping them against his chin. She wasn't sure if he was pretending to give her theory some thought, or if his FBI training was re-sorting and shifting the details in his head. Finally, he said, "If all our computer came up with were two female victims, then there is a chance the killing took place more than ten years ago." He glanced at the stack of files on his desk. "Unfortunately, cases with actual clues take precedence."

"Give me a conference room and back files and I'll go through them," Sam offered.

"No."

"That was way too quick."

"Why don't you just concentrate on you and the baby, okay?"

"Disappointment isn't healthy for me or the baby," she countered.

"Sam." Jake pushed his chair back and stood up. "Don't try to maneuver me into doing something I don't want to do."

She studied his chiseled features, ruddy complexion, the soft flecks of yellow in his brown eyes. Jake had a hardened look of someone who spent too much time exposed to the seedier part of life. The eyes are what smiled when his lips wouldn't and the gentle sound of his voice could sometimes send a rush of heat through her body. Sam felt that sudden rush, leaned across the desk and whispered, "Will you be home for lunch?"

He picked up the button and stared at her over his fingers, a glint of understanding in his eyes. "Abby going shopping?"

"Uh huh. Looking for more nursery furniture." Sam smiled back. "Does that mean you'll take the case?"

He handed her the button. "No, that means I'll be home for lunch."

3

S am greeted Jake at the front door, turned him around and covered his mouth with hers. Her hands gripped solid muscle.

"Sam," Jake mumbled around her tongue.

Her fingers struggled with his shirt buttons as she backed him across the quarry tiled floor. In a brief moment of surrender he wrapped his arms around her and returned the kiss. But just as quickly, he broke the embrace.

"Um, honey." He tried to ply her fingers free.

"I've got the Jacuzzi running and the candles lit." She grabbed fistfuls of fabric and yanked the shirt out of his pants.

Jake grabbed her by the shoulders. "Sam."

"Yes, yes, I'm hurrying." Shoes clicked on the foyer floor and Sam turned to see the last person she wanted to see.

"Uh, Dim Sum Duck, anyone?" Frank Travis held up two bags which leaked strong soy aromas. "Or is it Dim Sum *word that rhymes with duck?*" He broke out in a wide grin showing a mouth full of gleaming white teeth against dark skin.

Sam jerked her gaze back to Jake and a soulful whine caught in her throat.

"I'm sorry," Frank chuckled. "Were you expecting shrimp fried rice? Got that, too." He walked past the two tossing a wink at Jake.

"Jake." Her eyes pleaded as she watched him tuck his shirt back into his pants.

"We got a break on a case and we're having a quick bite while Frank waits for a call." He kissed the tip of her nose. "Go blow out the candles."

"The I.O.U. list is getting very long, Mitchell," she yelled at his back.

Food and files were spread out on the dining room table by the time Sam returned. Studying the contents of the takeout boxes, she told Frank, "This is a pretty high fat and calorie lunch you're having, Mr. Nutrition."

"I'll just spend three hours in the gym tomorrow instead of two." He pulled out a wax paper bag and dangled it from his fingers. "Fortune cookies."

"Boring," she mumbled as she stretched out on the window seat and stared at the acres of brown grass and withered stems where flowers once bloomed. She didn't like this time of year when Nature painted the landscape in only two colors—yellow and brown. At least if there were several inches of snow it would cover the dead plants.

"My contact said she'd call the minute she spots Ryerson," Frank said as he spooned fried rice onto his plate.

"Hope you're right. We can use a break."

"Is this the Silvy Serico murder you're working on?" Sam asked.

"Yes," Jake replied, "but no need..."

"To concern yourself," Sam said with disgust.

Silvador Serico had been another unfortunate victim caught in the crossfire of a drive-by shooting. Rumors were Lank Ryerson was the driver of the car but no one recognized the face of the shooter.

"Why don't you take up knitting or crocheting, Sam?" Frank suggested, a smile curling up the corners of his mouth.

Sam fumbled in her pocket and withdrew the brass button. "Jake tell you about the button I found?"

"Sorta."

"Sorta?"

Frank chuckled again. "Yeah, he said you saw a brutal murder taking place."

"Did he tell you where I found it?" Now it was her turn to smile. "Over at the new Briar subdivision."

Frank's smile slowly faded. "My subdivision?"

Her smile broadened. "Yes. And I think I found it on your driveway."

"My driveway?" Frank's eyes bulged and his head swiveled to Jake. "You didn't say anything about that."

"Drop it, Frank." Jake gathered up the empty containers and shoved them into the takeout bag.

"But it's my driveway." He jerked his head back to Sam. "You sure it's MY driveway?"

"Elliptical window, circular drive." Her hands drew a picture in the air. "It's the only house with a circular drive, right?"

"Damn." Frank pressed his hands against his shaved head. "I'm going to have a *Cemetery Mary* floating across my lawn?"

"I'm surprised you haven't spent your morning going through newspapers," Jake told Sam.

"I did. I mean, I am. You have been with CHPD for seven years and you don't remember anything. Scofield has been here ten years."

"I've been here twelve," Frank added, "and I sure don't remember that gruesome of a murder."

"All the old timers work at Headquarters and I certainly don't want to stop by and risk running into Chief Murphy." Sam stood with a smile and leveled her eyes on Jake.

"No."

"Why is it you say no so quickly and I haven't even asked the question yet?"

"I start asking questions, word will get back to Murphy. He even suspects you are working on a case and he'll make your life miserable." Jake carried the bags to the kitchen.

"I'm a private citizen," Sam called out.

Jake returned and stood across the table from Sam, his palms flat on the table. "No, Sam. You are a suspended cop."

Frank jumped when his beeper vibrated and he checked the number on the display.

"That her?" Jake asked.

"Yep." Frank pulled a cell phone from his pocket and dialed. "Granny Mae? It's Detective Travis." He smiled as he listened and nodded to Jake when he hung up. "It's show time."

Sam spent the afternoon visiting the *Chasen Heights Post Tribune* office hoping to find some seasoned veterans who might know the crime statistics and save her a lot of leg work. One lesson she failed to learn was not to visit a newspaper office during deadline.

Betsy, the bubbly receptionist, was busy typing one finger at a time. She giggled her way through two phone calls while Sam waited patiently to ask if they had an available log on crime statistics. Miss Perky was quick to point out that her name was "Betsy," like in "wetsy." She wasn't even blonde. "You can check our web site. We have an archives there," she offered.

"I have been on your web site. All afternoon." Sam strained to keep the irritation from her voice. Several desks away a group of Miss Perky lookalikes was clustered around a buff jock. While others hustled in deadline mode with papers flying and voices loud, these obvious interns were oblivious to the hectic pace.

"Nothing was detailed on the web site. I was looking for statistics, details."

The phone chirped, an irritating ring that sounded like a monster cricket. Holding up one finger, its long nail painted with a

Christmas tree design, Betsy signaled the silent wait-one-minute message and answered on the third ring.

The buff jock was standing and stretching, flexing his muscles to the delight of his admirers. Sam looked around for someone of authority but either they were all too busy or they just didn't care what the underlings did. Maybe paying seven dollars an hour wasn't sufficient incentive to put in a full day's work.

"Now, did you need anything else?" Betsy asked after hanging up.

"Is there anyone here that has at least twenty years seniority?"

"Twenty years?" Betsy's mouth twisted as though she had just bitten into a lime. "You mean like older than me?"

Sam turned on her heel and walked out. Maybe Jake was right. Maybe the murder had happened in another state.

4

The next day Sam headed for the library to look through back issues of the *Chasen Heights Post Tribune*. After one hour she came to the conclusion that all microfiche should have a warning label. She had felt the eyestrain after the first ten minutes.

Every time the door opened to the Circulation Department, Sam looked up with anticipation, hoping that an ancient librarian would come teetering in, someone with decades worth of gossip to share. But everyone who entered looked barely out of high school. One woman was dressed as Mrs. Claus. A notice on a nearby bulletin board announced that Mrs. Claus would be reading Christmas stories today in the children's library.

There was something about the eerie silence of a library that didn't sit well with Sam. It seemed unnecessary for one thing. Most people when they read at home have the radio or television set blaring. Why did they suddenly need absolute silence to browse through a bookshelf or thumb through a magazine?

The clock on the wall above the door said it was close to feeding time. Stifling a yawn, Sam popped out the film and returned it to the shelf.

An enclosed walkway led to the main library. Near the Information Desk Sam noticed a white-haired woman stocking books onto a rotating display. A cameo pin was fastened at the top of a starched collar. Her nametag read *Wanda*. She was taking books off of the shelves and replacing them with books from the cart.

"Anything new and interesting?" Sam asked.

The frail woman looked startled but recovered quickly. Sam couldn't help but notice how transparent Wanda's skin appeared and her eyes were drawn to the elderly woman's hairline where the sparseness resembled doll's hair.

"Didn't mean to interrupt you." Sam studied the titles of the books.

"What kind of mysteries do you like?" Wanda didn't wait for a response and quickly pulled down a book with a paw print in blood on the cover. "Have you read the Feline Series? Clever mysteries where the Siamese cat helps his master solve crimes." She set the book in Sam's arms. "And what about the Sister Sleuth Series?" Wanda piled three more books on top of the cat cover. "It's about a group of nuns who solve cases while running a home for wayward girls."

"Sounds like a real page turner."

"Course, all I read are cozies. I don't like a lot of blood and gore in my books. Don't like the King fella either." She pulled two more books off the rack and loaded them onto Sam's pile.

"So you've never read Patricia Cornwell?"

Wanda grimaced and fastened her gray eyes on Sam's stomach. "You shouldn't be reading those either. The baby will absorb all that nonsense. The world is full of enough evil without reading it to the baby."

By osmosis? Sam thought. "Have you lived here long?" Sam asked, trying to steer the conversation away from mysteries.

"All my life." Her pale fingers played with the cameo pin. "My brother was the pastor at Saint Michael's. He's been dead for ten years now." She turned back to her book shelving, checking spines for more recommendations. "I still help out at the church working as a part-time secretary. We need more of the Lord's work in our lives because Satan is everywhere." Wanda's eyes flitted down the hall and she waited for a mother and two daughters to pass. The girls were each clutching several selections. Once they were out of range, Wanda leaned in close and whispered, "There's enough evil in the world without hearing it on the news or reading about it in the papers. Close thine ears to depravity lest it conquer thee."

Sam's eagerness to discuss details of a multiple stabbing, rape, and decapitation was dwindling fast and she feared just mentioning such a crime would have the frail senior pulling out her rosary and flashing the crucifix before going into cardiac arrest.

Sam thanked her for the books and as she approached the check out, turned to see if Wanda was watching. She wasn't. Sam dumped the books through the *Returns* slot and fled the library.

The car screeched to a stop outside Braggio's, an upscale Italian restaurant just two blocks from the courthouse.

The stout valet came running over to the car and motioned frantically at the *No Parking* sign.

Frank grabbed Jake's arm. "I don't think we should do this."

"Then stay in the car." Jake pressed his badge against the side window. The pudgy-faced valet did a one-eighty and stalked away.

"At least take five minutes to calm down."

"Why waste a pissed-off mood." Jake stormed out of the car with Frank reluctantly trailing behind. They rushed past a fountain where the statue of a woman in marble was pouring water from an urn into a pool littered with coins.

Once inside the restaurant, Jake flashed his badge at the hostess. The detectives walked through the restaurant of power-suited lawyers, the country club elite, past an elaborate buffet, to a back room.

Where Judge Andrew Wise ate lunch was not public knowledge. But Jake knew who to call and what favors to collect. Against Frank's protests, Jake wasn't going to be satisfied until he heard from the judge why charges against Mo Williams had been dropped.

Judge Wise's fork of pasta hovered between his plate and mouth when Jake pulled out a chair and sat down. The fork returned to the plate and Judge Wise's eyes darted around the room.

"This is highly irregular, Detectives," Wise whispered, pressing a napkin to his mouth.

The private room held eight tables, half of which were occupied by men in starched shirts and Armani suits. A waitress walked up to the table.

"They aren't staying," Judge Wise told the young woman. His napkin was tucked under his chin and draped in front of his white shirt. A herringbone suit jacket hung on the back of his chair, the gray threads matching his hair. Fatigue glistened in his eyes and deepened the creases in his forehead.

He turned his attention back to the detectives. "Let me guess. This has to do with the Williams case."

Frank looked around nervously before sitting down, as if expecting a bouncer to toss their asses out on the street.

Jake started to speak but Wise held his hand up. The judge busied himself shaking cheese on his pasta while his eyes continued to dance around the room.

"You two are good cops and I know this case sticks in your craw." He took time to sip his coffee. "Felicia Moore's attorney refused to let me speak to Keesha alone. Needless to say, the girl changed her story completely. She definitely had enough time to be coached but the testimony of a six-year-old would have been weak at best anyway." Judge Wise wound pasta around his fork and shoved it in his mouth.

Frank leaned forward. "She's kept to her story for weeks."

"She was coerced. She's scared of Mo," Jake said.

The napkin flipped up again and Judge Wise patted his lips. "I cautioned Felicia Moore that one more call to the police about Mo and I will instruct the Department of Children and Family Services..."

"What good is that going to do?" Jake argued. "She'll just make sure she never calls and Mo will keep on beating." Judge Wise's back stiffened and Jake felt Frank's hand on his arm.

"Let me finish." The judge pulled the napkin from under his chin and tossed it on the table. "DCFS will make twice weekly visits. Mo has been instructed to attend counseling, as has Felicia. If ever I have seen a case of co-dependency, this is it." He signaled the waitress for his check. "This conversation is over."

Reluctantly, Frank and Jake pushed away from the table and stood. "Jake," Judge Wise said as they turned to leave. Frank looked sharply at Jake. "We can't win them all, no matter how hard we try."

Jake nodded.

"Okay, what was that about?" Frank demanded as they walked out into the crisp sunlight.

"Mo is free."

"Not that. What's the buddy-buddy *Jake* thing?"

Jake shoved his sunglasses onto the bridge of his nose and stared at his partner. "How about you drive." He tossed the keys over to him.

They climbed into the car but Frank hesitated before shoving the key into the ignition. He leaned back with a sigh and cocked his head toward Jake.

"No lectures." Jake pushed the button and the window rolled down.

"Ain't none coming. But the outcome shouldn't surprise you. What the hell did you think a six-year-old girl was gonna do?"

Jake clamped the cigarette between his teeth and struggled out of his leather coat. He flung it over the backrest and into the back seat.

"Go ahead. Clam up. Who the hell am I? Just your partner for the past seven fuckin' years. Ain't nobody important."

Jake turned his head slightly and peered through his mirrored sunglasses at Frank. He always said Frank should have his own pulpit.

"You don't think I'm skipping happy that ass got tuned up while he was in jail? Huh." Frank shoved the keys in the ignition and hesitated again. "That little boy was the same age as my son. Little kids can't defend themselves. People should have to be licensed to be parents, goddam right. Gotta have a license to drive, even to fish."

Jake stared out of the passenger window while his cigarette burned and Frank's preaching faded in and out. Instead, Jake was remembering the day an innocent three-year old died and the young mother who struggled with the decision whether to mourn the death of her son or valiantly support her boyfriend.

"Miss Moore, how long have you known Mr. Williams?" Jake asked.

"About a year."

"Has he ever hit the kids?"

"No."

"Ever hit you?"

"No."

Frank produced previous incident reports from a folder and laid them out for the young woman to see. "It's a shame that someone would mess up a beautiful face like yours," he said, letting his eyes drift over her face.

Felicia quickly responded, "I fell, that's all. Slipped on the ice. Another time I tripped over one of the kid's toys."

"What about the bruises you had our technician take pictures of and the warrant you wanted issued against Mr. Williams?" Frank challenged.

"I was only funnin' him. I was mad and wanted to get back at him. Don't mean nothin'. I dropped them charges."

"Did he ever hurt the children?" Jake asked. "Beat them?"

"No."

"Burn them with cigarettes?"

"No."

"Abuse them?"

"I told you, NO!"

When it was Mo's turn to be interrogated, Jake hovered over him like a storm cloud but the young bully didn't even flinch. Jake's six-foot-two-inch, two-hundred-plus-pound solid frame and the intense look in his eyes had little effect.

"Well, Maurice. What do you have to say for yourself?" Jake flipped the chair around and straddled it. Frank leaned against the door.

"About what, white boy?" he sneered. "The weather?" He clasped his hands together, fingers toying with a ring on his right index finger. The diamond horseshoe was anchored on a gold band. Jake figured the ring was stolen. It was too large to fit on Mo's ring finger.

Jake took a long reach across the table and grabbed Mo by the shirt, lifting his wiry body off of the chair until their faces were a few inches apart.

"Lose the chip on that shoulder, punk, or I'll knock it off," Jake whispered.

"Jake!" Frank pulled on Jake's arm until he released his hold.

"This is pole-eeze brutality," Mo sneered, but the sneer faded quickly when Frank received a phone call. Frank didn't hide the *gotcha* look in his eyes as he slid one hip on the table, and leaned in close.

"We just might have a problem, Mo," Frank said. "I just spoke to the policewoman who accompanied Keesha to the hospital. It seems the little girl is awake and telling our officer a completely different account of what happened. Now," he leaned in closer and whispered, "care to change your story?"

"…and just like my granddaddy always said, 'what goes around comes around.' Just got to be patient. Right?"

Frank's voice faded in as Jake felt a searing pain in his fingertips. He flung the burning cigarette butt out the window and rubbed his fingers.

"Also helps if you pay attention," Frank added.

Jake turned his mirrored sunglasses toward him and said, "Drive."

5

S moke swirled around the lights and drifted toward the ceiling fans. Sam wished the ceiling were higher. They were seated at a table in the back room of Izzy's, a hangout popular with the local men in blue and owned by a former cop. The bar wasn't fancy but it had great food. Its wooden floors were practical, the bar long, and drinks bottomless. Television sets were tuned to a variety of sporting events. A wall filled with autographed pictures served to separate the restaurant from the bar area.

Jake hadn't said much about Mo Williams' hearing. He didn't have to. Frank was doing all the talking.

"And Jake has to barge into the restaurant and interrupt the judge's lunch."

"Frank," Jake cautioned.

"You what?" Sam asked.

"And then I find out the two of them are on first name basis. What's next? Sleepovers at Judge Wise's house?"

Jake lit another cigarette while he glared at Frank across the table. He held the cigarette away from Sam and blew the smoke toward the ceiling. Sam glanced from Frank to her husband. No one spoke for a painfully long time.

"What time did you say he would be here?" Sam finally asked, changing the subject.

"Patience." Jake placed a hand on her thigh and squeezed. "I was told he stops by every night. Nancy will let him know we want to talk to him."

A roar erupted from the bar area prompted by one of the sporting events being televised. A child in a high chair at a nearby table placed her hands over her ears. Sam cringed at the crumbs under the high chair and tried to imagine her own kitchen floor littered with food.

"Gotta hand it to you, Sam." Frank picked up a packaged cracker from the basket in the center of the table and read the back, squinting at the small print. "One soulful look from a pregnant wife and Jake folds like any whipped husband."

She grabbed the crackers from his hand and ripped them open. "Either eat them or put them back. Don't play with them."

Frank drew back his hand. "Damn. Never get between you and food."

"Jake doesn't fold." Sam said, stealing a glance at Jake who was slowly twirling his beer glass in the rings of condensation. "My guess is I have sparked his curiosity." This elicited a one-sided grin from her husband.

A figure appeared in front of their table. "Bartender says you're looking for me."

Jake stood. "You're Jonesy?"

"John Jones but everyone calls me Jonesy." His flannel shirt was layered over a turtleneck and the buttons strained at the waist of his denim jeans. Once the introductions were made, Jonesy wasted no time sitting down and pouring a glass of beer from the pitcher.

"I understand you worked Homicide for a while," Jake said.

"From nineteen-eighty to eighty-five. Then I went to canine patrol. Always was good at training dogs."

Sam watched as beer dribbled down Jonesy's chin and wondered if he learned table manners from his dogs. She was itching to get a word in edgewise but Jonesy kept talking about the best breeds for training.

When Jonesy took time out to wet his whistle, Sam asked, "Do you remember any stabbing deaths in Chasen Heights near Briar Woods? Victim would have been around fifteen to twenty, female?"

"Oh, yeah. It wasn't my case but I remember the pictures being circulated. Would have thought a dog had been slaughtered. Couldn't tell it was human." He took another swig of beer and wiped his mouth with the back of his hand.

"So it's true?" Frank grimaced and stared at Jonesy's face, as though waiting for a laugh, some clue that it was all a practical joke. "It's really true?"

Sam could feel her pulse quicken but Jonesy's appearance kept her optimism at bay. His eyes were red and his words were a little slow in coming. She guessed he had started with a liquid lunch and continued through dinner. How much could she rely on his memory?

"One of my dogs had been hit by a car once," Jonesy said. "Looked the same way, covered with blood, difficult to tell where the injury was."

They spent another five minutes listening to canine talk when a familiar face strolled up to the table.

"Well, well. If it isn't the little murderer. I mean mother." Brandon Carter stood behind Frank, beer in one hand, eyes glazed. "What are you doing talking to a cop killer?" he asked Jonesy.

"What?" Jonesy looked around the table.

"What do you want Brandon, besides trouble?" Jake stood. The noise in the room was reduced to muffled chatter from the television sets.

Sam had felt the stares when they walked in but she was getting good at tunnel vision. Unfortunately, she hadn't seen Brandon when they passed through the crowded bar to the dining room.

"Yeah." Brandon jutted his dimpled chin in Sam's direction. "She's the one who shot Stu Richards in the back last summer and then spent a couple months at the funny farm claiming memory lapse."

"She's that cop?" Jonesy blinked, as if someone just shook him awake.

With that Frank stood. His chair wobbled and then crashed to the floor. Nancy, the bartender, muscled her way between the tables and jammed her fists onto her broad hips. She struck an intimidating pose, her large frame towering over Brandon.

"Cool it, all of you. Brandon, go back to the bar or out the door. I'll eighty-six anyone I feel like, starting with you."

"Just wanted Jonesy to know who he was talking to." Brandon made a finger gun and pointed it at Sam before strolling away.

"You'll have to get your information elsewhere." Jonesy staggered to his feet and retreated to the bar.

Sam felt her face flush and wished she had never let Jake talk her into meeting Jonesy at Izzy's where they were bound to run into Brandon.

Frank righted his chair and the silence in the room soon filled with a dull rumble. "Well, that was fun," he said. "I would have really enjoyed two minutes in a dark alley with Brandon."

"You okay?" Jake asked Sam.

"Fine." But Sam wondered if the stigma was going to haunt her for the rest of her life. It wasn't easy to pretend things were back to normal because too much had changed in her life.

Frank checked his watch. "Gotta go, guys. Promised the little guy I'd tuck him in." He stood and patted Jake on the back. "Pick you up at seven." He looked across at Sam. "Keep that chin up."

They watched him leave through the back door. Jake poured a cup of coffee as Sam played with her cup of lukewarm tea. She could sense his eyes on her and felt his arm across the back of her chair. But she avoided returning his gaze and prayed he wouldn't rub a hand across her shoulder or touch her hair or crook his finger under her chin to turn her face toward him. She was sure if that happened her hormones would kick into overdrive and she would be reduced to a blithering wreck.

A shadow emerged from the booth behind them and moved to the chair vacated by Jonesy. His face was round and pink and a ring of gray hair protruded from under the Santa's hat perched on his head. The furry white ball flopped against his ear as he nodded.

"Couldn't help overhearing." When blank stares greeted him, he added, "I'm Phil Cannon. Used to be the desk sergeant at the Fourth. The Sixth didn't exist back then." He nodded toward the pitcher of beer. "Mind?" Jake shoved the pitcher closer to Phil whose gaze drifted to Sam. "I'm retired myself. Don't matter to me none what anyone thinks of who I talk to."

They made small talk while he sipped his beer. Phil Cannon was a widower. His only daughter and grandson lived with him. During in-climate weather, he played around in his greenhouse, babying a prize peony that he entered every spring in the local flower show. Once the waitress brought more coffee and hot water, Sam asked Phil about the stabbing. She pulled a notepad and pen from her purse.

"Seventeen years ago, a warm July night," Phil started. "I remember it like it was yesterday. Catherine DeMarco. She was the same age as my daughter back then, sixteen." Phil took a swallow of beer and then continued. "It was an unincorporated area at the time with an unfinished street running parallel to the woods. Dispatcher received an anonymous call so we sent out a patrol car. The rookie found what he thought was a dog. She was so butchered he couldn't tell at first that it was human. Throat was cut so deep she was almost decapitated."

Sam shuddered as she remembered her vision, how lifelike when the killer had sliced the knife across the teenager's throat.

"You'd a thought he was tenderizing meat. He just kept stabbing and stabbing. Bastard raped her, too. Horrible. Many a cop had a sleepless night after that one."

Sam thought back to the details she had seen and asked, "Did the knife have a pearl handle?"

Phil thought for a moment. "Come to think of it, it did. But how did you...?"

"I take it they caught the killer," Sam said. "Wy-chin-sky?"

"Wy-chin-sky?" Phil wrinkled his brow. "Never heard of him. Taggart. Jimmy Taggart's who killed her. He's gonna be executed next month."

6

"You seem shocked, Sam," Phil said. "Where did you come up with the name *Wydachinski?*"

"Wy-chin-sky," Sam repeated. "I'm not sure how it's spelled. The name didn't come up at all in the trial? Was he even a suspect?"

"Open and shut case. Taggart was drunk and passed out about fifty yards from the body. The knife and the girl's blood were on him and it was his semen inside her. He pleaded innocent. Didn't remember nothin' from that night other than he had a lot to drink. Vaguely remembers seeing Catherine."

"I don't understand." Jake pulled the carafe of coffee closer and filled his cup. "If this Taggart is going to be executed soon, why hasn't the case been rehashed in the papers? The press doesn't miss a beat when it comes to sensationalizing a case for ratings."

"That's right." Sam flagged their waitress down and asked for another tea bag. "I would think the papers would have reactions from every politician and friends and relatives of the victim."

Phil rested his elbows on the table and leaned closer, dropping his voice to a whisper. "People would just as soon forget that someone that sick could be born and bred in this town. Seventeen years ago the worst crime you would read about was the theft of a wallet at the local food store. Even as crime increased to car jackings and home invasions, the city would never live down the murder of Catherine DeMarco. They were trying to convince people to move here, safe town to raise a family. So once Taggart was found guilty, it was rare to hear a word whispered about that horrendous crime. And politicians have probably done their best to keep Taggart's name and the DeMarco case out of the papers as the execution date nears."

Phil leaned back and wrapped his hands around the beer glass. Tables were emptying and the noise in the room had been reduced to the clatter of dishes from the busboy.

"What about the anonymous call?" Jake asked. "Anyone trace it?"

"Nearby pay phone. Male caller. No witnesses. We just figured it was someone driving by who just didn't want to get involved. And once we had Taggart, there was no need to look elsewhere."

"Who was the detective on the case?" Sam asked.

Phil smiled as though remembering a childhood friend. "Pit Goddard."

"Pit?" Jake echoed.

"Yep. Paul *Pit Bull* Goddard. He was like a dog with a bone the way he attacked his cases. Best damn detective I ever worked with." Phil took another long swallow of beer, then scratched his head through the Santa hat, the furry ball flopping back and forth. "You know, that case never did set too well with him. As I recall, he had a feeling in his gut that all the pieces of the puzzle just fit too damn well too quick."

"Where is Mr. Goddard now?" Sam asked. She noticed Phil's smile fade and the sparkle in his eyes dim. It would be just her luck that Goddard was dead.

"Pit had a lot of problems. Shot and killed a thirteen-year-old boy by accident. Kid was a gang member and shooting at him from the shadows. Big enough to pass for eighteen but to Pit he was still just a kid. That's why I kinda know how some things just aren't the way they appear," he added, referring to Sam and the shooting of Officer Richards. "Pit never forgave himself. Started drinking a little too much. Department put him on medical leave for a while, then shifted him around from precinct to precinct, job to job. He finally quit five years ago. Never really did stop drinking.

"His wife left him three years ago. Took their six-year-old daughter. They were driving out to Phoenix to live with her parents when a semi hit them head on. Pit's life took a spiral. People have seen him late at night shopping at the grocery store. I used to stop by once every other week to see how he was. Got to the point where he just didn't bother answering the door or the phone."

"I take it he still lives in the area," Sam said.

Phil nodded. "The insurance money paid off the house and provides him with enough money to keep his pantry and bar supplied. Tried P.I. work with another firm, then opened his own, so I hear. But after a while just didn't take any cases that I've heard of. Neighbors take care of his yard. They've called the cops a couple times. They'd hear a gun shot from his house. Cops arrive. There'd be a bullet hole in the ceiling and a drunken, unbathed, unshaven Pit, sitting on the couch, his .357 Magnum lying in his lap."

Sam shuddered at the thought of how much pain it would take to drive someone to suicide. "Where does he live?"

"Ash Street. Five hundred block. Can't miss it. He has a penguin for a mailbox. His wife was into penguins." Phil cocked his head and looked at Sam curiously. "You're not thinking of getting that bastard out, are you?"

Sam shoved the notepad and pen in her purse, saying, "I just want to make sure the right bastard is in."

7

He stood in front of the bookcase holding a picture in a brass frame. An attractive brunette smiled back at him—short hair, hazel eyes, deep dimples punctuating her smile. A mirror of her sat in her lap. They wore the same green velvet dresses, patent leather shoes, and sat in a chair next to a Christmas tree.

Years worth of dust clung to the bookshelves, except for the space in front of the picture. Nothing had changed in three years. He hadn't moved any of Megan's stuffed animals from her bed or given Colleen's clothes to the church rummage sale, clothes he was supposed to ship to her after she arrived in Phoenix.

He dragged the picture off of the shelf with his left hand while his right hand gripped the Magnum. The reflection in the brass frame showed a face sunken and creased, bloodshot eyes, and a three-day growth of beard. He had watched his weight drop from one-hundred-and-eighty-five pounds to one-hundred-and-sixty. That was thin, even for his height. But nothing he did worked. He couldn't starve himself to death, couldn't drink himself to death. Hadn't even been able to keep the barrel of the gun in his mouth. Always pulled it out at the last minute. But not this time.

He carried the picture to the couch and sat down. This was how he wanted to remember them. Youthful, innocent, beautiful, alive.

His hand shook as he slid the barrel into his mouth. Tears welled as he looked at his wife and daughter for the last time.

Sam studied the penguin that stood vigil by the curb. The house was a split-level, vinyl siding, country blue trim. The lawn had been carefully edged and fertilized for the winter. Evergreens were shaped, flower beds weeded. Phil was right...Paul Goddard had exceptional neighbors.

She pressed her finger to the doorbell and heard its response echoing back. After several seconds she pressed the buzzer a second time, a third, each time a few seconds longer than the previous.

"Damn," she muttered under her breath. Her blanket coat felt stifling and she cursed herself for not leaving it in the Jeep. Nine o'clock in the morning and the sun was already beginning to burn through the morning chill. Her hair was still damp but it was the only way she could coax it into a French braid.

Deciding to take drastic measures, she opened the storm door and pounded continuously with a closed fist. The door was jerked open in mid-pound. If she hadn't halted abruptly, the next pound would have been on the man's throat. She had seen worse figures on State Street waiting for the soup kitchens to open. Maybe not. He wore a sweat-soaked tee shirt and blue jeans. His face was haggard and had enough stubble to sand a hardwood floor. Damp, stringy hair hung past his collar and clung to his moist forehead.

Sam's gaze drifted down to the .357 Magnum clenched in his right hand, the knuckles white. Her eyes traveled up his arm, the muscles tense and twitching. His jaw was set and there was a look of contempt in his eyes, either reserved for his intruder or life itself.

Sam took a deep breath and pushed past him saying, "Can you put your plans on hold? We have work to do."

"Who the hell are you?"

Sam wrinkled her nose. "Phew. It smells like a men's locker room in here." He hadn't moved away from the door. Just stood there, gun cocked and ready. Sam held out her hand. "Casey. Sergeant Sam Casey. Sixth Precinct." When he still didn't respond, Sam said, "You must be Pit Bull Goddard."

"Pit Bull?" He shook his head as though trying to remember where he had heard the name before. "Damn, I haven't been called that in..." The door slid shut as he leaned against it. He looked at the Magnum as though wondering who placed it in his hand, uncocked it, and set it on the coffee table.

"Phil Cannon said to say 'Hi.'"

"Phil?" He shook his head again in an effort to jog his memory.

Sam's eyes took in the room with its stacks of newspapers, empty beer cans, smudged glass tables. She noticed the picture on the couch and picked it up. Pit yanked it from her grasp and set the picture back on the bookcase.

"Phil said you worked the Catherine DeMarco case seventeen years ago."

He shook a cigarette from the pack on the coffee table. "I'm not with the police department anymore." Touching the match to the tip of the cigarette, he studied her through the smoke.

Sam lifted newspapers off of an armchair and sat down. "What a coincidence. Neither am I." He raised his eyebrows. "I'm on suspension," Sam explained. "Little problem with a murder. Long story."

"I don't care to hear it."

"Good, 'cause I don't care to tell it. I'm here about Jimmy Taggart. Phil said you never were one hundred percent sure they had the right man. I don't think they do either."

He took a long drag from his cigarette, sat down on the couch and draped his legs on the coffee table. "In a few weeks no one will have to worry about guilt or innocence. It will be over. Not my concern any more. You want to go on a crusade? Help yourself, lady. I have more important things to do."

Sam gazed up at the ceiling where a number of holes verified Phil's account. "Most important thing is to get to the shooting range. If you really wanted to kill yourself, you wouldn't have missed so many times."

He pulled his legs off the table and stood up so fast, Sam thought he was going to lunge at her.

"What the hell do you know? Who the hell are you to come into my house, lady, and dictate to me?" His voice was hoarse but loud. His breath smelled of stale cigarettes and a three-day hangover. She calmly let him spout off until he got to the part about losing a loved one.

Sam stood and jabbed an index finger at his chest. "Just hold it, buster. At the age of five I watched my father get blown into pieces no bigger than your beer can. Don't tell me I don't know about pain, about nightmares. What makes you think you cornered the market on suffering?" She reached into her purse, pulled out a business card and flung it on the table. "When you're through pitying yourself and feel like doing something worthwhile like getting an innocent man out of prison before he's executed, give me a call. If not, you can add one more person to your nightmares."

"I just hope I didn't push him over the edge." Sam coasted to the railroad crossing, glanced both ways, then drove across.

"I wish you would pull over when you call, Sam. I prefer you keep two hands on the wheel."

"Jake, I have two hands on the wheel. I'm using the hands-free toy you purchased. Why don't you just hire a limo driver for me?"

"Don't think I haven't thought about it. Where are you?"

"Just leaving the court house. I had hoped to get a copy of the court transcripts from Taggart's trial but the one and only person who makes the copies isn't in until tomorrow."

"Sam, the damn thing is going to cost you two bucks a page. Check with Taggart's lawyer. He should have a copy."

"Good idea."

"You can call from home."

"No. I'm on my way to Benny's to take a look at the autopsy

report on Catherine DeMarco. What are you and Frank up to?"

"We may be burning the midnight oil. Ryerson gave up the shooter's name. Word is he might be hopping a flight tonight so Frank and I are staking out the airport."

"Want me to bring dinner out to you?" She could hear a breath catch in his throat as he took his time mulling over the proposition.

"Maybe I'll stop by for lunch," Jake offered in response.

"Oh sure. Like the lunch we enjoyed with Frank?"

8

"Seventeen years ago?" Benny pulled open a file drawer and sifted through folders. "DeMarco. Here we go." Sam followed the colorful Hawaiian shirt down the hall. "What are you looking for?" Benny asked.

"Pieces of a puzzle." She pulled out a carton of orange juice from Benny's refrigerator. "You wouldn't happen to have any chocolate chip cookies lying around, would you?" Sam asked.

"Sorry. There should be some in the vending machine upstairs, though." He poured himself a cup of coffee and ushered Sam to the oblong conference table. Ceiling fans droned overhead, softly rippling the posters of Hawaiian sunsets thumb tacked to the walls.

"That's okay," she said with a sigh.

"Have a new client?"

"Unfortunately, no. Just my own damn curiosity."

Benny laughed and shook his full head of coal black hair. "That's what I have always liked about you, Sam. Your curiosity." Benny Lau was the Chief Medical Examiner for Chasen Heights and one of the few people who understood her *gift*. She assumed it was because of his own native customs and traditions that gave him more of an open mind.

Benny opened the folder and pulled out a stack of pages and color photographs.

"Jack Olsen was the medical examiner back then." Benny picked up the police and pathology reports and studied them for a few minutes. "Let's see. White female, well-developed."

"Why do men have to put that in a report?"

Benny peered over the top of his glasses. "That's a clinical term, Sam, pertaining to the stage of development. Is that baby sucking out all the brain matter?" He returned to the report. "Found lying on her back five yards from an unfinished asphalt road. A hunting knife with a seven-inch serrated edge was found fifty yards away lying near a white male who appeared to be passed out due to intoxication. The victim was found at approximately twelve-fifteen in the morning and pronounced dead at the scene at twelve-forty."

Sam studied the pictures and felt a chill. It was definitely the face she had seen in her vision. Phil was right. The body was so butchered it vaguely resembled a human. She felt her breakfast rising and reached in her purse for crackers.

"Multiple stab wounds?"

"Twenty-one to be exact." Benny skimmed through the detailed autopsy report. "The wound that did the most damage was the ten-centimeter long cut below the left mandibular angle along the highest portion of the neck which severed the left carotid and right interior jugular."

"Killer was right-handed?"

"That would be my guess. There were ten cutting wounds of stab characteristics on the upper back between the base and upper quarter thoracic cage."

"She must have turned around," Sam thought aloud. "Probably tried to run away."

"The ten cutting wounds were post-mortem."

Sam looked up from the picture. "After her throat was slit?"

Benny shrugged. "Someone was pretty pissed."

"What about a toxicology report? Any sign of drugs?"

"Just alcohol."

That would explain the stumbling and dazed look, Sam thought. She shifted through the pictures again and found the ones of Catherine DeMarco on the examining table, the dried blood cleaned off, exposing the stab wounds more clearly.

"What's on the chain around her neck?"

Benny handed her pictures of personal effects. "Looks like two items on one chain. One is a small key. Haven't a clue what this one is."

Sam studied the picture. "I've seen small keys like this one used to open jewelry boxes and diaries. And this one, I'm not sure." The charm was sterling silver and resembled a tree hanging upside down with items suspended from the branches. "Looks like a knife, moon, snake, and a flower."

Benny pulled his glasses off to get a better look. "Tough to tell what kids were into back then."

"Do you have an extra photo of these items?"

"Sure."

Sam glanced over the report again. "Phil Cannon mentioned that she had been raped but there's no indication in this report of any forced entry, only the presence of semen. Someone with such rage should have left some type of bruising, wouldn't you say?"

"That's what I would expect." He then peered over his glasses at her, almost expecting her next comment.

"If it was rape."

In lieu of the court transcripts, Sam had settled on copies of newspaper articles she had finally located. With a cup of hot tea in her hand, she stretched out on one of the window seats in the dining room. Jake never showed up for lunch as promised and she was beginning to feel like the proverbial neglected wife.

After reading the articles, Sam felt the case was just as Phil had described...open and shut. The papers had nineteen-year-old Jimmy Taggart tried and convicted before the trial even began.

After all, it had been his prints on the knife and the victim's blood on his body. The jury had recommended death by lethal injection. The sentence was to be carried out on New Year's Day.

Sam prepared a list of names on a pad of paper. Anne and Howard DeMarco had lived on Paxton. At the time of Catherine's death, Anne had been a beautician and volunteered at the hospital. Howard had worked for the post office.

Maggie and Bill Taggart had lived on Newell. Maggie had been a homemaker; Bill had owned a butcher shop. Sam's first guess was the couple probably split town as soon as possible after the trial.

Rose Chavez, a girlfriend of Jimmy's, had sobbed hysterically on the stand that Jimmy was innocent. She hadn't known about Jimmy's relationship with Catherine. And Jimmy hadn't known that Rose was two months pregnant.

Paul Goddard had given expert, detailed testimony of how and where Jimmy had been found. A lot of man hours had been spent on this high-profile case.

Doctor Jack Olsen gave a gruesome account of the condition of the body. Every drop of blood had drained from the multiple stab wounds and especially from the severed carotid artery.

Sam rubbed her eyes and stared past the flagstone patio to the one hundred acres of land. It was by sheer misfortune that Sam lived in a five-bedroom, five-bathroom house, and not a penny owed. All inherited when her father and Melinda died.

Material things aren't worth much if you're dead. They don't do you any good in the afterlife. From reading the articles it was easy for Sam to see that so many people lost so much. The DeMarcos lost their only child; the Taggarts were about to lose a son; Rose lost her true love; and her child lost years that he or she could have spent with its father.

What if she was wrong? What if Taggart was guilty? Would she be doing more harm than good stirring up the pot again? Sam felt a hand on her shoulder.

"You are having doubts," Abby said as she sat down next to her daughter.

"I was just going through these articles. All the evidence points conclusively to Taggart."

"Sometimes trails are made to look like they lead somewhere."

"I know. I guess I'm afraid that if I start digging, I'm going to stir up a lot of pain for a lot of people."

"There's only one person's pain you should be concerned with. If the wrong man is executed, her pain will never be eased. She will never be at rest."

9

it was up earlier than usual the next morning. He didn't toss
and turn for the typical reasons. Last night the facts from the
Taggart case tumbled and rolled in his head. He had told
himself to leave it alone, don't get involved. Lord knows he had
enough problems of his own.

Three times this morning he had walked to the closet in the
spare bedroom, the closet where the boxes containing Colleen's and
Megan's clothes were stored. But he just couldn't bring himself to
turn the doorknob. He lost count of the number of times in the past
three years he had called Goodwill to rid himself of the painful
reminders of his wife and daughter and then called back to cancel
the pick-up.

Returning to the kitchen, he poured himself another cup of
coffee and sat at the table in the breakfast nook, the little alcove
overlooking the backyard. A square patch of sand marred the
otherwise manicured lawn. He wasn't sure what happened to the
swing set. All he remembered was the fit of rage that prompted him
to rip the thing out of the ground years ago. If his neighbors
removed it, they must have done so under the cloak of darkness.

Pit lit a cigarette and stared at the business card in front of him.
Samantha Casey, Investigator. How the hell could she be a P.I. if she

was still a cop? And she would have had to work two years with an existing firm before getting a license. Suspended. He wondered what that was all about. It pays to read the newspapers rather than let them pile up. And what kind of information could she have about the Taggart case?

He set the cigarette in the ashtray, returned to the spare bedroom, and stood in front of the closet door. He would be a fool to get involved, he told himself. He had better things to do. But a voice in his head said, *Like what? Like feeling sorry for yourself?* That's what Sergeant Casey had said.

Pit wrapped his fingers around the doorknob and yanked. The five boxes sat on the floor inside, all taped and labeled, ready to go. Ready to LET go. But he wondered if he ever would be ready. A brown file box rested on the top shelf. With a forceful tug, he had the box in his hands and a swirl of dust circling his head. He carried the box into the kitchen.

What could he have missed? His gut had told him seventeen years ago that something wasn't right but he couldn't place his finger on it. Why would he think he could figure it out now? *Not your problem, leave it alone,* another voice in his head said as he lifted the lid and started pulling out the files.

The DeMarco house was a brick split-level with a side driveway leading to an unattached two-car garage. It was in the middle of a well-kept residential block of cookie-cutter houses with Christmas wreaths hanging on front doors and elaborate holiday displays in front yards. Sam was dreading this meeting which is why she decided to show up unannounced.

"Can I help you?" The woman was out of a Norman Rockwell picture. She wore a solid pink bib apron over a floral shirtdress. Her face was flushed and framed in short, gray hair. The smell of furniture polish mixed with pine cleaner escaped from the open door. Sam handed her a business card.

"Detective Sam Casey, Mrs. DeMarco. I'd like to talk to you about Catherine."

"Catherine?"

"Who is it, Anne?" From behind Anne a stocky man appeared. He was a head taller than Anne with thinning hair and small, pale eyes.

Sam stepped into the living room of hodge-podge furniture. Soft, metallic dings from the grandfather's clock to Howard's left ticked off ten o'clock. The wall behind the clock was covered with a cream and green flocked wallpaper. On the wall were countless pictures of Catherine...in a pink tutu for a dance recital, her first communion picture, school cheerleading, prom. Surrounding each picture were crucifixes in a variety of sizes.

"So, you're with the Chasen Heights Police Department?" Howard asked. "Pardon our being a little jumpy. We weren't expecting anyone from the police department."

Anne motioned her to a side chair. Howard took a seat next to his wife on the sofa. Their fingers interlocked and a look of anxiety crossed their faces.

"They make such cute clothes these days," Anne said as she admired Sam's maternity outfit. "Nothing like what we had in my day." Her voice trailed off and she stared nervously at her hands. "Can we get you anything to drink?"

"Tea would be nice." Anne left Sam alone with Howard, who fidgeted with the buttons on his sweater. Sam tried to focus on the white artificial tree in the window with meager presents underneath. It looked as though the holidays in the DeMarco house had lacked enthusiasm for probably seventeen years. She pulled her notepad out of her purse and flipped it open just as Anne returned with a tray. Once her tea was poured, Sam settled back and met two sets of nervous eyes.

"How long have you lived here?"

"Twenty-two years," Anne replied. "We liked the schools." Anne hesitated and looked quickly at Howard.

"Did you have some information?" Howard asked.

"Did Catherine ever mention anyone named Wy-chin-sky?"

"Wy-chin-sky?" Howard thought for a moment, then looked at Anne. "I don't believe so."

"Did she date a lot?"

"Sergeant, all these questions were asked seventeen years ago," Howard pointed out.

"We're just trying to tie up some loose ends." Sam showed them the picture of the key and charm Catherine had worn at the time of her death. "Did this charm have any significance?"

"Catherine was always buying charms. She had a charm bracelet. Every girl did," Anne replied.

"What about the key? Did it perhaps belong to a diary?"

Anne jammed a hand into her apron pocket and withdrew a hankie which she promptly proceeded to ply and twist with her fingers. Howard studied Sam's business card again.

"It says here you're a private investigator. Just who is it you are working for?"

Sam took a deep breath. Her hopes of getting at least ten minutes of their attention were quickly fading.

"There's a possibility that Taggart didn't kill your daughter."

"Oh my god." Anne's hand clamped over her chest.

Howard rose slowly. "Get out of my house, NOW. We want nothing to do with anyone who is looking to get that demon a last minute appeal." Anne started sobbing.

Sam stood reluctantly, trying desperately to delay her departure. "Mrs. DeMarco, don't you want to make sure your daughter's killer is punished? The real killer?"

Howard rushed to the door and pulled it open. "Detective, as far as we're concerned, they have the killer. Now don't you ever set foot on our property again."

"I didn't mean to upset you."

"OUT," Howard yelled.

Sobs seeped from the house and followed Sam to the curb. This hadn't been one of her better ideas.

Sam recognized the woman with the full head of dark curly hair entering the restaurant. Jackie Delaney, one time high-priced call girl, part-time informant, was now owner of a very successful lingerie shop. *Jackie's Boutique* was where Sam had purchased most of her tasteful nightgowns.

Jackie raked her long nails through her hair and searched the restaurant. When she spotted Sam, Jackie rushed as fast as her short, tight, skirt would allow. Although her black silk blouse was conservatively high cut, she had a massive bustline that stretched the fabric to the limit. She waved in a *yoo hoo* motion and called out, "Sam, honey."

Heads swiveled as they watched the attractive black woman maneuver on five-inch stacked, ankle-wrap heels.

Sam slid out of her side of the booth and they embraced like childhood friends. Jackie patted Sam's stomach. "How soon till you pop that little bun?" She slid into the booth and flashed her best Whitney Houston smile.

"Four more months."

"Four?" Jackie's eyes widened.

"I know, I look about seven months."

"Healthy baby, darlin'." She picked up a menu and said, "I am starving."

Baker's Square was beginning to fill with customers, constant chatter, and crying kids. The high-backed booths managed to tame most of the noise level. The restaurant was across the street from the Three Oaks Shopping Center and was a favorite among shoppers. They ordered the moment they caught the attention of their eyebrow-pierced waitress.

"How's business?" Sam asked. Jackie also had a very prosperous business in the back building that involved a sex talk phone service and scantily clad female dancers.

"Wonderful. Runs like clockwork. I just sit back and collect the money. Of course, I do all of the ordering and meet with the sales-people."

"You always had good taste in clothes, Jackie, not to mention knowing what, uh…"

"What men like?" Jackie's head flipped back like a Pez dispenser as she let out a full-throated laugh. "That I do, sugar."

Their order came and after the waitress left, Jackie said, "Speaking of men, how is that hunk you are married to?"

Sam smiled.

"Ahhh." Jackie pointed her fork at her. "That smile speaks volumes. Your mother probably has the right idea. Arranged marriages can have their advantages. Although I could never have trusted my mama. She was married four times. Couldn't get it right with her own life." She organized her plates as though the food had some specific order.

"It wasn't exactly arranged," Sam said. "Arranged is more like when mothers get their heads together when their children are infants. Mine was different. Abby saw someone with qualities she liked and selected my husband, much to my dislike, at first."

"But mother knows best."

Sam smiled again.

"Yes she does." Jackie emitted another throaty laugh.

"I'm still trying to get my bearings with Jake. There are so many things he keeps private."

"Strong, silent type. Women love men who are quiet and brooding. Every woman thinks she is the only one who can get him to open up. Don't play that game." Jackie attacked her food with zest.

Sam watched Jackie's fork move in synchronized stabs. Back

and forth. It amazed her the amount of food her friend managed to pack away and still stay thin.

"Is that all you are going to eat?" Jackie pushed her empty plates away and searched for the dessert menu.

"Just soup is fine. I find I do much better eating lots of small meals rather than three large ones." Sam's attention was drawn to the pictures of the pies in the menu Jackie held.

"You're going to have some, right?"

Sam shook her head. "I'd feel guilty."

"Since when?"

"I just would, trust me." Sam pulled a photograph from her purse and unfolded it. "Do you have any idea what this is?"

Jackie dragged the picture across the table and studied the charm design. Sam explained the DeMarco case.

"Were you in town then?"

Jackie shook her head. "I was in high school in Seattle." She thought for a moment. "Or was it California? Hard to tell," she added with a shrug. "I think that was when mama was with hubby number two who was in the Army and we moved around a lot." She squinted and studied the items dangling from the limbs of the tree. "This looks like a snake and this one is a rooster head. Uh oh."

"Know what it is?"

"Suweeet mother of gawd!" Jackie's sudden outburst brought stares from customers at nearby booths.

"What?"

Jackie leaned in and mouthed, "Witchcraft!"

10

Pit pushed away from the kitchen table, stood, and stretched. The clock above the stove read three o'clock. He had been at this most of the day and the acid from the endless cups of coffee on an empty stomach was making him nauseous.

"What on earth could you possibly discover that I couldn't, lady?" He remembered his visitor yesterday. She was determined, a little too smart-mouthed for his liking, but sometimes police work will do that to you. She was pregnant and he had been ready to physically throw her out of the house. What had he become? A recluse with no use for friends or neighbors, pissing away his time trying to build up the guts to end his life.

Jimmy Taggart's life was about to end. And Pit hated those nagging doubts, the ones that had kept him up half the night after Taggart's arrest and conviction. And the ones that had kept him up last night. Sam Casey had managed to rekindle those doubts and force him out of hibernation, all in a matter of five minutes.

He remembered she had said she was suspended. Why? Probably opened her mouth to the wrong person. But she had mentioned something about murder. He carried the box of case files into the living room and set it on the coffee table. Next he pulled a black bag from under the oak secretary and carried it into the kitchen.

"Let's see what the newspapers have to say about you, Sergeant." Pit pulled the laptop from the bag and plugged it in. While the computer booted up, he popped a frozen potpie into the microwave and grabbed a can of beer from the fridge. With his finger under the pop-top, he hesitated, then returned the beer to the refrigerator and poured himself a glass of orange juice.

Sam checked the answering machine on the kitchen wall phone. One blinking light. "Finally." Expecting a message from Pit Goddard, she pushed the PLAY button. But the call wasn't from Pit. It was a message from an Agent David Brackin with the FBI. Puzzled, she replayed the message to make sure it was for her and not Jake. The agent hadn't left a number, just a message that he would try back.

Hearing voices in the study, she walked in to find Abby and Alex adding ornaments to the Christmas tree. There were two trees in the house. The one in the study was decorated with multi-colored lights, animated ornaments, and a porcelain Santa treetop dressed in a fur-trimmed velvet coat. A Lionel train set that had been her father's sat in a corner waiting to be assembled under the tree. Many of the ornaments were antiques and spending the day decorating the trees with Abby had always been a tradition. A second tree in the sitting room by the front door had special meaning. All of the decorations were handmade by the children living on the Eagle Ridge Reservation. It was trimmed in raffia and feathers and topped with a miniature feathered headdress.

"The trees have been up for a week, Mom. What could you possibly add?" Sam fingered a ceramic ornament shaped like a birdhouse.

"Your mother was watching Martha Stewart again." Alex dug through a large bag with something less than enthusiasm. He set Abby's latest purchases on the couch.

"You shouldn't be doing a lot of climbing, Samantha. Alex is helping."

"Hmmppf," Alex snorted. "You would do a much better job, Sam. Your mother complains when I put identical ornaments too close together."

Sam tightened the band around Alex's gray ponytail and straightened the silver conch at the top of his shirt. "Why don't you make a pot of tea and I'll help Abby finish."

His bronze skin crinkled when he smiled. "Saved."

Sam climbed the step stool and draped the honeysuckle vine garland across the top branch of the tree. The lit candles on the bar emitted the fragrance of evergreen throughout the house. Abby loved a real tree but ten years ago she had developed an allergic reaction to the tree sap. So she bought an eight foot artificial tree for the study and a twelve foot tree for the sitting room.

Abby circled the tree with the garland and handed it back to Sam. "Do you have any idea what we can buy Jacob for Christmas?"

"He could probably use a new leather coat. His got ripped by an uncooperative prisoner." They worked in tandem, each taking one side of the tree laying the vine across the branches.

"Alex and I had something else planned," Abby said as Alex set the tray of cups and a teapot on the bar.

Alex grumbled. "He won't like it. He'll feel like he should be in a dogsled race."

"You remember a few people on the reservation are raising alpacas to make coats and jackets," Abby said. "Wait til you see them, Samantha."

Sam stepped down from the stool and walked over to the bar. "One with a hood?" She tried imagining Jake in a rust and cream patchwork coat with a fur-trimmed hood and found herself agreeing with Alex. Jake was always hot and she couldn't imagine him bundled in a heavy Sherpa coat made more for a Siberian winter.

"What did he wear this morning?"

"His trench coat," Abby said. "I guess we could buy him a new leather coat but the ladies on the reservation do such a beautiful job with the alpacas."

"No use trying to replace his stolen one. He'll be stubborn, want to pay for it himself," Alex said. "Doesn't seem to want to take anything from you, Sam. Like he wants you to know he can pay his own way. *Wankeya.*" Ridiculous.

"Reminds me of someone else." Sam winked at Alex. She stepped back and admired the tree. Lights were tucked in close to the trunk and reflected off mirrored and crystal ornaments. Porcelain Santa heads with flowing beards were clamped in place. Bouquets of silk mauve poinsettias were tucked between the branches.

"It's beautiful, Mom."

"You say that every year."

Sam set her teacup down and pressed a button on the fifteen-inch Santa on the bar. He was seated and holding a book. The animated figure proceeded to read *Twas the Night Before Christmas.* Sam flitted around the room as she did every day, pressing the button on each of the animated figures and soon the room was filled with music and voices as carolers sang and music played.

"You guys really get into this stuff." Jake stood in the doorway, eyes drifting from figures on the floor to the bar to the train Alex was busy assembling.

"Isn't it wonderful?" Sam wrapped her arms around his waist.

"We do love decorating," Abby said with a sigh. "There is nothing more joyful than seeing a child's eyes the first time you turn the tree lights on. I have been collecting the animated figures since Samantha was old enough to walk."

Alex rolled his eyes. "Should have bought stock in Eveready batteries."

Jake gave the tree a cursory examination. "Not bad." He folded his arms, fingers clenched around a newspaper, and glared at Sam. "Did you touch my poinsettia plant?"

Sam's face flushed as she gulped out, "Only a tap."

"I don't think even Abby's green thumb can revive this one." Jake unfolded the early edition of tomorrow's paper and handed it to her. "You made the headlines, sweetheart."

Sam glanced over the headline and read a portion of the article out loud.

> *Detective Sergeant Sam Casey has found something new to while away her suspension time—finding ways to grant James Taggart a last-minute appeal. Anne and Howard DeMarco have confirmed that Sergeant Casey has tried to interview them regarding their daughter's murder. Perhaps Sergeant Casey should spend more time clearing her own name first.*

"Well, that didn't take long." Sam folded the paper and tossed it on the bar.

Eighty miles away Lonnie Dahlkamp was watching the news on the television set in his trailer home in Plymouth, Indiana. He almost tripped running to turn up the volume.

"Damn." He smiled slowly revealing stained teeth as large as Chiclets. "More, I want more," he yelled at the screen as the newsman cut away to the weather. Lonnie grabbed the channel changer and clicked repeatedly looking for similar reports on other stations. Stained sweatpants hung on his narrow hips. The cold linoleum floor stung his bare feet.

He fumbled his way to the couch, stumbling over stacks of old

magazines and bags of used clothing. Continuing his channel surf-
ing, he sank back onto the limp cushions. Fingers with nails chewed
to the quick picked at tufts oozing from a tear in the armrest. Matted
hair stuck out as if someone had been picking similar tufts out of his
head.

"Lady Luck finally come my way." He jumped from the couch
and ran into the bedroom. "Where did you put it, Mama?"

The one bedroom trailer didn't afford him the luxury of his
own space. Emma Lou Dahlkamp had passed away a month before
Lonnie was released from prison. It had been quick. A massive
heart attack during bingo at the local American Legion. Emma Lou
had plopped face down on her twenty-four bingo cards taped
across her section of the table. A parade of two-inch-high troll
dolls stood vigil over Emma Lou and her cards while Hank Butler
kept spewing out bingo numbers. It wasn't until five minutes after
someone yelled "bingo" and Hank's wife was walking around selling
raffle tickets that someone noticed Emma Lou wasn't napping.

Lonnie ran a hand through his unruly hair and studied the
boxes stacked to the ceiling in all four corners. Emma Lou had
been a garage sale junkie. The boxes were filled with glassware,
cookie jars, cheap jewelry, empty perfume bottles, and every other
useless piece of junk most people dump in the garbage. Each item
was wrapped in newspaper.

"Aw, shit! How the hell am I gonna find anything?" Emma Lou
had cleaned out Lonnie's apartment and brought his belongings to
her trailer after his last excursion to prison. He hadn't thought
twice about what he owned nor had she asked any questions.

Lonnie opened the closet door and grimaced. He hadn't given
much thought to the envelope in years. "Oh, lordy, I hope she didn't
throw it out." He pulled boxes down from the shelf and ripped them
open. Frustrated, Lonnie returned to the living room and moved
through the sea of clutter, tearing at boxes and moving aside
glassware and old cookie jars.

After thirty minutes of pushing his way between stacks, Lonnie studied the gap between the wall and the back of the couch. Kneeling on the tattered cushions, he poked his head in the space and found a dark plaid suitcase. It was worn and faded. Lonnie recognized it as one Emma Lou had purchased for him at a yard sale.

He pulled the suitcase onto the couch and unsnapped the locks. In it were towels, sheets, a thin blanket, old magazines, and junk mail…items from his apartment. Lonnie dug through the suitcase until he came to the bottom. The brown envelope lay flat, its corners bent. He sat down and pulled out the contents. Everything was there.

11

S am held the brass button up to the light and studied the design. What could *MB* stand for? The obvious answer was a designer. But her search through the Internet of just the initials or a list of designers left her with a dizzying list of possibilities.

The music from *Nightline* filtered in from the study. She assumed Jake was sitting on the couch, one eye on the television set, the other perusing any one of a variety of newspapers. It was as though the ten o'clock news wasn't enough. Then again, he could be brooding over the fact that DEA had the airport staked out the other night and claimed jurisdiction over the drive-by shooter.

Tightening her fist around the button, Sam tried to conjure up more details of that fateful night seventeen years ago but her mind was a blank. She pushed away from the kitchen counter and stood. Maybe she had to be back at the construction site. She peered through the pass-through into the dining room. Her purse wasn't on the table. Neither was it in the kitchen.

Damn. It had to be in the study. Now the trick was getting past Jake. She would have to wing it. Pausing in the doorway, Sam spotted her purse next to the stack of newspapers on the coffee table. As usual, Jake was lounging on the couch, legs crossed at the ankles and propped on the coffee table, his attention riveted on the television. A fire crackled in the corner fireplace providing the only light other than the Christmas tree.

"What?" Sam smiled serenely as she entered. "No bed time cigarette?"

"Ran out. I forgot to stop and pick some up on the way home." His index finger tapped repeatedly on the remote, searching through the stations until he found CNN.

"No problem. I'll go get you some." She whisked her purse off the table and took several long strides toward the front door when a muscular arm shot out and Sam was pulled gently down onto Jake's lap.

"That was too damn easy." His finger tapped the remote and the television clicked off. Slowly he leaned sideways until Sam was lying on the couch, her legs across his lap, Jake's elbow propping up his head. "Want to tell me what you're up to?" His right hand roamed up the back of her leggings.

Sam blinked. Jake's FBI training had served him well. Always suspicious. Even at the office his eyes swept his surroundings, searching shadows, rarely leveled at the person talking to him, as if some sniper were lurking in a corner. And he was doing it now. His gaze glossed over the bookcases, the computer desk, and then retraced her steps from the doorway. His gaze made a similar sweep of her features, his breath hot on her neck.

"Cat got your tongue?" His mouth hovered over hers.

"Tough to concentrate when you've got your hand on my ass," she finally replied.

"No problem," he whispered as he slowly moved his hand under her top and gently caressed her breast. His left hand played with tendrils of curls spilling around her head. He clasped a length and inhaled its fragrance.

"No fair," she whispered back, her voice hoarse as she felt his lips on her ear. Thoughts of leaving the house were a fleeting memory.

"Where did you say you were going?"

"Ummm." Sam gasped as she felt his tongue flick her earlobe.

"You were planning to sneak back to the construction site, weren't you?"

Damn. "Thought did cross my mind."

"No," he whispered.

"Jake," Sam protested, trying to ignore what his right hand was doing. She struggled to sit up but he was as immovable as a slab of granite.

"It's late and it's cold."

"I have a coat."

His mouth trailed down the side of her neck. "I can think of something better to do."

She stopped struggling and spent a few pensive moments. "How about a compromise?"

Jake lifted his head. "I'm all ears."

"Shine the light over here." Sam pointed to a section bordering the asphalt.

"Honey, we've been over this section three times already." Jake stooped down and ran a hand rake through the dirt. "They've already paved the driveway. What did you hope to find?"

"I don't know. Something...anything." Gravel crunched under her boots as she made her way to the drive. "Do you know an Agent Brackin?" She told Jake about her phone call from the FBI.

"No. What did he want?"

"Didn't say. Didn't even leave a number. Just left a message that he'd call back. Thought maybe he meant to call you." She watched him weave the rake through the dirt and debris. His trench coat barely looked warm enough to stave off the night air. "You really need something heavier to wear."

"I already ordered a new leather coat. Should have it in a couple days."

"You sure don't leave anything for Santa to bring." She watched him through the glare of the flashlight and wasn't surprised when he said he had everything he needed. Alex was right.

Jake pulled the collar up on his coat and stepped over to the driveway. "There's nothing here, Sam. And don't even think about chopping up the asphalt."

She sighed. He not only didn't find anything else in the area where she had located the button, he also wasn't going to give any hints of what he wanted for Christmas.

Looking up into the evening sky, she easily picked out the constellation Orion. Her breath came out in wisps of frosty air. It had been a wasted trip and all she could think of was the warm fireplace back home. She turned and faced the clearing, remembering the young girl who had stumbled out of the woods only to encounter a deadly fate. While her fingers twirled the button in her pocket, she slowly walked to the clearing.

She kept waiting for the crescent moon to change to a full moon and the chilly air to become hot and muggy. With a sigh of disappointment, she picked her way toward the woods. Dark shadows danced among the trees as she approached and deep pockets were swathed in ethereal fog. Her head told her to turn around and go back to where Jake was, where there was more light. Instead, she wrapped her fingers tightly around the button and trudged on, dried weeds slapping against her boots.

The tree line loomed ahead like a majestic mountain and she waited for her eyes to become accustomed to the dark. Sam tried sorting out in her head details from the police report as to where Jimmy and Catherine had spread their blanket and engaged in heavy breathing. Fifty yards from the body. That was what was written in the report. Sam had already covered twenty yards so she mentally walked off twenty more paces, her eyes easily picking out a path. After twenty paces, she was at the edge of the woods. She gathered her blanket coat tighter and picked her way cautiously around gnarled underbrush. Thinking back to the morning of her walk, she vaguely remembered a smaller clearing somewhere to her right. That would put it about fifty yards from where Catherine's body had been found.

A dead branch snapped somewhere close by followed by the scuffling of dried leaves. She held her breath. Was it animal or human, she wondered. A shadow moved in the distance and Sam strained to make out a shape.

The sweater coat felt heavy and hot and Sam's mind started playing tricks. Did she just feel hot because of her heart slamming in her chest? Or has the button clenched in her fist brought her back to that fateful night seventeen years ago and she is seeing the killer lurking in the bushes?

Once her heart stopped pounding in her ears and she didn't hear any more rustling ahead, she continued down the path. Branches reached out like bony fingers and after a few more feet, Sam found herself in a small opening in the woods.

A thin mist swirled around the forest floor, snaking around the trees. She felt as if she were on the grounds of some gothic castle waiting for the drawbridge to lower. The thought of gothic castles brought images of vampires, bats, and ghosts, sending a chill up her spine.

Another movement rustled several feet from her and suddenly a bright flash popped in front of her eyes. Sam let out a scream and within seconds, a flood of light appeared to her right. She let out another scream, shielding her eyes.

"DON'T MOVE. POLICE!" Jake bellowed.

"Don't shoot. Don't shoot." A youth dressed in black jerked his hands up and turned to face Jake. "I have identification," the youth stammered.

"KEEP YOUR HANDS UP." Jake's Sig Sauer was leveled on the young man.

"You okay?" Jake asked Sam as he handed her the flashlight.

"He just startled me, that's all."

"Up against the tree," Jake ordered. The youth faced the tree and Jake patted him down, located his wallet in the back pants pocket. Keeping the gun trained on him, Jake flipped the wallet open with his left hand. Sam shined the flashlight on the driver's license.

"Larry Matlock, Matteson, Illinois. Little far from home, Larry," Jake said.

"I wasn't trespassing. Just getting some photos of the crime scene for the newspaper," the youth blubbered. His hair was shaved except for a bowl-shaped swatch at the top which was long and gathered up in a ponytail.

Several business cards for various newspapers as well as a press pass were tucked under one of the flaps. "You can put your hands down," Jake said.

"I'm a freelance photographer. I thought I'd get pictures of the crime scene, you know, taken at night, around the time of the crime. Thought it would be more real, you know?" He stole glances at Jake's gun while sweat glistened on his forehead. His face was pudgy and seemed out of place on his thin frame.

Several feet away a blanket was stretched out on the ground. Jake placed a hand on Sam's wrist and directed the beam to the area. A camera on a tripod stood nearby. Jake shoved his gun back into its holster, walked over to the tripod, and fumbled with the camera. He removed the film and placed it in his pocket. The last thing he wanted was for any newspaper to have a picture of Sam.

Larry didn't say anything, just let his doe eyes blink from the camera to Jake's pocket.

Jake studied the blanket again, then the tripod. With a piercing gaze toward the youth, he demanded, "Where's the girl?"

"Huh?" Larry blinked quickly, jerked his head to the blanket. "I'm here alone."

The realization of what Jake was alluding to hit her. "Oh how sick," Sam blurted.

"You can come out now," Jake shouted into the woods.

Larry's face reddened as bushes rustled and a husky blonde emerged. Her eyes were ringed in black and she lumbered from the woods like an overweight raccoon.

"I told you we'd get caught," the blonde hissed.

"Recreate that night, right. Get your things," Jake ordered. "You're trespassing."

Larry gathered up his tripod as his girlfriend pulled the blanket off the ground.

"Where's your car?" Jake asked as the two started to walk toward the construction site.

"I have it parked at the sub shop a block away." The youths continued walking.

"That was really sick." Sam shuddered in the dark thinking of the two romping on the blanket while the camera on a timer clicked snapshots. She could imagine the picture in a tabloid paper. Two figures groping on the blanket, faces hidden, and a headline that read, *What really happened that fateful night?*

Jake turned to Sam and pulled up the hood on her coat. She lowered the flashlight to avoid seeing the scowl that was forming. He pulled the flashlight from her and led the way back to the construction site. Once they were clear of the trees and bushes, he wrapped a protective arm around her and pulled her close.

"Why did I let you talk me into this?"

"I have you wrapped around my finger?"

After a few beats, Jake said, "I needed a pack of cigarettes."

12

S am was thrilled to see the visitor at her door the next morning cradling a cardboard box in his arms. "Mr. Goddard. I'm glad you reconsidered."

"I passed your gate three times. Didn't think this place could possibly be yours," he said as his head tilted up, eyes taking in the cathedral ceiling and the potted poinsettia plants lining the staircase. His gaze drifted from the pottery on the fireplace mantel to handmade rugs and wall hangings as he followed Sam down the three stairs.

"It's homey," Sam replied with a smile, knowing to some people it was more than just homey.

He set the box on the dining room table and shrugged out of his baseball jacket.

Sam studied her visitor for a few seconds. His hair, glistening with threads of gray, had been cut short and smoothed back. The stubble was gone, leaving skin pink and raw from a long-overdue shave. "You clean up rather nicely." He flashed an uncomfortable smile and she noticed he had those basset hound eyes, eyes that turned down at the corners. And the blue seemed pale against skin that was in dire need of sunlight.

Abby entered with a tray and Sam made the introductions.

Pit's eyes riveted on the pastry and fruit. Abby asked Sam, *"Tan yan nistima he?"* Did you sleep well? They walked arm and arm into the kitchen and shared a laugh.

"What were you speaking?" Pit asked Sam when she returned.

"Lakota," Sam replied. "We're Sioux. Well, at least half of me is, but all of Abby is." She nodded toward the tray of sugar-coated bread. "Fry bread is a Native American tradition."

His eyes danced from her feathered earring down to the medicine bundle hanging from her neck. Pit shifted from one foot to the next and his hands moved repeatedly from the box to his pants pockets.

"Could you please sit down? You make me want to check you for an on/off switch." Sam pulled out a chair and looked eagerly at the folders in the box. Pit finally took a seat and busied his hands pulling out file folders. "Wonderful, you have a copy of the court transcripts." She also noticed copies of newspaper articles on some of her prior cases and especially the Stu Richards case.

Pit's face flushed. "Sorry. After you stopped by, I accessed back issues of the *Chasen Heights Post Tribune* on their web site to find out more about you."

"No problem."

"Is the shit in these articles true?"

"Guess you have a chance to find out." She reached into her pocket and pulled out the button. Setting it in the middle of the table, Sam watched Pit's reaction. "What brought you here?" she asked. "You didn't seem interested when I met you."

"Curiosity. After seeing the articles I was curious why this seventeen-year-old case caught your attention." Pit picked up the button and examined it while Sam explained how she found it and its significance.

A deep crease formed between his eyebrows. "This is it?" He turned the button over in his hand, then tossed it on the table. "I thought you might have something a little more concrete, like a prisoner who talked in his sleep. What the hell am I supposed to do with that?"

Sam wasn't too surprised at his reaction. It was the same doubt Jake and Frank displayed when she first worked with them. "You already knew from the newspaper stories how I do my work. I find it hard to believe that you expected something more. How do you explain how I knew all the details? I even knew what Catherine looked like."

"I don't know." Pit sank back in his chair and poured a cup of coffee with a shaking hand. "Guess I was hoping the press was just sensationalizing your cases. This is all pretty new to me."

Sam wondered how long it had been since Pit had left his home. He was a far cry from the man with puffy eyes who was in desperate need of a shower and shave. Yet he seemed jittery out of his comfort zone.

"Tell me, Sam. Did Phil tell you about me or did it all just kinda' come to you?"

"Phil told me. But I deal mainly with dead bodies."

He stared at her with those sad, puppy eyes as his fingers danced around his shirt collar, then under his v-neck sweater. He pulled out a pack of cigarettes and tossed them on the table. "I guess old-fashioned police work didn't do it before. I'm game to try anything."

Sam smiled. "Great. First thing I'd like to do is read the trial transcripts."

He passed a stack of papers across the table. "I highlighted the important areas."

She nodded toward the tray. "You eat while I read." It was obvious by the look on his face that he had never seen fry bread but he took a cautious bite and mumbled his approval. Sam asked, "If the case was considered closed, why did you hang onto all these files? Phil said that something bothered you."

"Gut instincts, I guess. I don't know. Everything seemed too perfect. The trail of blood led to Taggart. The knife, the finger-prints. I've been led too many times down a flowery path and boy did I feel led by a bullring on this one. Everything pointed just a little too neatly to Taggart."

"But no other suspects."

"None."

Sam sifted through papers and came across the picture of Catherine's necklace. "What about these charms? Mrs. DeMarco claimed Catherine didn't have a diary."

"I heard about your trip to the DeMarcos. I'm sure their response didn't surprise you," Pit said.

"Not really. Maybe they wouldn't have been so quick to throw you out since you're a familiar face."

"I doubt it. They've been in denial for seventeen years. I wouldn't be surprised if they still had Catherine's clothes in her closet and her bed made." He stopped as he realized he was describing how he treated his own wife's and daughter's possessions. "What's this about a diary?"

"When I told Mrs. DeMarco that the key Catherine wore might have belonged to a diary, she got very agitated. I think I might have hit on something. If Mrs. DeMarco lied about it to you, maybe it's because there are some things Catherine wrote that they didn't want known. Maybe we both can go back tomorrow."

"I'd rather try to set up a meeting with Art Bigalow, Taggart's attorney."

"What about Olsen, the former medical examiner?"

"Died last year," Pit replied. "Forrest Eckart, who was the intern who assisted with the autopsy, now owns the Eckart Funeral Home."

Sam returned her attention to the photo of the charms. "I have a friend who thinks the other charm is a Wiccan symbol of some sort."

"Witchcraft?" Pit shook his head. "There wasn't proof of any type of bizarre rituals, if that's the road you are heading down. There were a few instances of animal sacrifices and strange ceremonies in the woods during Halloween but witchcraft had nothing to do with Catherine's death."

"It still might be worth checking out."

13

"I don't tolerate no parties, no drug use, and no overdue rent." The old man's mouth caved in when he stopped talking. His lips seemed to disappear into a sinkhole, filling the empty spaces where his teeth used to be. "I require two months rent up front and then the fifteenth of the month after that." J.D.'s lips disappeared again.

Lonnie counted out two hundred and fifty dollars. He wasn't going to argue. It was the cheapest place he could find in such short notice. His gaze drifted over his new digs. A couch, recliner, coffee table, and television set were crammed into the living room. Lonnie wondered if the television set was color or black and white. The green carpeting was worn in spots, the walls in need of paint. But what did he want for one-twenty-five a month? A cheap apartment over a packaged liquor store sure beat prison.

"Any questions?" J.D.'s eyes regarded the one suitcase Lonnie had set on the floor and then settled on his new tenant.

"Yeah. Where is the nearest bank?"

"American National over on Sibley."

Lonnie handed J.D. the cash. The old guy took his sweet time counting, then folded the bills neatly in half and stuffed the wad in his shirt pocket.

Once J.D. left, Lonnie carried the suitcase to the bedroom and set it on the double bed. He had packed what few toiletries and clothes he owned. His stay would be short and sweet and, hopefully, profitable.

There was barely room to walk between the marred dresser and the foot of the bed. Digging through the suitcase, Lonnie located the envelope and pulled it out. First order of business was to get a safety deposit box. Next would be to find a phone. No sense wasting too much time in town.

After checking some contacts, Jackie had come up with the name of a local Wiccan store. Sam asked her friend to tag along. They stood in front of a quaint shop called *Bell, Book and Candle.* The windows were decorated in a menagerie of black silk, candles, and flowers. The two women entered and were immediately assaulted by an array of odors. A wall to their left was filled with books on Wiccan, spells, chants, candlemaking, and meditation. Racks of scented candles, tarot cards, and crystals were scattered throughout the store. Jars of a variety of ingredients were shelved behind the cash register.

"Should I have worn my crucifix?" Jackie whispered.

Sam laughed as they dodged two young shoppers dressed in black, nails and lipstick to match. The girls sported matching pierced eyebrows and tongues.

"Wiccan is just a small segment of Paganism," Sam said. "And if you stop to think about it, being Native American, I'm Pagan. It encompasses Egyptian and Celtic, too. It's basically the spiritual belief in the Universe through Nature."

"You are very well informed."

The two women turned to see a porcelain-skinned woman with black hair, spiked and frosted in mint green. Sam wondered how much gel it took to get hair to stand on end like that. A black lace choker circled her neck and several beaded necklaces hung in varying lengths. Crystal-beaded bracelets traveled up each arm.

Sam pulled out a business card and handed it to her. "I'm looking for Tina Zagone."

The woman studied the card. Her body was draped in a black gauze fabric with an uneven, tattered hem. In a previous life, it might have covered someone's window. What was most striking about Tina were her eyes. They were the same color as the green tinting in her hair.

"You've found her, Detective." Tina's eyes swept over Sam's face. Her fingers played with the third earring of beads and feathers that touched Sam's shoulder. "Nice." Her gaze continued down Sam's frame and settled on her bulging stomach. She reached out and placed a hand on the bulge. "How sweet. A little boy. He's going to be big, like his daddy."

Sam smiled nervously and looked at Jackie.

"Now you know how you make us feel, girlfriend," Jackie said, arms folded under her massive chest.

"You've got a gift," Tina continued. "Very strong powers."

Sam was beginning to feel uncomfortable. It was funny how she easily accepted Abby's powers and especially her own but felt uncomfortable witnessing anyone else's.

"Listen, Miss Zagone," Sam started.

"Tina." She seemed to float around to the back of the counter.

Sam found herself checking to see if Tina had wheels for feet. A drapery of beads served as a door to a room behind the counter and an odor of incense drifted from behind those beads. Sam pulled the photograph from her purse and laid it on the counter.

"Can you tell me what this is?" she asked the store owner.

Tina picked up the photo and examined it closely. "It's a Cimaruta, known as the Spring of Rue charm." She slid open the glass door under the counter and brought out an identical charm.

There was something soothing and mesmerizing about Tina's

voice. It had a slow, hypnotic cadence. It was difficult to tell her age. But if she owned the shop at the time Catherine died, Sam guessed she had to be in her forties. She didn't look a day over twenty.

"It dates back centuries and was worn by Italian witches as a sign of their ancient faith."

"You mean the damn thing knows if you're Italian or French?" Jackie flicked one long talon between the charms and looked up at Tina's smiling face.

"When were you born?" Tina asked.

"Valentine's Day. A day of looovve." Jackie flashed her Whitney Houston smile. "But I ain't giving the year."

"Aquarius. I should have known. You are very confident, a self-starter, successful at most everything you do. Water and air." Tina looked at Sam. "No wonder you two get along so well."

Sam felt hairs on the back of her neck lift. Now she truly understood what people felt whenever she unveiled her own insights.

"Did you know Catherine DeMarco?" Sam asked.

"DeMarco? Don't think I have any regulars by that name."

"This would have been seventeen years ago. She was sixteen at the time of her murder. Did you own the shop seventeen years ago?"

"Murder? Oh my." She studied the charm again. "Yes, I did own the shop back then. These charms were the rage of the teens in the eighties. I haven't carried them in years."

"Is there any particular reason why someone would buy this particular symbol?"

"Rue was believed to be a magical herb," Tina explained. "People would carry some of the herb in a bag or wear a sprig of rue as a protective amulet. They would sprinkle it around their homes or bathe in it to break spells. But many did believe it was a love potion."

Jackie perked up. "Love Potion Number Nine." She started to show more interest in the charm.

Tina continued, "In the olden days women would burn the herb with lavender flowers and place it in a man's left shoe. They believed it to be a love spell. Of course, serious shop owners would not make any such claims. A true Cimaruta is four inches wide. These duplicates are just charms. See?" Tina turned the charm over. "The crescent moon depicts waxing or waning so the wearer can reflect the current phase of the moon." She returned the charm to the showcase. "Interest in Wiccan was minimal back then. Not until *Buffy* and *Charmed* did business pick up big time. Seventeen years ago they bought charms because they were unique or cute, not because of what they symbolized." She handed the photo back to Sam. "Wish I could be of more help."

"But you have been." Sam thanked her and turned to leave.

Tina said, "Be careful, Detective. I see a dark cloud hovering over you. You have an enemy."

"Weird." Jackie mumbled from the passenger side of Sam's Jeep. "Don't tell me you wouldn't have peed your pants if you looked at her driver's license and discovered she was over a hundred years old. Probably got some youth potion that keeps her looking ageless."

Sam laughed. "Thought you didn't believe in hocus pocus."

"There is only one Queen of Hocus Pocus." Jackie paused for a few beats, then added, "Of course, there is your mother. Either way, why didn't you tell me you were having a boy?"

"The doctor hasn't told me if it's going to be a boy or girl. And, truthfully, I don't want to know."

Jackie was silent for a moment as the impact of her words hit her. With a slight hesitation in her voice, she squeaked, "Lucky guess?"

After dropping Jackie off at her boutique, Sam checked the next name on her list. The Eckart Funeral Home resembled an English

Tudor gingerbread house spreading over two acres. The interior was tastefully decorated, colors not too drab or too cheery. Plush cranberry and cream-patterned carpeting greeted visitors in the foyer. A staircase of rich, dark mahogany led to the upstairs.

Forrest and his brother Jeb were a cross between television evangelists and members of the *Munster* family. They had soft-spoken, hand-over-your-wallets and save-your-soul voices, yet sinister eyes set in deep sockets. They wore matching dark blue pin-stripe suits and navy ties. Sam felt their eyes sizing her up for a casket.

Jeb closed the office door leaving Sam alone with Forrest. She was offered coffee but felt as though she needed a taste tester. Every nerve cell in her body was crying for open spaces. She was sure she was just guilty of watching too many horror movies.

Forrest sat down behind his spotless desk and asked, "How can I help you?"

For some reason the Bates Motel sign flashed in her head. Sam pulled the autopsy report from her shoulder bag and placed it in front of him. "I need to jog your memory a bit. You assisted in this autopsy."

Forrest picked up the report and looked at the date. "Oh, yes. It's hard to forget this one. She was so young, so beautiful." He thumbed through the pages. "What did you need to know?"

"Anything you can remember. I know from experience that some details are omitted from a report, unintentionally, of course. Such as the chain Catherine wore." She pointed to the pictures of the two charms.

Forrest gave the picture a passing glance. "Wasn't important. They were just charms. All the girls were into similar trinkets back then. The necklace, watch, and rings were all given to the girl's parents.

"What about the fact that she was raped? There was no mention that she was or wasn't a virgin yet it was mentioned repeatedly during the trial."

"Girl that young, coming from a prominent Christian family, attending a Christian school, there was no question that she was a virgin."

"Uh huh," Sam said doubtfully. She tapped her pen on her notepad.

"Why do you feel that an error was made? And why all the questions after seventeen years?"

"Department likes to tie up loose ends."

The intercom interrupted their conversation and, by the look on Forrest's face, Sam had a feeling Jeb was filling him in on the real reason for the visit.

"I do have another appointment, Sergeant." He handed the report back to Sam. "But feel free to call if you have any other questions." He picked up her business card and studied it. "Are you here on department business or as a private investigator?"

"Both."

Forrest smiled as he handed her back the business card. "I had a sister close to Catherine's age. I would have killed the bastard with my own hands if I had the chance. I still would."

So much for the evangelist persona.

14

"**D**oes your mother-in-law always cook like that?" Pit held the lighter for Jake.

"Usually on Sundays or when we have company." Jake clamped the cigarette between his teeth as he zipped up his jacket. They were outside on the patio, bracing against the crisp night air. Inside Sam was setting out cups and saucers while Alex helped Abby load the dishwasher.

Pit asked, "Who is this Alex guy? Hardly said a word all evening."

"He was sizing you up." Jake jammed one foot on the three-foot-high brick wall surrounding the patio and leaned his elbow on his knee. "But don't let him bother you. Alex Red Cloud claims to be Abby's protector. Abby says he's her confidante. Sam says he's a rain dancer. I say he's a little smitten with Abby." He took another long drag off his cigarette and tapped the ashes into a beer can. "He's the all-around handyman. Does the gardening, orders around the landscapers, makes herbal medicines. He likes to speak in Lakota when strangers are around. It's his way of making you feel like you don't belong."

"Rain dance." Pit smiled in amusement and pulled up his jacket collar. "Thought those were only performed out west."

"Alex is a man of many talents. He lives out back in the gate house. Even built himself a tipi."

"Tipi?" Pit's smile broadened.

"There's also a sweat lodge back there."

Pit fixed his gaze on the darkened yard. "You really picked yourself one helluva family."

"Never a dull moment."

"When did you meet Sam?"

"About seven months ago."

There was a slight lift to Pit's eyebrows as he seemed to make mental calculations.

"What can I say? She put a spell on me."

"I can understand that."

Jake jerked his gaze back to Pit and studied him. What he saw was a far cry from the suicidal wreck Phil had described. If anything, he seemed talkative during dinner, as if he had stored up words for three years and had to get them all out in one night. But he did recognize a certain look in Pit's eyes—torment. He had seen the look in other agents' and cops' eyes, men who had spent too many years on the job seeing the ugly side of life. Sometimes he saw that look in the mirror. He was sure Pit was still tormented by the death of his wife and daughter, and probably the thirteen-year-old he had shot.

"What interested you in this case again?" Jake asked him.

Pit gave a casual shrug. "I actually wouldn't have given it a second thought if it hadn't been for your wife. The execution would have come and gone. I did what I could. Thought I gave it my best shot." He inhaled long and deep, trailing the smoke out slowly through his nose. "I thought about the case a lot seventeen years ago, questioned what I might have overlooked." He glanced over at Jake. "Sam said you worked with the Bureau for a few years." Jake nodded. "Well, how would it feel if you thought, 'It would be great to get a good set of prints,' and bingo, there are the prints. Next you think, 'would be great to have a weapon,' and bang, there's the weapon all neat and tidy, practically tied in a ribbon with a great set of prints. And to top it off, you have a prime suspect right near the crime scene with a DNA match."

"You never thought once that Taggart was guilty?" Jake dropped the cigarette butt into the beer can.

"Sure, but have you ever worked a case where you felt every-thing was too easy? As if someone were yanking your family jewels by a string?"

"Guess I've had a few of those." Jake shoved his hands into the pockets of his jacket. His breath billowed out in plumes and he started missing his leather coat. "How did Sam convince you to take up this cause?"

Pit's gaze drifted toward the window box where he could see Sam standing at the island counter in the kitchen.

"She was so convincing," Pit admitted with a smile. "She's tough to say no to."

This brought a chuckle from Jake. "It's not that tough. It's just living with the consequences that's hard."

Pit laughed. It was a hearty laugh that lit up his face and erased the sadness in his eyes. They were silent for a while, staring off toward Lake Michigan at the Chicago skyline. The Sears Tower resembled a lighthouse beacon in the distance.

"How long did it take you to understand the..." Pit nodded toward the house, "...you know?"

"Never said I did. I like proof I can see and feel. Something that will stand up in court."

"So most of the time you are just pacifying a pregnant woman."

A slight smile tugged at the corner of Jake's mouth. "Something like that."

"And what about that other two or three percent?"

Jake thought back to the cases he had worked with Sam and her uncanny abilities to pluck information out of thin air. The chilly air sent a shudder through his body.

"My sentiments exactly," Pit said. He watched the interaction between Sam and Abby. Sam appeared vibrant and full of life. The love in her eyes for her mother was evident.

"Tell me, Jake. How would you feel if you lost it all tomorrow?"

Jake followed Pit's gaze. Sam was hugging Abby. She was a mirror of her mother except for her hair and eyes. There were times he wanted to turn Sam over his knee. She was a handful, to say the least.

"I almost did once," Jake replied.

"That was the car bomb which killed Chief Connelley?"

Jake nodded. "We all thought Sam was in the Jeep. I don't think I ever want to go through that again." But would he seclude himself in a house for three years not seeing or talking to anyone? Or bury himself in his work? "Do me a favor, Pit. Sam has a habit of acting before thinking. Don't be afraid to say no or to give me a heads up if she gets to be too much to handle."

"No problem."

Sam pressed her face to the screen door. "Dessert's ready."

They filed back into the dining room.

"I'll take a pass on dessert." Pit eyed the chocolate cake with thick frosting. The aroma got the best of him and he accepted a piece.

Sam watched Abby pass slices of cake down the table. Whiffs of chocolate filled the air and she could feel her mouth watering.

"I have your dessert, dear." Abby disappeared into the kitchen, then reappeared setting a dish of Jell-O in front of her.

Sam gave the dish a tap and watched the contents wiggle. "Lime," she said dully.

"Don't like it?" Jake asked.

"If anyone ever wanted to discourage me from eating dessert, all they would have to do is make it lime or put coconut in it." Sam pushed the dish away, her gaze drifting across the table, watching the bite of chocolate cake oozing in frosting disappear into Alex's mouth.

Abby placed a hand on her daughter's arm. "I'm sorry. That's the only flavor I had. Did you want something else?"

Sam watched Alex cut himself another piece of cake. She felt her head shake "no" but mentally counted how many pieces remained.

"How were the DeMarcos?" Jake asked.

"Guarded. Very guarded. And you should have seen their house," Sam replied. "It looked like the shrine of Saint Catherine's."

"What's your next move?"

"We meet with Rose Chavez at eight o'clock tonight."

"I hope this isn't too late for you," Rose Chavez said. "I wanted to wait until Emilio left. He went to a friend's house to use his computer for a study project. Please have a seat."

The two-bedroom apartment was on the third floor near the Chasen Heights High School. Rose was dressed in her nurse's uniform and apologized as she picked up clothing and gym shoes off the floor.

"Boys, they are so messy." She was soft-spoken, not overly attractive but not plain either. "Coffee?"

"Nothing, please. We just finished dinner, dessert, and a pot of coffee," Sam explained. She and Pit took a seat on the couch across from Rose. On the end table was a framed picture of a younger Rose in cutoffs and a tank top, her hair cascading down her arms. She was sitting in the lap of someone Sam assumed was Jimmy Taggart. His hair was sun-streaked and fell across his forehead. There wasn't so much a cockiness to his smile as roguishness. It was in the eyes. Jimmy's arms were wrapped protectively around Rose and Sam had a difficult time seeing anything but love and devotion on Jimmy's face. Certainly not the face of a killer.

"We don't want to take up too much of your time," Pit said. "I take it Emilio doesn't know about Jimmy."

"Actually, he does." She massaged the lotion into her rough, dry skin as she spoke. "I've never kept anything from our son. I've told him all about Jimmy, especially how I was sure of his innocence. I have always focused on his good points. How kindhearted he was, always a gentleman, respected his parents, respected me, how he has always been good at woodworking. That armoire is one of the first shop projects he completed in high school." Rose pointed to a mammoth oak cabinet standing in the corner. It had intricate designs on the panels and doorframes.

"It's beautiful," Sam said.

"But Emilio has your name, not Jimmy's," Pit pointed out.

"I can't hide the fact that having Jimmy's name would have caused Emilio problems. I have tried to shield him from that." She studied the armoire and smiled with pride. "Emilio has his talent." She grew silent for a while, then looked at them with doe-like eyes that were quick to tear. "Do you think there's a chance?"

"We won't make any promises, Rose," Sam said as she looked toward Pit, "but for now we need you to tell us anything you can."

"About what? I said everything hundreds of times."

"I know, and we apologize for making you repeat yourself," Pit said. "I know just about all of your statements but Sergeant Casey is working on it from another angle so if you could indulge her for a few minutes, she just needs you to verify a few things."

"Let's start with Jimmy." Sam could see Rose's eyes tearing at the mention of Jimmy's name. "Tell me about your visits."

"At first he wouldn't see me at all. Then I started mailing him pictures of the baby, his baby. I'd write. Then he started asking about Emilio. Finally he asked me to come visit and bring more pictures. Jimmy hadn't changed. He was still the sweetest guy, so thoughtful. The closer it got to his execution date the more withdrawn he became. About six months ago he asked me not to come anymore."

"Did you know Catherine?" Sam asked.

Rose shook her head. "I knew who she was but I didn't know her personally." She pulled a tissue from her pocket and dabbed her eyes. "We went to different schools. But kids talk. Guys said she was easy. She would sleep with anyone."

"To your knowledge, did Jimmy ever date her?"

"She flirted with everyone. Like all the guys, Jimmy was awestruck with her body. Jimmy laughed it off because he told me no one like her would ever give a guy like him a second glance. He worked in a gas station and she liked college guys who drove fast cars and had lots of money."

"Did you repeat any of this in court?"

Rose squirted more cream into the palm of her hands and worked it into her cuticles. They were nurses' hands...clean, nails trimmed and clear. The more she spoke, the harder she rubbed. "They stuck to specifics about Jimmy in court. Plus, anything I tried to say about Catherine I was told was hearsay."

"In all of your trips to visit Jimmy over the years, has he remembered anything about that night?" Sam asked.

"No. They even tried hypnosis before the trial but it was useless. He was too full of booze and pot that night. He had a bit of a wild streak, but he definitely wasn't violent."

"You were baby-sitting your neighbor's children the night of the murder, is that correct?" Sam asked. Rose nodded. "Did you have any idea Jimmy was meeting Catherine?"

"No, he was going out with friends. They hung out at Briar Woods, smoked a little, drank a little. Girls sometimes showed up but Jimmy never cheated on me. Never. He gave me his class ring the week before. Does that sound like a guy who still wanted to play around?"

"But Jimmy did have sex with Catherine that night," Pit reminded her.

Rose looked away, the hurt still fresh, a hurt she couldn't hide.

"She seduced him. He wouldn't lie to me if he remembered every-thing that happened." A brief flash of anger washed over her face. "She took advantage of him when he was too drunk to know what he was doing. Girls like that..." she stopped herself and looked over at the detectives. "I'm sorry. It's been a long day."

Sam showed her a picture of the two charms Catherine had worn. "Do you recognize either of these?"

Rose studied them for a few seconds and shrugged. "Many of the girls wore all kinds of charms. I couldn't afford any." Resentment clouded her eyes. Rose twisted the tissue and smiled apologetically. "I haven't really added much to my story. I don't know how anything I have told you can help Jimmy."

"One last question." Sam stood and slipped into her sweater coat. "Have you ever heard of the name "Wy-chin-sky?" Rose shook her head without hesitation. Sam, too, was beginning to wonder how anything she was learning was going to help Jimmy.

15

"What are they trying to do to my little girl? They just won't leave you alone, will they?" Anne DeMarco gathered her coat around her as she knelt in front of her daughter's tombstone. Clouds hung low in the sky, obstructing the morning sun.

Chapel Hill Cemetery was on the outskirts of Chasen Heights. Some of the tombstones dated back to the early 1920s. A brick archway led visitors to the newest section where a pond and walkways were supposed to make visitors feel as if they were walking through heaven's gates.

"A lot of weeds in here." Howard worked the trowel between the dead plants.

"They are all weeds. Look at them." Anne angrily touched the dead leaves of a princess rose bush. Visitors streamed in carrying blanket wreaths and poinsettia plants. She noticed buds sprouting and crocuses blooming at other gravesites. Like the trees, the plants had also been fooled by Mother Nature's spring-like weather. She returned her gaze to her daughter's desolate grave.

"I brought some fertilizer." Howard patted his wife's shoulder and walked back to the car.

Anne continued to pluck at the weeds while trying hard to keep from swearing at the plants that refused to grant her daughter one bud of color. A shadow crept over the tombstone. Anne sat back on her heels and gazed up. The woman wore a blanket shawl over a colorful blouse and long skirt. Her dark hair was pulled back in a long braid. And she wore the most stunning turquoise necklace Anne had every seen.

"Maybe it's still a little too cold to plant flowers," the woman said. She studied the tombstone. "Your daughter?"

Anne nodded. "By all rights, the crocuses and daffodils I planted should be coming out. Everyone else's are. But nothing. Nothing ever blooms here. They are all as dead as..." She muffled her sobs with a hankie. "Everything we have planted has died. Her favorite rose bush, azalea, and day lilies. Even potted plants I bring are shriveled up by the next day."

"My ancestors would say that your daughter is not at rest. That is why nothing will grow. Something in her past is unsettled, unresolved. Her spirit has not been in its final resting place since her death."

Anne slowly rose, eyes wide, her fingers continuing their torment of the lace hankie. She heard her husband's footsteps behind her. "Howard?" She turned and ran toward him. "This woman, Howard, make her stop saying those things."

Howard blinked against the morning light and looked over his wife's shoulder. "Who, Anne? What woman?"

Anne looked back and quickly scanned the surrounding area, but the Indian woman was nowhere to be seen.

"I take it you saw the papers?" Lonnie Dahlkamp sat huddled in his Chevy Impala at a Mobil gas station, the morning paper folded on the passenger seat.

"Who is this?" The voice on the other end was cautious.

"You know who it is," Lonnie said with a smile.

After a brief silence the voice said, "I thought you had left the state."

"I did...for a while. But now I'm back." He guffawed, a snorty laugh that had stayed with him since high school. "Lucky you." He snorted again.

There was a hissing on the other end of the receiver. Lonnie pulled the phone away and stared at it as if he expected something to crawl out. Pressing the phone back to his ear, a voice calm and in sudden control told him, "I'm not concerned. Everything will be taken care of soon. Our business is over. Don't call again."

"Not so fast." Lonnie unfolded the paper. "I'm sure you read the article on page three." There was another brief silence. "Certainly would be baaaad timing for information to come out about..."

"What do you want, Mr. Dahlkamp."

He laughed, pulled out a cigarette and lit it, savoring the taste and enjoying having the upper hand for once in a long time.

"Why, the American dream, of course. Money is what makes the world go round. Right?" His gaze wandered from the rear view mirror to the gas pumps, keeping his movements and reactions to a minimum so as not to draw too much attention. He turned the heat up and directed it to the floor. His feet felt like two blocks of ice.

"How much, Mr. Dahlkamp? How much this time?"

He learned a lot from the other inmates. Always ask for three times what you hope to get. That's what lawyers always do because they know the jury or opposing lawyers will chop it down to eventually the amount you were hoping for all along. He would be happy with twenty-five thousand dollars, but why stop there?

"One hundred thousand. I like round figures."

A boisterous laugh came from the receiver. "You are out of your mind."

"Well, inflation is an ass kicker. That ten thousand didn't last long. With the value of the dollar and all..."

"Twenty-five thousand, not a penny more."

"Fifty thousand and you'll never hear from me again."

There was silence on the other end of the receiver. For a while Lonnie wondered if the call had been disconnected. Finally, the voice said, "I need time."

Lonnie checked his watch. "Banks are open till five o'clock."

"You think I can get my hands on that kind of money without arousing suspicion?"

"I think you have a very creative mind and can do just about anything you want. Have the money today. Meet me at midnight at the Miller Car Wash on Torrence Avenue. And don't be late." He folded the cell phone and set it on the seat. Settling back, he let out a shaky breath and waited for his heart rate to calm down. Then he slowly smiled. It had been easier than he thought. "Oh yeah. They won't call me Lonnie Dumbkamp any more." That had been his nickname all through school. Kids would sing it on the playground. Wasn't his fault he had to repeat third and fifth grades.

Things would be different this time. He had pissed away the ten thousand on drinking and gambling. Always looking over his shoulder. Afraid someone was coming after him even though he had run as far away from Chasen Heights as his money could carry him. But the other towns had been boring.

He watched a biker pull his Suzuki up to a pump. The bike was equipped with saddlebags and a luggage box. Lonnie's eyes brightened like a kid standing outside a toy store. A nice cross-country trip, something he had always wanted to do. Fifty thousand dollars should last him a long time, if he stayed away from the bars and casinos.

Social Security checks had provided the majority of Lonnie's income most of his adult life. He no longer attended his AA meetings but he also no longer drank himself into a stupor. At forty-nine, he couldn't handle the hangovers any more.

A luggage box would be big enough to hold his belongings. He had never owned much. A few pairs of pants and shirts hung in his closet. Clean clothes and showering had never been a priority until his first stay in a downstate jail. Lonnie had itched the entire time and could swear body lice were more numerous than roaches. After his release he had spent hours taking steaming hot showers and washing every piece of clothing in bleach.

His wants were few, his goals in life non-existent. Just took it one day at a time. But if an opportunity ever crossed his path, like it did seventeen years ago, he would never pass it up.

"I don't believe you understand the severity of..." Pit started.

"I understand quite well. What you don't understand is that my son died seventeen years ago when he was arrested for the murder of that young woman and again sixteen years ago when a jury found him guilty of that murder."

Sam sat at the island counter peeling a banana while Pit paced in front of her. They had turned her kitchen and dining room into a makeshift office. Bill Taggart currently lived in Seattle, Washington. Taggart's voice was deep, strong, and she imagined him to be a fairly large man. He did nothing to hide the resentment in his voice. She took a bite of the banana and glanced over at Pit. His hands were doing their dance, looking for a place to rest. She wasn't sure if they wanted to grasp a cigarette or a can of beer.

"What about Mrs. Taggart?"

"She died two years after Jimmy was sent to prison. It killed her. In her mind, the sun rose and set on that kid and to have this happen, it..." He took a shaky breath. Sam could hear the creaking of chair legs as if Bill Taggart finally sat down after determining this was not going to be a quick phone call. "She was never the same after all that had happened. Her friends wouldn't talk to her. She was shunned at her bridge club. There wasn't one of our friends or neighbors who would give us the time of day."

"Mr. Taggart," Sam started, "in your testimony you had described Jimmy's childhood. Could you repeat it for me in your own words?"

They heard him scoff as though just talking about Jimmy wasn't worth his energy. "He was trouble, nothing but trouble since he was about seven. Had no attention span, always in trouble at school, cutting class and talking back. I caught him smoking at the age of twelve."

"What about the shoplifting charge when he was thirteen?" Sam asked as she tossed the banana peel in the garbage can under the sink.

"Those charges were dropped. Supposedly a friend of his slipped something into his pocket."

"No other arrests?"

Bill scoffed again. "Isn't one enough?"

Sam leaned her elbows on the counter and shook her head. She held back the urge to scream at the phone and tried to control her tone.

"Mr. Taggart, at any time did you believe your son was innocent of the murder of Catherine DeMarco?"

Without hesitation he replied, "No." Sam's muffled, "jezzus," did not go unheard. "Maggie and I made a good home for that boy. We were there for him for homework, little league, PTA meetings, you name it. And look what he gave us in return. Don't you go prejudging me. He was my flesh and blood. But, my god, the evidence was overwhelming." He stopped to catch his breath. "That poor girl."

Pit shook his head and mouthed the words, "hasn't changed."

"Mr. Taggart, let's forget the charges for a moment," Sam said. "As a child, did Jimmy show signs of violence? Did he kick the family dog? Light the neighbor's cat on fire? Throw rocks at birds?"

"No," he replied. "Just the opposite. He kept bringing stray pets home. Even found an injured raccoon in the forest."

Sam let him digest those words, hoping to leave him with that image of his son.

"Could you do me a favor, Mr. Taggart? I really believe your son was framed and I might be able to prove it."

"Think? Might?" Taggart spit the words out with an air of cynicism. "Where were you seventeen years ago?"

"Actually, I was only nine years old." Sam laughed, hoping to ease the tension but only a response of dead silence seeped through the telephone. "Mr. Taggart, I need to speak to Jimmy but he isn't accepting visitors. I was wondering if you could call him..."

"Are you out of your mind?" The creaking of the wooden chair accompanied his response. Sam imagined he had just shot out of his chair. "I wouldn't give him the time of day."

"I'm not asking you to do it for you, or even for Jimmy. I'd like you to do it for his mother."

Her comment was met with silence again. Sam looked over at Pit and smiled, thinking Taggart was perhaps mulling over the request. Several seconds later they heard a dial tone.

Pit filled a glass with water and leaned against the sink. "That was brutal."

"Gee, I thought I was being subtle."

"I warned you he was a tough cookie. And he hasn't changed much in seventeen years." He popped two pills into his mouth and washed them down with the water. Sam must have had a quizzical look on her face because he suddenly said, "Vitamins."

"I wasn't asking." Sam felt her face flush.

"Not verbally." He downed the rest of the water and set the glass in the sink. "I'm sure I didn't make a good impression the first day we met. But believe me, I get drunk on three cans of beer and bow to the porcelain god after five. How do you think I lost all this weight?"

Sam remained silent, hoping the crimson color on her cheeks was enough of an apology.

"You obviously haven't lost your talent for detecting," Sam finally said. "Anyway, Bill Taggart certainly didn't describe the angel who respected his parents that Rose did last night."

"Rose is in love with Jimmy. She only wants to see the good."

"I assume you checked into Rose's alibi the night Catherine was murdered."

Pit smiled. "You're putting a lot of names on your suspect list. Yes, Rose was babysitting that night."

"Did the Taggarts show any support at the trial?"

"They both sat like two wooden statues. She seemed in denial and shock most of the time and he just stared straight ahead."

Abby appeared in the doorway by the dining room, her hair pulled back in a long braid, a shawl over her shoulders. "I'm sorry to interrupt. Will you be home for dinner?" Before Sam could answer, Abby turned to Pit and said, "You will be joining us again." She didn't make it a question.

"I really don't want to intrude," Pit said.

"Yes," Sam told Abby. "Pit will be here." She checked her watch. "Could you or Alex do us a favor, Mom?" Sam scribbled dates on a piece of paper and handed it to her. "Could you stop by the library? We need copies of some Chasen Heights yearbooks."

16

The office reeked of smoke although neither the white-haired woman behind the desk or the young girl at the copier was smoking. Sam and Pit took a seat on the fabric chairs and waited for the older woman to finish her phone conversation. The name plate said Loretta Stern.

Sam's eyes shifted from the boxes in the corner to the dried-out plants on the windowsill. The tan carpeting was worn threadbare and stained with spills.

Sam whispered to Pit, "The smoke must be in the drapes and carpeting."

Pit took a deep breath. "I don't smell anything."

"Of course not. This place smells better than your house."

Loretta hung up the phone and smiled at their visitors. "Can I help you?" Her fingers brushed crumbs off the front of her pullover.

Pit stood saying, "Paul Goddard. Detective Casey and I have an appointment with..."

"Oh, yes. He's expecting you." She walked around her desk saying, "This way."

Art Bigalow's office was worse than Loretta's. One wall of shelves was crammed with books. The other wall was lined with boxes containing file folders. Pictures and certificates hung askew on the walls. Art Bigalow stood in the middle of the room peering over his bifocals at the golf club in his hands.

"Art," Loretta called out, "your one o'clock is here."

"Have a seat," Art bellowed without looking away from his putt. The ball bounced up a ramp and landed in the hole. A few seconds later, the ball was spit out and rolled back to the lawyer's feet.

Loretta steered Sam and Pit to an octagon-shaped conference table. She closed the door behind her.

"Well, it's been a long time, Detective Goddard," Art said as he lined up his next putt.

"This is Sergeant Sam Casey," Pit said as he made the introduction.

"Please." Art motioned with a nod for them to be seated. "Hard to believe it's been seventeen years." The next putt careened off the end of the cup. "Damn," he muttered. "Have to tell you, though. Jimmy still refuses to see anyone, not even Rose." He leaned the putter in the corner and crossed the room.

"That's it? As his lawyer you can't force him?" Sam asked, somewhat bewildered.

"Can't force anyone to do anything these days. Even prisoners have rights, Sergeant."

"Can't you file a motion on his behalf? File an appeal based on new evidence?" Sam asked.

"Evidence?" Art snorted. "What? I show them a button and tell the court that you saw some vision? I'd be laughed right out of the courthouse." He grabbed a thick file and sat down.

Pit studied his short list of new evidence. "Exactly how concrete of evidence do you need?"

"At this point?" Art opened the folder and pushed his glasses up on his nose. "A confession from the real killer would be nice."

Sam and Pit stared at each other from across the table. He lifted his eyebrows as if to say, "What next?"

"If I might make a suggestion," Sam started, "Jimmy should be placed under hypnosis again and asked about the button and a guy named Wy-chin-sky. Don't ask him his permission. As his attorney, you should strongly suggest it and don't take no for an answer."

Art looked at Pit. "Is she always like this?"

"Her husband tried to warn me," Pit replied.

"And have Rose visit him to add a little pressure. Maybe even take Emilio with her," Sam added.

"Scratch Emilio. Rose has tried but Jimmy refuses to allow the kid anywhere near the prison." With a heavy sigh, Art reluctantly started taking notes. "I don't take murder cases anymore. Jimmy's case sort of cured me of any taste for the criminal element."

"As I recall," Pit said, "you didn't seem too enthused."

"Court-appointed and I had to pull a high profile case that had me blacklisted in this town. Now I get real estate closings and wills. Thought it would only take a couple years for people to forget but my name was tarnished permanently." He waved a hand around his office. "I clutter it up so clients think I'm busy. Fact is," Art nodded toward the golf club, "I spend more time practicing my putting."

Sam relayed their phone conversation with Jimmy's father. "What was your impression of Jimmy when you first met him?"

Art placed his glasses on the table and rubbed his eyes with his fists like a two-year-old. He shook boredom from his eyes and rested his clasped hands on the table. "Polite, quiet, scared. I believed him that he didn't remember that night. And he started to believe the press reports about himself. He took whatever beatings the other prisoners dealt out." Art looked over at Pit. "He really took a liking to you. Thought you were the only one looking to find the truth, not looking to nail whoever was convenient."

"Well, I tried. Jimmy was, is, easy to like."

"Did he take any college courses in prison?" Sam asked. "Has he been a model prisoner?"

"Likes working with his hands." Art turned his hands over and studied the pink, pudgy flesh. "These hands wouldn't know which end of a hammer to hold. But that kid is good. Made a lot of the bookcases for the prison library, even taught classes. But he's run the emotional gamut. He went from feeling guilty to a period of resentment. He got hardened, pissed at how he was being treated, started working out in the prison gym and started fighting back. Figured he wasn't going to get out for good behavior so why try to be a model prisoner. Now his emotions have swung back to surrender, giving up. That what-the-hell attitude and just living out the last of his days with his own quiet thoughts."

Sam pushed away from the table and stood. "I'd like to shake up those quiet thoughts of his if you'd just get me in there."

Prior to the construction of the Three Oaks Shopping Center, downtown Chasen Heights had flourished. The seven-story Goldblatt's building had been the focal point. A stream of buses delivered shoppers from all four corners of town, dropping them off a half-block away in front of the Edward G. Minas building. The major retail stores had been supported by shoe stores, a bakery, accessories shop, costume shop, courthouse, bank, law offices, and several restaurants. For five years downtown struggled to hold onto what few faithful shoppers it could but one by one businesses moved, filed bankruptcy, or were victims of suspicious fires.

Goldblatt's had been leveled and replaced with a few trees, benches, and a godawful free-form art sculpture some people thought resembled an erect ant on steroids. The few stores that chose to tough it out changed hands five and six times and now offered visitors a coffee shop, shoe repair store, lottery office, and deli. Several buildings were barely able to stand, their walls gutted and windows boarded. The courthouse had moved two miles away and the former building was currently used as an unemployment office.

The five-story Minas building had been renovated into one of the better kept apartment buildings. Windows on the first floor were dressed with bars and a sign flashed in one window, *Office*.

"I think we'll blend in," Frank said as he straightened his beret.

"Face it. We look like two cops trying not to look like cops." Jake zipped up his jacket and shoved his hands deep inside the pockets. The baseball cap hovered low over his mirrored sunglasses and although the look was casual, it was far from downtrodden. Next to him, Frank's gait had taken on a hip-hop step, like a man with a rock in his shoe.

"You've really got that hip-hop step down pat."

"Just a homey goin' to buy a lottery ticket."

They walked past the entrance to the unemployment office where a number of nicotine addicts were inhaling their afternoon dose. Through the window the detectives could see bodies crammed in lines snaking toward the entrance.

"Can certainly tell the steel mills are closing," Frank said, a sound of disgust rolling around his words. He added an extra bounce as they turned the corner and headed toward the cigar shop. The line at the unemployment office paled in comparison to the line waiting to buy lottery tickets. Discarded instant tickets littered the sidewalk along with broken bottles and food wrappers.

"Do you know that Chicago is the Twinkie capital of the world?" Frank said as he kicked at an empty wrapper. "They eat more Twinkies there than in any other city. Them folks sure like their cream filled cakes."

"I've noticed one hanging out of your mouth on occasion."

"Just during a moment of supreme weakness."

On a bench in front of Adolpho's Cigar Shop sat a reed of a man, skin as dark as chocolate, eyes hidden behind pitch black shades. He was dressed in a mix of plaids and stripes but his spats were buffed to a shine. Resting against the bench was a cane and between his feet sat a metal cup stuffed with coins and bills.

Behind that cup and relaxing under the shade of the bench was a large mutt, black and white in color but with too many mixtures to lay blame to one breed. A large head was supported by equally large paws and one of its milky brown eyes was ringed in black.

"Nice day today, Hershey." Frank gave a nod to the beast under the bench. "How are you doing, Patch?" The milky brown eyes lifted lethargically.

"That you, Franklin?" Hershey flashed a smile that filled his thin face and revealed a gold-capped tooth.

"How's biz?"

"Better now that you boys moved me here. Winners are pretty appreciative. Think either me or Patch brought them good luck."

"You just watch yourself. The losers might get desperate enough to swipe your money."

"They wouldn't dare. Not with my attack dog here."

With that, Patch rolled over on his side and closed his eyes.

Frank skirted out of the way as a woman charged from the cigar shop. "Dangerous place." He sought the safety of the bench and sat down next to Hershey.

"I know the Boss Man is here. I can hear the pounding foot-steps as the scourges of society go running." Hershey flashed white and gold and patted the seat next to him.

"Not all of them, Hershey." Jake sat with a heavy sigh and kept his sunglasses focused on the apartment building across the street.

A blue and yellow bus rumbled past spewing a toxic cloud of exhaust. When it screeched to a stop at the corner, a knot of people erupted from the bus and headed down the sidewalk. One elderly woman stopped in front of Hershey and fumbled with her change purse. Coins jingled in the cup.

"Bless you." Hershey nodded his head toward his benefactor who disappeared into the shop.

Four youths ambled off the bus tossing a tennis ball back and forth and speaking in a street lingo. They wore matching jackets and pants that could only be hanging on by certain body parts. One of the teens wore a do-rag with a sports team logo blazoned across the front.

Out of habit the detectives watched the youths. It was a school day, they didn't have book bags, and their eyes shifted, looking for a mark.

"We got a real United Nations coming," Frank said. "One yellow, white, black, and brown."

"How nice the homeys play together," Hershey laughed.

Jake hated this part of undercover work because if something happened they would end up blowing their cover. So they watched in silence as the ball bounced dangerously close to Hershey's feet.

"Sorry, man." The youth with the do-rag reached for the ball but passed his hand over the cup.

Two things happened simultaneously. Patch sprang to life and snapped at the hand and Hershey's cane smacked down with lightning speed.

"YOW!" The youth clutched his hand. "You ain't blind."

"I don't need eyes to smell a thief a mile away," Hershey said.

Jake watched the four race across the street. He told Hershey, "I should haul you in for assault with two deadly weapons." He pulled a pack of cigarettes from his pocket and tapped out two.

"Yeah. You and what third Army?" Hershey flashed gold again and held up his hand so Jake could place one of the cigarettes between his bony fingers. Hershey took a long drag and exhaled a stream of smoke.

Jake waited for the few stragglers off the bus to pass. With a final hiss and a belch of blue smoke, the bus pulled away. He leaned forward, forearms on his knees, and tapped an ash on the ground.

"Anything?" Jake asked.

Hershey mirrored Jake's position. "Been quiet. Mom takes the kid to school. Comes home with groceries. While she's gone, your suspect gets picked up at ten each morning by a dude driving a silver Lexus. License plate number MOJO34. Returns home 'bout two o'clock, then leaves again at four-thirty for that security job."

Next to Hershey, Frank was busy writing the information on a pad of paper. Frank closed the pad, slipped it back into his pocket, and with a nod to Jake, walked into the cigar store.

The apartment building across the street was where Mo Williams and Felicia Moore resided. Jake didn't think it would be long before Mo fell back into his routine. The neighbors didn't want to get involved and if the police department did the surveillance, Mo's lawyer would call it harassment. So Jake employed the help of an ex-con who had served five years for conducting crap games in his eighteen wheeler. Now Hershey was a snitch for the CHPD. His wife picks him up and drops him off. Between her and Patch, they play the dutiful seeing eye to a guy who has perfect 20/20 vision.

Jake pulled a fifty out of his wallet, folded it in thirds, and slid it under the cellophane wrapper. Then he slipped the pack of cigarettes into Hershey's jacket.

Frank strolled out of the store and patted Hershey on the back. "See you around."

"Sorry I can't say the same," Hershey said with a loud chuckle.

17

Sam heard the back door click shut and footsteps echo along the hallway by the laundry room. Then nothing. Abby was upstairs inspecting Alex's work on the nursery.

"Anything yet?" Pit asked.

Sam closed the yearbook, shoved it aside and grabbed the next one. "Nothing. No Wieczynski. Just a lot of Walens, Wests, Wimples, Woods."

"At least you were able to get the proper spelling."

"Thanks to Abby. She asked our Polish cleaning lady and Tillie rattled off the spelling as if it were as simple as SMITH or JONES."

Pit stood abruptly. "Did you check the telephone listings?"

Sam motioned for him to sit. "No Wieczynskis listed." She listened for sounds from the study. She didn't hear footsteps on the staircase. Jake usually changed clothes after work, sometimes took a shower depending on what alleys or dumpsters he might have been crawling through. But there weren't any sounds from the foyer, nor did she hear the television set.

Footsteps clambered on the staircase and Sam and Pit moved to the kitchen. Abby cleared off the island counter to set out dinner. Voices were raised in the study and carried down the hallway.

"Forty acres and a mule. Hell, you just have to give me half of your property," Frank laughed as he motioned toward the backyard.

"Not mine to give," Alex countered. "Besides, three hundred years? Stand in line behind my people."

"Alex and Frank have been having this discussion on retribution for slavery for the past six months," Sam explained to Pit.

Jake ambled in and headed for the refrigerator. He pulled out several cans of beer.

Frank declined the beer and invitation to stay for dinner. "You know, when I was a kid, my parents were too poor to buy a crib." He trailed behind Alex, grabbing a green olive from the relish tray. "I slept in the bottom drawer of a dresser."

Alex turned a scowl on him. "At least you had a dresser. We slept on a hard floor, used our clothes for pillows."

Pit watched with amusement at the barbs being tossed back and forth. "This happen often?"

"You should have been here during the last election." Abby shook her head as if it were a memory she would just as soon forget.

"Alex and Frank always argue over whose ox has been gored the most. As if that matters to someone like Anton Moore," Jake said.

"Don't worry. Mo Williams even breathes wrong, we'll hear about it," Frank said. "It probably won't be long until he has Felicia turning tricks for him. Poverty makes people desperate."

"Poverty is a poor excuse for killing. Mo wanted to lord his power over Felicia by showing her who was boss. And what the hell is she doing having her first kid at sixteen?" Jake popped the top on the beer can and took a long swallow. "Bet neither Mo nor Felicia attend counseling. I can tell you now. He isn't going to change. He'll kill again."

"What's that?" Pit motioned toward the television set on the kitchen counter. On the screen were Anne and Howard DeMarco standing in their doorway, a microphone shoved in their faces by a female reporter with long dark hair.

Sam grabbed the remote and turned up the volume. The interview had to have taken place earlier in the day since the DeMarcos were standing in bright sunlight.

"Do you think there's a chance Jimmy Taggart will be a free man?" the reporter asked.

"Not as long as I'm breathing," Howard replied.

"With all the details of your daughter's murder being dredged up again, Mrs. DeMarco, do you feel like it was just yesterday that she died?" The reporter moved the microphone from Howard's face to Anne's.

"Get away," Anne screamed. "How dare you come here." Howard struggled to pull his door closed while Anne, visibly shaken, started crying.

The reporter remained unshaken by the parents' reaction and turned toward the camera. She moved away from the house while she concluded her report. "Will the mad killer of Chasen Heights be freed to kill again? Will young women in our city ever be safe to walk the streets?" She paused for effect. "This is Erin Starr for WABC News. Back to you, Jack."

"Erin Starr?" Pit laughed. "Gotta be a made-up name."

Sam shook her head. "How on earth does the media get their information?"

"Cops at headquarters," Frank said. "Press has feelers everywhere. And with that short dress she was wearing, I doubt that reporter would have trouble getting cops to talk."

Sam turned the television set off. "Well, scratch my chances for ever getting to speak to the DeMarcos again."

"Anne? Why aren't you in bed?" The bedsprings sighed as Howard sat down next to his wife on their daughter's bed. The pink floral bedspread looked as new as the day Anne had purchased it. The clock on the nightstand was set for six-thirty in the morning, the time that Catherine used to get up to go to school. Pictures on the wall were an extension of the pictures in the living room.

Anne's hand stroked a red book in her lap, Catherine's diary. Her other hand held the key. The diary had been kept locked and stored all these years in a box on the top shelf of Catherine's closet, a closet still filled with dresses, blue jeans, sweater tops, and Catherine's favorite terrycloth robe.

"Sweetheart? Are you okay?"

Slowly, Anne shook her head no. "She was a good girl, wasn't she, Howard?"

"Of course."

"Maybe we were a little too strict, but I did respect her privacy. I wasn't like some mothers who demanded to know where their children were every hour of the day." Anne clutched the diary to her chest and looked at her husband. "Was it wrong of me not to hand over her diary after she died?" she whispered. "I didn't think it was right for anyone to read her private thoughts."

Howard answered with a squeeze of his wife's shoulder.

"You know, no matter how many years go by, nothing seems to change." Anne pressed a corner of her apron against her eyes. "I come in every day hoping to see the bed unmade or clothes on the floor, hoping everything was just some bad dream. They say life gets easier. But it doesn't, Howard." She sighed heavily and squared her shoulders. "Maybe that woman was right."

"What woman? The reporter?"

"No." Anne looked into his face and for the first time in years felt positive about what she wanted to do. "No," she repeated. "The woman in the cemetery."

Lonnie's dark green Chevy Impala turned into Miller's Car Wash. The sign was a beacon in bright orange, the full name obscured by numerous burned out bulbs. Water pooled around the stalls and glistened in the chilly air.

He drove around back and pulled up next to one of the vacuum cleaner units. The ten-year-old Chevy Impala coughed and sputtered to a stop as Lonnie shoved the gearshift into PARK. Emma Lou had known very little about car maintenance and Lonnie never wanted to waste time or money fixing a car that was in need of a major overhaul. He raised his arm and strained to read his watch. It was two minutes before midnight. Beyond the front windshield darkness seeped from the forest preserve. It was hard for him to keep his eyes on the rear view mirror and also watch for anyone approaching from the woods. But who would be stupid enough to try trekking through the woods in the middle of the night?

He punched up the heat and pulled a can of beer from the six pack on the floor behind the driver's seat. A phantom tune played in Lonnie's head as he drummed his fingers on the seat. Also on the floor in the back was a gym bag he had found at the bus station. It had been left in the bathroom so he didn't consider it stolen. Now Lonnie wondered if the bag was big enough. Exactly how much space did fifty thousand dollars take up? And was he being paid in hundred dollar bills or smaller denominations? Maybe he should have specified. He tried to remember how big a wad the ten thousand had made but it had run through his fingers so fast that the incident was a blur.

The passenger door opened and Lonnie jerked back in his seat. "'Bout time you showed up." The dome light was broken so Lonnie didn't see the shiny object being raised toward his head until it was too late. The look of surprise was frozen on Lonnie's face as the back of his head blew against the driver's side window. His last thought wasn't of the money or a cross country motorcycle trip. The only word that flashed through his head was Dumbkamp.

Sam gathered her robe around her and stepped out of the bathroom. Light flickered in the gas fireplace. Jake had stayed up to read the paper and brood. She had learned months ago that pushing and prodding never accomplished much. Jake bottled up a lot of his feelings and emotions. It didn't take a genius to know there was a reason why Jake took such an interest in child abuse cases. She had seen the scars, one quite visible on the top of his forehead at the hairline. The ones not visible were the ones most painful to see. They crisscrossed his back like the ancient carvings in Narca.

A dot of red from the balcony caught her attention. Jake was smoking a cigarette, forearms on the railing, head gazing up. He had brushed off her prodding again for an explanation on how Judge Wise seemed to know Jake personally. She had little patience when her curiosity was getting the best of her. That was something she needed to work on. Jake was too tight-lipped when it came to his personal life. That was something he had to work on.

She turned to the mirror behind the headboard and surveyed her shape. The balcony door slid shut. Placing one hand under her bulging stomach and another across her breasts, she struck a pose.

"Do you think I could make the cover of *Vanity Fair?*"

Jake slid her arm away from her breasts and replaced it with his own. "You're beautiful," he whispered. His hands were surprisingly warm considering he had just came in from the night air. "And if your breasts get any bigger, you'll make Jackie jealous."

Sam laughed and turned to face him. "Far from it. But enjoy them while it lasts. I won't be pregnant forever." Her robe drifted from her shoulders as his hands continued to explore. Somehow while the room grew warmer, Jake's clothes managed to disappear yet she never felt his hands leave her body.

Sex could be a great release valve. There were times in cases like Mo Williams that Sam knew Jake needed an outlet. She could measure his frustration at work with the intensity of their lovemaking. Anything to help him relieve the tension was fine with her, especially when it meant intense, wall-banging sex. It was the kind of intensity that soaked the sheets in sweat and required a shower with more touching and groping. Then they would climb exhausted into bed where blissful sleep came easily. This was far better than the nights she would awaken to find Jake staring at the ceiling, mulling cases over in his head.

But blissful sleep tonight was interrupted at four-thirty in the morning when the phone rang. Jake groped for the phone on the ledge above his head.

"Yeah." He slowly propped himself on one elbow, straining to see the time on the clock radio. Jake sighed heavily. "Pick me up in twenty." He set the phone back on the ledge.

"Frank?" Sam murmured from her cocoon of covers.

"Yeah." Jake turned to find Sam snuggled against him. He fingered the knot of curls her hair mysteriously created during the night.

"Want my help?" Sam whispered.

Jake chuckled in the darkness. "It's thirty-seven degrees outside."

"On second thought." She snuggled closer.

His mouth hovered over her lips. Twenty minutes he had told Frank. He thought better of it and moved his lips to her forehead.

"Gotta go. We've got a homicide at the car wash on Torrence."

18

"The deceased is Lonnie Dahlkamp, male Caucasian, forty-nine years old," the officer reported as he met the detectives at their car. "The car is registered to Emma Lou Dahlkamp but she passed away last June. DMV gives her last known address as Plymouth, Indiana. Appears Mr. Dahlkamp was shot once in the head."

They followed the stocky beat cop to the back of the car wash. They stayed outside of the yellow and black tape while Benny conducted the examination and the crime techs scoured the area. Flood lights lit up the back lot where a green Chevy was parked.

Frank pulled the flaps down on his hat saying, "I don't care how stupid this looks. I'm freezing my ass off."

Jake found a thermos of coffee and several cups in the open trunk of Benny's car. He gave the hat a passing glance while he poured the coffee.

"I figured you wouldn't last one winter with that Michael Jordan haircut. You'll be growing it back by January." He handed a steaming cup to Frank. "You look like something out of the movie *Fargo*."

"I can handle this. Just gotta get used to it."

They took a seat on the bumper of Benny's car as the beat cop flipped open a notepad, the cover battered and soiled.

"Give us the scoop," Frank told the officer.

"I was patrolling the area around oh-four-hundred hours, when I noticed a vehicle parked in the rear." Eilerman gave a nod toward the Chevy. "I directed my headlights and spotlight on the area and approached the vehicle on the driver's side. It was then that I noticed the shattered window and the victim in the car and on the vacuum unit." He grinned at his gallows humor but the smile vanished when he saw the stoic reaction on the detectives' faces.

"Did you open the car door?" Frank asked.

"No, sir. Didn't want to disturb any fingerprints. I went to my radio and called it in to the desk sergeant. I also ran a check on the license plate which is how I came up with a possible identification." He dug around the inside of his jacket. "I took these. Always keep a camera in my car." He handed them Polaroids of the crime scene.

"Good thinking," Frank said. They took their time studying the photos. They knew Eilerman was an amateur photographer and was sometimes called out to assist CID when there was a back load of cases.

One of the crime techs walked over and held up a small brown bag. He poured the contents into his gloved hands and held it out to the detectives.

"Looks like a nine millimeter," Frank said, peering into the tech's palm.

The tech placed the bullet back in the bag and walked to the Criminal Investigation Division van.

Benny waved them over. They snapped on latex gloves as they approached. A low mist seeped in from the woods and the chill forced Frank to pull up the collar on his wool coat.

"Nice hat," Benny said. "Reminds me of *Fargo*."

"You got your damned car bugged or something?"

They approached the driver's side first. The vacuum unit was just as Eilerman had described. The words *No Music Please* were distorted by what looked like brain matter.

"Saw Sam the other day," Benny said. "She is really getting big."

"She saw you about the DeMarco murder?" Frank asked.

"We went over the autopsy report together. Pretty gruesome."

"I don't know why the heck she's on suspension. We should just rent her out to other police departments. You know, like a rent-a-mystic," Frank said. "Department's always looking for ways to bring in money."

Jake rolled his eyes.

"What is it you don't like, Jake?" Benny asked. "The fact that she's right or the way she gets her information?"

"Our job would be a hell of a lot easier if all we had to do was touch a dead body," Jake said. It didn't bother him when someone was right. What mattered to him was that the criminal is taken off the streets. "I've learned not to question how she does it. What bothers me is the publicity. The more the wrong people find out what she can do, the more her life will be in danger. I can't concentrate on doing my job if I have to worry about her safety." He had had this discussion with Abby before. In her infinite wisdom Abby had simply said that there are others who watch over Sam. Jake had little faith in people he couldn't physically see.

Frank opened the back door of the vehicle and leaned in while Jake walked around to the passenger side.

Benny said, "We have an entrance wound just above the left eye. I'd say it was pretty close range. Killer was probably sitting in the passenger seat."

The victim's eyes were open in mock surprise. His jacket was covered in blood. Most of the blood splatter marks, as well as hair, flesh, and bone, were contained on the driver's side seat, window and door. The sweet, metallic odor of blood blended with the smell of death and human excrement. An unsettling combination any time of the day.

"He had time for a beer." Frank held up the six-pack with the tip of his pen, the five cans tethered with plastic.

"Got an open can in the front seat," Benny said. The can and six-pack had a dusting of powder residue.

Jake pulled the gym bag from the back seat and unzipped it. "Empty bag. He was probably waiting to fill it or someone relieved him of the contents."

Benny handed Jake a clear plastic bag. "Take a look at those goodies."

The bag contained items the crime techs discovered in the car. Jake studied the contents through the plastic. "Seems the victim liked the off track betting parlors." He counted out seven ticket stubs. He looked closely at another receipt. "Two hundred and fifty dollars for something purchased at Tombstone Liquors in Harwood."

"That's one hell of a pricey bottle of liquor," Benny said.

"Harwood is right over the state line," Frank said.

The detectives stepped back as a tow truck pulled up behind the green Chevy. "What do you think?" Frank asked as his shoulders hunched inside his coat.

"The nearest building is a used car lot five blocks away. No witnesses, not much traffic. No nearby houses with insomniacs who might have heard shouts or shots." Jake shoved his hands deep inside his coat pockets wishing he had taken the time to zip in the lining. "And there's one other thing."

"What's that?"

"Most drug business is done near the state line or close to the expressway. Easy off, easy on," he said.

"True. So maybe he went to the casino and was supposed to split the winnings but his partner wanted it all."

"But there aren't any maps or handwritten directions retrieved from Lonnie or his car."

"Point being?"

"Our boy seemed to know his way around town."

19

"House, oh yeah." Frank peeled his dark sunglasses off and stared at the mobile trailer park. "Don't you just love it when they attach the name Estates onto a slum? It's like calling The Projects the Chasen Heights Country Club."

"Guess home is whatever you can afford." Jake studied the cramped trailer park as they waited in the car for the Vista Mobile Estates manager and Plymouth police to show up. The drive through Plymouth to the trailer park had been a stark contrast. Plymouth was a small town of 7,800. Streets were pristine. Aged trees along the parkways stood like majestic sentries. Houses seemed like remnants from eras gone by.

The trailer homes barely measured up. Some owners had made a reasonable effort to keep their property neat and tidy, adding flowers, patio stones, and keeping their shrubs trimmed. The Dahlkamp home, however, had weeds snaking up the siding and jutting between landscaping rock. The green striped awning was torn and listing to one side, and the lawn was littered with cigarette butts. It reminded Jake of every place he had ever lived as a kid. The home had always been rented, and his father never lifted a finger in the upkeep. Evan Mitchell felt that was what he was paying rent for...to have maintenance-free living. Truth was, any kind of work got in the way of Evan Mitchell's drinking.

A squad car lumbered up the street and parked behind the black Taurus. Jake and Frank climbed out and approached the emerging couple. The officer hiked up his belt and unzipped his jacket.

"If his name is Gomer or Barney, I'm going to lose it," Frank whispered.

"Howdy, boys." The officer jammed a hand toward the two detectives. "I'm Officer Mason Gallows." Frank smiled. "It's okay," Gallows said. "I get a lot of jokes about gallows humor." He turned to a portly woman with flaming red hair. "Sparky here is the manager of the park." Gallows wedged his cap under his armpit and raked a hand through his straw-like hair.

Sparky gave a "hi ya" and led them to the Dahlkamp home. The three men stood in the doorway and gaped at the stacks of boxes, newspapers, magazines, and knickknacks.

"Not exactly *House and Garden* material, is it?" She led them to the kitchen. "Probably the only place we can all sit together."

"How the hell are we going to go through all this?" Jake shrugged out of his sportscoat and hung it on the back of a kitchen chair.

"Actually needs a backhoe," Gallows added.

"Emma Lou was a junk dog," Sparky explained. "Hit every garage sale in town. She'd stop by and show me all her bargains. It was bad enough she never threw any of her own stuff away, then she had to add everyone else's junk to the mix. Unfortunately, her lazy son didn't do much cleaning after she died."

They gathered around the kitchen table. Frank pushed condiments and junk mail to one side, then set out a tape recorder.

"Gotta tell you," Gallows started, "don't surprise me one damn bit Lonnie got himself kilt."

"He was nothing but trouble, according to Emma Lou," Sparky chimed in.

"How long did they live here?" Jake opened one of the cabinet doors above the sink and jumped back. Boxes of pudding and cup cake papers fell into the sink. He hated to think how crammed the other cabinets were.

"Emma Lou moved in about fifteen years ago. You wouldn't believe the stories she'd tell me." Sparky shrugged out of her parka and clasped her hands on the table. Sunlight danced across the freckles that dotted her face. Sparky and Gallows proceeded to fill the detectives in on the Dahlkamp life story.

"Ain't no daddy," Sparky started. "Left when Lonnie was fifteen. Lonnie was always in trouble in school. Detention, suspension, you name it. Don't think he ever did graduate. Even the Army didn't want him. Was arrested for forging checks, spent time. Of course, Emma Lou blamed the kids he hung around with. They'd call him Dumbkamp behind his back. Guess that was bad for his self-esteem or some damn shit." Sparky pulled a pack of cigarettes from the pocket of her shirt. "Mind?" She cranked open the kitchen window next to her.

Jake squatted to check the bottom cabinet. It was crammed with canned goods and bags of flour and sugar. Emma Lou could have opened her own general store.

"No living relatives?" Frank asked.

"None I'd ever heard of." Sparky took a long drag which gave Gallows time to get a word in edgewise.

"Lonnie was only good for working odd jobs but tired of them pretty quick. The guy liked to gamble...lottery, horses, sporting events."

"He promised Emma Lou he would straighten out," Sparky added.

"Sure it had nothing to do with the broken arm and leg he received from a bookie's henchmen," Gallows said with a chuckle.

"What kind of gambling debts are we talking?" Jake asked.

"About eight thousand dollars is what Emma Lou told me," Sparky replied.

"That's when they moved here to Plymouth but the bookie found him." The radio on Gallows belt squawked. "What have you got, Mabel?" he barked into the radio.

"Luke's prize heifer's on the loose again."

"I'm gonna be tied up here a bit. Give it to Sammy."

"Ten-four."

Gallows set his radio on the table. "That's the biggest job we've ever had...chasing down cattle. Until Lonnie came to town."

Sparky patted the Sheriff's bulky arm. "You tell them about the car." This produced a chuckle from Gallows. It seemed as though the sheriff hadn't stopped smiling since he stepped out of the squad car. Word one hadn't left Gallow's mouth and already Sparky was squirming like an impatient pre-schooler. "You're gonna love this," she squealed.

Frank flashed a wide smile. Sparky's enthusiasm was infectious. Jake listened intently as he inspected the contents of the kitchen drawers.

"Well," Gallows started, his chuckling now at full throttle, "old Lonnie got himself a job at Billy Bob's gas station. Since his bookie was leanin' on him quite heavy, he knew the only way to score some big money was to rob a store. But he didn't have no wheels. So he took one of the cars that was in for service."

Sparky's giggle was high-pitched and tears formed at the corners of her eyes.

"So he headed north but only got about four hundred dollars from a convenience store. Drove on a little further and walked into this store. They thought he'd come to apply for a job. And, Lonnie thinks, 'yeah sure.' After all, what better way to get his hands on the cash drawer, right?"

Jake stopped his searching and leaned against the sink, arms crossed.

"Lonnie thinks he done hit the jackpot. He's got his money and off he goes. Spends a little on the way back, drops the rest into his savings account at the bank. Now all he has to do is get the car back to the service station."

Sparky's chubby hands slapped palms down on the table several times as she let out a bellyache of a laugh.

Gallows laughed and coughed and waved one hand to signal he

wasn't through yet. A soft rumble erupted from the back of Frank's throat.

"Oh yeah. Next morning cops come a knockin' at the door. Emma Lou claims Lonnie was home all night. What on earth could they want with her boy? But they traced the plates from the robbery." Another hefty laugh erupted from Gallows and he had to calm down before coming to the punch line. With tears forming in the corners of his eyes, he announced, "The dumb ass stole the mayor's car."

Now it was knee-slapping time as tears ran down the sheriff's and Sparky's faces. Frank's laugh rumbled along with them. Jake couldn't help but chuckle.

Jake asked, "How much time did he serve for that one?"

"Ten years," Gallows said, wiping the tears from his face. "Emma Lou visited him every day. When he got out he was back to his drinking again. Mom went with him to AA meetings. But then the idiot solicited an undercover vice cop for a Super Bowl bet. Back into prison."

"I love that story," Sparky said, finally catching her breath.

"Did Lonnie live with his mother the entire time they lived in Plymouth?" Jake asked.

Gallows shook his head. "At first. Then he had his own apartment for a bit, at least until his last incarceration. Emma Lou took care of cleaning out his apartment, before it got bulldozed."

"When's the last time you saw Lonnie?" Jake asked Sparky.

"Two days ago. Left with a suitcase. Said he'd be gone for a few days."

The sheriff rapped his knuckles on the table. "So you want me to give you a hand going through all this crap?"

Jake gave the living room a long, hard look. "How many men do you have?"

20

Abby pressed the button to open the front gate. She wasn't surprised to see Sam's visitors staring at her through the monitor.

When she opened the front door, a shocked Anne DeMarco gasped, "It's you!" Anne turned to her husband. "It's her, the woman from the cemetery."

"Please, come in." Abby closed the door behind them and offered to take their coats. Anne and Howard preferred to keep their coats on. "Would you like something to drink?" They declined. Abby left them in the sitting room where Alex was changing a burned out bulb on the Christmas tree.

Anne asked Alex, "Who is she?"

"Abby Two Eagles. She is Sam's mother."

"Mother?" Anne's ears picked up the faint sound of flute music. She looked over at Alex again and said, "I mean, who is she really?"

Alex regarded her briefly as his fingers snapped in a new bulb. "I take it you have met *wicasa wakan* before."

Puzzled, Anne said, "I'm sorry?"

Alex watched the bulb light up. Satisfied, he turned the lights off. "*Wicasa wakan,* medicine woman."

"Medicine...?" Anne looked at Howard.

Sam was pleasantly surprised to see the couple.

"Have you eaten?" Sam asked the DeMarcos.

They shook their heads. "Your mother stopped by the..." Anne started.

"Yes, she told me she saw you in the cemetery."

"I really don't know why I decided to call you." Anne's hand shook as she wiped away a tear. "I just..."

"Please, won't you have a seat?"

Anne shook her head. "We really have to get going. I never meant to keep anything from the police. I just thought some things were private, you know?" She stared for several seconds at the floor.

Howard nudged Anne's elbow. "It's best we just get it over with, dear."

Reluctantly, Anne reached into her purse and pulled out a book. She studied the treasure before pressing it to her chest as though parting with it was the most difficult thing she ever had to do.

"Anne," Howard whispered.

Reluctantly, Anne handed Sam Catherine's diary.

"A nine millimeter can do some major damage at close range." Benny led the detectives to his office and handed them each a copy of his M.E. report on the body of Lonnie Dahlkamp. "No needle marks, no bruises. Had a fast-food cheeseburger for dinner about two hours before meeting his maker and then half a can of beer for a snack right before the bullet for dessert. Definitely the gun shot was the only culprit."

Jake and Frank sat in adjoining chairs and studied the report. "Like your shirt," Frank told Benny. The black tee shirt had white lettering that said, *I See Dead People,* a phrase from the movie, *The Sixth Sense.*

"Close range?" Jake asked.

"Depends on what you mean by close." Benny peered into his coffee cup and turned toward the window, lifting the cup high. Turning back to his desk, he grabbed his copy of the report. "I'd say he was shot from no more than three feet away."

"So the killer was in the car?" Frank asked.

"That would be my guess."

A young man dressed in green scrubs entered the office carrying a steaming pot of coffee. "Thanks," Benny said and pointed a finger at the detectives as if to ask if they wanted any coffee. They both declined. "You guys have had a long day. What did you find out about our guy when you went to Plymouth?" Turning to the intern, Benny said, "Bring in the tray, Ace."

"Dahlkamp may have had a gambling problem, but his mother was a major pack rat," Frank replied. "And we still haven't gone through every box of crap in that trailer home. We left that to the Plymouth P.D. They are kinda bored chasing cattle around anyway. Found nothing so far belonging to the deceased, other than some old junk mail in the garbage."

Ace set a tray on the conference table and the three men waited for him to leave before sifting through the contents. Inside the container were Lonnie's clothes, shoes, the change from his pockets, and a key ring.

Jake picked through the keys...car, house, and a long slender key. "There weren't locked mail boxes at the entrance, were there, Frank?"

"Nope." Frank examined the thin piece of metal. "Looks like a key to a safety deposit box."

"Speaking of key," Benny said, "has Sam found out anything new on that murder?"

"She called earlier and said the DeMarcos stopped by with a diary that belonged to their daughter," Jake said. "But evidence-wise, if you ask me, Jimmy Taggart doesn't have a prayer."

* * * *

The steel door slammed shut with a heavy, sucking sound. Locombe State Prison, affectionately referred to as *LOCO* by the inmates, was a two-hour drive south of Chasen Heights. The cinder block walls were painted steel gray and prisoner uniforms were a faded orange, as though they had gone through too many cycles in the laundry room.

Jimmy stood in the hallway and waited for Moses to unlock the door. The elderly black man had lived most of his life at *LOCO*, which is why the inmates called him Moses. No one knew his real name. Whenever his parole hearing came up, he always refused to express remorse for his crime. No remorse meant no parole, which was fine with Moses. He didn't know what he would do on the outside.

"Gotcha a phone call, Jimmy." Moses hobbled to the wall phone under the watchful eyes of the burly guard stationed at the end of the aisle. Moses's leg never did heal right after the steely eyed store owner had beat him and his wife with a rake handle, all because they were stealing milk for their kids. Moses had offered to pay him back after he got a job but the rotund man with the *Love It or Leave It* tee shirt told him and his wife the world would be better off without them reproducing. The store owner had unloaded a string of racial slurs before pulling out a 357 Magnum. Moses had tried to wrestle it away but the gun went off into the flabby guy's chest. His wife died two days later of massive head injuries.

"Who is it?"

"Don't know," Moses replied. "He don't say but the warden said to make sure you get the call."

"Thanks." Jimmy watched Moses hobble away and wondered who was better off—Moses, who was stuck in this hellhole for the rest of his life, or Jimmy, who wouldn't have to look at it again.

Jimmy didn't expect his attorney to call so soon. He had

already instructed him not to allow visitors. He pulled the stool out, sat down, and lifted the receiver.

"Hello." There was a pause on the other end but Jimmy knew someone was there. He could hear breathing.

"Jimmy?" A voice finally said.

Jimmy hesitated. The voice sounded familiar but where had he heard it before? Somehow his subconscious must have known because he felt his throat constrict.

He couldn't get the words out of his throat and the silence stretched on until the caller said, "Jimmy? It's Dad."

21

"How far are you?" Pit asked with a nod toward the diary.

"Makes for very interesting reading. Catherine was not a wallflower by any stretch of the imagination." Sam pushed the sleeves up on her gray fleece pullover and studied her notes. "I'm guessing Catherine received the diary when she was thirteen. That's when she started making entries."

"You're not going to read the whole thing to me, are you?"

"You might learn a thing or two. However, we don't have that kind of time. I did write down some notes." Thumbing through the pages, she said, "I started with her last entry and worked back. She was supposed to meet someone she referred to as 'B' at eleven o'clock the night she was murdered. I went back to when she first mentioned 'B'. That was six months before her death."

"Jimmy's name certainly doesn't begin with a 'B'."

"She had a fender bender in December. We should check accident reports during that time period to see if one was filed. Maybe her mystery man is the one who hit her car." She turned back to her notes and continued. "She knew 'B' for a few weeks before they had sex." Sam turned the diary and pushed it toward him. "She gets pretty explicit in her descriptions. I don't think I want to read any of it out loud."

Pit gave her a puzzled look and then started reading. His eyes widened and his cheeks appeared flushed. "I don't think she learned any of this in Bible School." He turned a page and continued reading. Sam thought she saw beads of perspiration forming on his forehead. "She obviously didn't think anyone would ever read this."

Sam said, "Prior to meeting 'B,' she used to charge twenty-five dollars to perform oral sex on the members of the football team."

Pit looked up from the diary. "No wonder Mrs. DeMarco wanted this diary kept in the dark."

"I don't think her parents ever read one sentence, although I think they may have suspected their daughter of having overactive hormones." Sam stifled a yawn and shook the fatigue from her head.

Pit pushed the diary back across the table. "If it's all the same to you, I prefer the shortened version."

Sam returned to her notes. "They met at least twice a week. She mentions that he had a car, but she didn't say what school he attended, so I think Rose might be right that Catherine liked college guys. She mentions someone named Rachel Stowe. Sounds like she might be a close friend. Hard to tell though if she told Rachel her mystery man's real name."

"Did Rachel go to her school?"

"Only for one year. She was three years older."

Pit wrote down the name. "I still don't understand why the medical examiner and doctors claimed Catherine was a virgin."

"I bet if we dug deep enough we might find that Doctor Olsen, Forrest Eckart, or maybe even both, knew the DeMarcos personally. May have belonged to the same church and wanted to preserve Catherine's virtue."

Sam's cell phone twirped. Pit located it in his jacket pocket. It was Art Bigalow calling to let them know that Jimmy had agreed to meet with them.

"We're on," Pit announced. "Seems Bill Taggart came through. Bigalow will call back with a day and time."

* * *

"Have we eaten yet?" Frank asked, patting his stomach.

"Not since our drive-thru late breakfast of fat and cholesterol." Jake turned his back to the faint breeze and lit his cigarette. They were standing outside Tombstone Liquors. After calling earlier to check on the receipt found in Lonnie's wallet, it was discovered that Lonnie rented an apartment above the liquor store in Harwood, a mid-sized town on the Illinois/Indiana state line. A patrol car eased up to the curb and two uniformed cops climbed out.

"Sergeant Mitchell?" An olive-skinned beat cop approached and reached out to shake hands. "Hector Vasquez." He motioned toward his partner. "John Marquette."

John pulled papers from his jacket and handed them to Jake. "The search warrant, sir."

Jake scanned them quickly. "They look in order." He handed them back to John. "What about the landlord?"

"He's in the store." Hector opened the door and stuck his head in. "Yo, J.D."

A wisp of a man emerged from the liquor store, flipped a *Closed* sign on the inside of the door and locked up. He drew his bulky cardigan around his thin shoulders and turned toward the cops.

"Yeah, yeah. Follow me," J.D. growled as he barely glanced at the search warrant John held up. He opened the side door and led the officers up to the second floor.

"I don't know much about the guy. He just rented the place a couple days ago." J.D.'s voice was raspy and his clothes reeked of smoke. His nimble fingers worked the key in the lock, pushed the door open, and drew back the heavy curtains.

Frank asked, "Did he pay in cash?"

"Yeah, but I checked the bills. Weren't counterfeit. I can usually tell a drifter so I asked for two months rent up front. Guess I'm just glad he wasn't killed in my building. I'd never hear the end of it."

"Did Mr. Dahlkamp give you a place of employment?" Jake asked.
"Nope."

"Thanks for your time, J.D.," Hector said. "We'll let you know if we need you." He patted the older man on the back and steered him out of the apartment.

Jake gave the living room a quick scan. After the trash they had waded through in Emma Lou's trailer home, it was a relief to find Lonnie's apartment rather bare. Even the worn furniture was a welcome relief from the wall-to-wall clutter Emma Lou had accumulated.

"Can you give us some background?" John asked.

Frank gave brief details on Lonnie Dahlkamp and was bursting at the seams to repeat the story about Lonnie's stolen car escapade. They enjoyed a laugh and then they each took a room.

A double bed and four-drawer dresser were crammed into the bedroom. Clothes were balled up in the suitcase as if Dahlkamp hadn't bothered to unpack. In the kitchen there were just three cans of beer and a jar of instant coffee in the refrigerator. Two cans of soup were on the counter, the labels faded and yellowed with age.

After an hour, the four filtered back to the living room.

"Anything?" Jake asked. They shook their heads.

There was a knock on the door. Frank crossed the room and pulled the door open with a strong jerk.

"Thought of something," J.D. wheezed. "The young fella asked me for the name of a bank close by, one that had safety deposit boxes. I told him American National on Sibley."

Jake checked his watch. "We might be able to find a judge to get a search warrant."

"May as well wait til tomorrow. Can't get into the bank until then," Frank said. "Chief's gonna pitch a fit when he sees the overtime we're racking up."

"We'll get the warrant tonight and then go to the bank first thing in the morning." Jake turned to J.D. "No phone here?"

"I've got a pay phone in the store. There's also a few up and down the state line."

"Hector," Jake started.

"Yeah, we'll get a subpoena for the phone records."

The ranch-style home of Judge Andrew Wise sprawled across three acres in an upscale section of Chasen Heights. The European-style furniture and expensive artwork on the walls reflected someone's taste and appreciation for the finer things in life.

"He'll be with you shortly." The woman who showed them to the study spoke with a thick accent. Heavenly odors of meat and potatoes followed her into the room, reminding the detectives that it was long past dinnertime.

They heard a soft whining in the distance, gradually increasing in volume. A figure appeared through the doorway. In a motorized wheelchair sat an elegant woman dressed in a powder blue cashmere dress. A large pin in the shape of a bird nested in the scarf around her neck. The light caught the myriad of colors in the gems. The woman sat rigid, giving the appearance that if she were able to walk, she would probably stand just as straight.

"Marjorie, perhaps the gentlemen would like something to drink."

The maid turned back to the men.

"No, nothing, thank you," Jake and Frank replied.

Once the maid left, the woman held out her right hand. Her long nails were carefully manicured and several fingers were adorned with elaborate rings.

"Eleanor Wise." They each shook her hand. "Andrew is just finishing up a phone call." She broke the uncomfortable silence by explaining, "An unfortunate fall down the stairs many years ago left me paralyzed." Her fingers played with a wisp of auburn hair that was swept up in a French twist. "My mother always told me a Duncan never cleans house or washes windows. She told me I went to extremes to assure that I kept that family tradition." She emitted a throaty, Lauren Bacall-type laugh. The two men smiled.

"Charming them already, Ellie?" Judge Wise walked into the room and kissed his wife on the head. "Gentlemen." He shook each of their hands.

"I'll leave you to your work. It was nice meeting you." The wheelchair hummed as Ellie maneuvered out of the room.

Judge Wise poised his reading glasses on the end of his nose and unfolded the papers Jake handed him. "We have been seeing a lot of each other lately, Sergeant Mitchell." He walked over to an antique roll top desk, sat down, and spread the papers in front of him.

"I apologize again for interrupting your lunch," Jake said as he moved past the fireplace. He noticed a picture of a younger Eleanor and Judge Wise with a teenage boy who had Eleanor's eyes and nose and the judge's thick hair and solid build.

"I admire your tenacity, Sergeant Mitchell. Cases like Mo Williams' are sometimes lost in the system. You and Detective Travis are a credit to your profession."

"Thank you," Frank responded for both of them.

Judge Wise studied the papers thoroughly and asked, "You think the victim's safety deposit box might reveal something?"

"It's a little suspicious when a drifter obtains a safety deposit box the minute he arrives in town," Jake explained. "We won't know until we get in there exactly what he felt was so valuable."

Judge Wise brought out a pen from his shirt pocket and signed the papers. He folded them up and handed them back to Jake.

"There you go, gentlemen. I wish you luck."

22

The next morning Anne and Howard DeMarco agreed to let Sam take a look at Catherine's room while Pit was at the precinct going through accident reports. Sam waited until the parents left before studying the room. The first thing that struck her was how meticulous it was. Even the windowsills were dust free. The odor of fresh flowers drifted from the vase on the dresser and sunlight streamed in through the windows. The wallpaper had a rosebud pattern which matched the bedspread and curtains.

The room appeared to have been left exactly the way Catherine kept it seventeen years ago. There were stuffed animals on the dresser along with a collection of crystal elephants enclosed in a glass case. A dollhouse filled the entire top of a card table. The three-sided structure had been expertly built to scale. Sam wouldn't have been surprised if Howard had made it for his daughter. The miniature furniture had plush upholstery and tiny Persian rugs dotted the floors.

Sam wondered whether if she had toured Pit's house she would have found his daughter's bedroom in the same condition, with her toys and clothes still in place as though the child were just outside playing and would be back soon.

There was a clock radio on the nightstand set for six-thirty in the morning. The closet contained Catherine's clothes with shoes lined up neatly on the floor. Hats were stacked on the shelf above the clothes along with a tennis racket and pom poms.

Sam fought back tears as she realized the pain the DeMarcos felt every time they walked into their daughter's room. No wonder they couldn't let go. She turned away from those reminders but was faced with more. The toes of pink house slippers peeked out from under the bed, ready for their owner to slip into at the first buzzing of the alarm clock.

Turning, Sam noticed a white jewelry box under the clutter of animals on the oak dresser. She opened the jewelry box and a tinny tune played briefly, then died out. Her fingers roamed through a collection of dainty earrings, pierced, in all colors, neatly arranged in the divided storage compartments.

She walked over to a rocker where a large, stuffed white rabbit sat. Cradling the rabbit in her arms, she sat down and pulled the button from her pocket. Sam held the rabbit as if it were a baby. "May as well practice," she whispered. Slowly, she rocked. The rabbit was soft and plush and was about the size of a six-month-old. She closed her eyes briefly and felt the gentle rock.

*Hush little baby don't say a word...*Sam smiled at the whispered singing and could hear herself humming along with the tune. Four more months and she'll be singing to her baby. *Mama's gonna buy you a Mockingbird. If that Mockingbird don't sing...*Sam slowly stopped rocking. She had the sudden realization that she wasn't the one singing. Her eyes snapped open and she found the room dark, the walls gone, and the humidity stifling. She was back at the murder scene, sitting in the rocker at the edge of the clearing. Catherine was taunting her killer, singing the song as she swayed in a drunken stupor. Then Catherine said, *the rabbit died.* This time when the knife struck down, Sam saw something else, a detail that moved past her eyes too quickly.

Sunlight returned to the room as quickly as it had left. Her fingers clutched the rabbit tighter. Sam was beginning to dislike these unannounced jaunts through time and space. Details of the autopsy report came flooding back as she thought about the location of the stab wounds. She slowly rose and returned to the living room, the rabbit still clutched in her arms.

Pit had returned from the precinct and was sitting on the loveseat. Anne stood and stared at Sam with anticipation.

Sam didn't know how to put it delicately so she just blurted it out. "Why wasn't it ever brought out in the trial that Catherine was pregnant?"

Anne's hands flew up to her face. "Oh, my god." She reached a hand out to Howard who wrapped a protective arm around his wife and guided her back to the couch.

Anger washed over his face and he glared at the two detectives. "For crissake. Why does it have to be brought up now?"

"Why did it have to be hidden then?" Sam asked. "And how did you ever convince Jack Olsen and Forrest Eckart to cover up that important piece of information?"

"Important to who?" Anne screamed. "Who would it hurt to keep it a secret? Our girl was a good girl. There was no need for that to come out." She clasped her fingers in a tight fist until the knuckles turned white. After several moments of muffled sobs, Anne calmed down and in a low, halting voice, asked, "Did Catherine mention in her diary that she was pregnant?"

Sam shook her head no. "I was suspicious when I read the autopsy report. Many of the stab wounds were in the abdominal region. And," Sam paused, averted her eyes to Pit, "I felt it in her room. I heard her laugh and say, 'the rabbit died.'"

"Heard?" Anne muffled another sob.

This was always the most difficult part of Sam's job—explaining how she knows what she knows. Skeptics far outnumbered the believers but families of victims desperately searching for a clue to the death of a loved one sometimes clung to Sam's words like a lifeline. And sometimes she didn't even have to explain.

"The rabbit died?" Howard finally murmured.

"You heard her voice?" Anne whimpered.

Sam nodded. "She was also singing a lullaby."

Pit shifted uncomfortably in his seat and glanced quickly from Sam to the DeMarcos. "Was there anyone she might have told?" he asked. "Maybe the girl she mentions in the diary, Rachel Stowe?"

Anne and Howard exchanged glances. "I think the pot of tea should be ready, Howard." When Howard left for the kitchen, Anne said, "Rachel was several years older than Catherine. We didn't much approve of her hanging around with a college girl but they seemed pretty close. She might have told her."

"Where did she go to school?"

"Northern Illinois in DeKalb. They spent a lot of time on the phone and, much to our disapproval, Catherine spent weekends with Rachel at the college." Anne twisted the hankie between her fingers, then untwisted it and dabbed at her eyes. "Of course, at the time she told us she was at a slumber party at Rachel's home. We didn't know she was going to DeKalb."

Howard came back with a tray and set it in the middle of the coffee table. Anne filled four cups.

"Where does Rachel live now?" Pit asked. He opened a spiral notepad and pulled a pen from the spine.

"Oh, my." Anne looked up toward the ceiling in thought. "Out East I think." She turned toward her husband. "Howard? Do you remember?"

"I know her parents moved to California years ago. Jerry, I think was her father's name. He worked for one of those space technology places, a government job."

"Do you know if Rachel is married?" Sam asked.

"No, I'm sorry. Once Catherine died, there was no reason to keep track of her friends," Anne explained.

Sam asked Pit, "What did you find out at headquarters?"

"If Catherine was in an automobile accident the December before her death, it wasn't filed with the police department."

"What about that time someone knocked the rear bumper off of the car, Howard? Wasn't that during the winter?" Anne turned to Sam. "Catherine said it happened in the mall parking lot. The driver of the other car already had two tickets and pleaded for Catherine not to call the police."

"Yes, I remember," Howard said. "The young man was supposed to pay her something every month. It cost us two hundred dollars to have it fixed. She had his name and phone number, but he never came through with any money."

"Do you remember his name?" Sam asked. They both started shaking their heads before she even finished her question. "According to her diary this was about the time she met someone she called 'B'. Would either of you know who 'B' was?" Again, they both shook their heads. "She alluded to another woman in her diary and felt 'B' loved her more. I think Catherine may have gotten pregnant on purpose."

"Oh, god," Anne muffled a sob. "My poor baby." Then her eyes widened as though details were finally falling into place. "Do you think the father of her baby killed her because he wouldn't marry her? Can they get DNA from..."

"No," Pit said. "It's been too long; the chance of confirming the baby's father is impossible."

"The baby still could have been Jimmy Taggart's, though. Right?" Howard asked.

"He testified he never had any physical contact with Catherine before that night." Pit set his cup down, wondering how anyone could drink this stuff all day long. He patted his pockets but didn't see any ashtrays lying around.

"What about that name that you mentioned?" Howard asked.

"Wieczynski?" Pit asked. Howard nodded. "Unfortunately, we haven't been able to come up with anyone by that name. He could be living anywhere now."

"If he's still alive," Sam added.

23

"Sergeant Mitchell?" The sound traveled through the lobby and bounced off the marble walls. Patrons in the bank flinched and the detectives turned to find everything the voice had promised.

"He's Sergeant Mitchell," Frank said, pointing, as if blaming Jake for whatever they were guilty of. Jake handed her the search warrant.

Mrs. Shavers rocked from her toes to heels, mouth in permanent scowl and eyes like laser beams as she examined the search warrant.

"Hmmppf," she huffed as she took her sweet time.

Jake deliberately splayed his hands at his waist, opening his jacket so the bank manager could see his gun and badge. She caught the size of the Sig Sauer and slowly met his eyes. Jake had *cold* and *heartless* down to a science.

"Anything Judge Wise needs to amend?" Jake asked, putting the onus on her to question a judge's authority.

She huffed as she handed the papers back to Jake. Making a crisp 180-degree turn any drill sergeant would be proud of, she barked, "Follow me."

She led them through the Customer Service Department of the two-story building. It was the oldest and largest bank in Chasen

Heights. Wrought iron and marble teller cages looked out of place next to modular workstations and state-of-the art computers.

A security guard with a name tag of *Hobbs* stood slowly as Mrs. Shavers approached. She whispered something to him and Hobbs grabbed a set of keys.

"This way, gents," Hobbs said as he hobbled and groaned his way through a glass enclosure and into a room with drawers from ceiling to floor. "What have you got?" Jake handed him the key. Hobbs located the box at the far end of the room. He inserted both keys, slid the box out of its chamber, and led them to a private room. Frank closed the door to a room just large enough for one narrow table and two chairs. The detectives sat down, pulled on latex gloves, flipped up the catch on the box, and opened the lid. The box was as sparse as Lonnie's apartment.

Frank frowned. "Damn. No wads of cash or tons of jewelry. I expected our boy to surprise me."

Jake lifted out a receipt stamped *359*. "Dillon's. Ever hear of it?"

"No."

Jake studied the receipt closer. It listed the item number *19389*. "I can barely make out July. Nothing more."

Jake lifted the flap on the evidence envelope and pulled out a log sheet. He recorded the receipt and carefully placed it in the envelope while Frank lifted the remaining item from the box. It was a brown envelope, no markings. Jake shoved the safety deposit box aside while Frank pulled out the contents. The newspaper clippings were yellowed around the edges and he carefully unfolded them, scattering them around the table. Frank pushed his chair back as an irritating rumble started in the back of his throat. It grew in intensity as he noticed Jake's reaction.

"Don't you just hate it when Sam's right?" Frank cackled.

Jake heaved a loud "shit."

* * *

With fingers laced and elbows propped on the desk, Captain Robinson rested his chin on steepled fingers. Dark eyes scanned the newspaper headlines. "I'm hoping like hell this is some fluke coincidence." On his desk were the original newspaper articles on the Catherine DeMarco case and the subsequent trial. These were the items found in Lonnie Dahlkamp's safety deposit box.

Jake was silent and tried to ignore the Cheshire grin Frank had been wearing since they opened the safety deposit box. A headache was building in intensity behind his eyes.

Robinson picked up the claim ticket and studied it. His gaze flicked back to Frank. "What the hell have you been grinning at, Travis?"

Frank clamped a hand on Jake's shoulder and nudged him. "Just watching pure logic butt heads with mysticism."

"What do you mean?" Robinson's broad head swiveled on his shoulders. Somewhere between his loosened tie and chin there was a neck. He had a tight-hugging Afro from which Nature saw fit to omit a patch on the top of his head. People joked behind his back that it was from years of scraping ceilings when he walked.

Jake groaned and clasped his hands behind his head. Leaning back, he painfully retold the story of Sam finding the button at the construction site and how it lead to her search for someone named Wieczynski.

Robinson listened intently, then a decisive "hmmpph" erupted from his throat. Robinson didn't just fill a chair...he wore it. It fit him like a diving suit. His clothes had to be special made allowing for his mammoth frame. He was still waiting for the arrival of an office chair, which had also been special-ordered.

"You guys know me. I'd listen to Svengali if it meant catching a guilty person. And with the public leaning against capital punishment because of innocent people being incarcerated for years, I would just hate for us to find out weeks or months after Taggart is executed that we killed the wrong man." He sank back, the chair creaking and groaning against the assault from the former college linebacker. "Shit!" The utterance was identical to what Jake had blurted out at the bank. "Any human body to go with the Wieczynski name?" The two men shook their heads. "Mayor ain't gonna like this." His deep, Barry White voice resonated off the walls and vibrated the papers on the desk. He looked at the two detectives. "Talk to me."

"There's still the possibility that drugs or gambling were involved in Dahlkamp's death," Jake said. "At one time he owed the wrong people eight thousand dollars. There's a possibility he might have racked up some more debts."

"And we have the claim check. Gotta be something important if he went to the trouble of getting a safety deposit box the minute he popped into town," Frank chimed in.

"And what do you make of him squirreling away these newspaper clippings?"

"Honestly, I don't know what to make of it," Jake admitted.

Frank shrugged. "I'm sure if we asked Sam, she'd say Dahlkamp was rejuvenated by the recent publicity over the case and Wieczynski killed him." He fought it but a wide grin again forced its way across his face.

"I think we should keep these articles and any reference to Sam's opinions out of the papers for now," the Captain suggested.

"I agree," the detectives said in unison.

"What about phone records?" Robinson asked.

"Harwood PD should have them by tomorrow," Frank reported.

"What about the owner of the car wash?"

"John Miller?" Frank asked. "Never heard of Lonnie before. Never had trouble at his car wash. Fine upstanding citizen, and he wants the police department to pay for the clean up of his vacuum unit."

"Tell him not to hold his breath." Suddenly, Robinson started gathering up the newspaper clippings and shoving them back into the envelope. He slipped the envelope under his right elbow and looked up, just as his door was pushed open.

"Gentlemen." Chief Dennis Murphy stood in the doorway, beady eyes taking in the furnishings of his former office, smug in the knowledge that he now had an office three times the size. "Jake," Murphy started, "can't tell you how disturbing it was to read about your wife's involvement in the DeMarco case." He moved to the side credenza and leaned against it, hands gripping the edge, shirt cuffs riding over his Rolex watch.

The three men remained silent. Robinson swiveled his chair to face Murphy, his elbow pressed firmly to the brown envelope.

"You can imagine how Mayor Jenkins feels about this," Murphy continued. "After all, he was the state's attorney who sent Taggart to prison. Can't begin to tell you what it meant to the residents of Chasen Heights when Jenkins was instrumental in putting that killer behind bars."

"I believe you mean voters of Chasen Heights," Robinson said.

"A high profile case like that, of course it was what catapulted him to mayor. Now to see Sam's efforts undermining the mayor's victory does not reflect well on this department." Murphy turned his broad smile to Robinson. "Does it, Captain?"

"As yet our department hasn't been involved, Chief," Robinson said, his words honey-lacquered and chosen carefully. "I will certainly keep you apprised if the situation should change."

Chief Murphy pushed away from the credenza, his fingers buttoning his suit jacket and straightening his silk tie.

"Let me repeat." Murphy's gaze scanned each of their faces, his smile not reaching his eyes. "The mayor wants to see this execution go off without a hitch." He pulled the door open amid chatter and chaos in the outer office as reporters and cameramen rushed to greet Chief Murphy. It wasn't unusual for Murphy to make sure his handlers let the press know where he was at all times.

Robinson handed the envelope to Frank. "I didn't see this. We didn't have this conversation. These assholes would keep their own mother in jail if it meant getting their faces on the front page." Turning to Jake, he said, "Tell Sam she has my blessings. She reports to you and you are to inform me of any progress. I don't want anything leaked to the press."

Frank leaned forward, the noise from the outer office making it difficult to hear. "Captain, if you hide this from Murphy and Jenkins, they'll have your ass in a sling."

Robinson wedged himself out of his chair and stood slowly, unfolding his six-foot, six-inch frame. "I say they better have a pretty big sling."

Frank trailed Jake into his office. "Sure would like to be there when you tell Sam about Dahlkamp's safety deposit box."

"When hell freezes over."

Frank cackled and collapsed into one of the chairs, hands applauding.

"I don't know why you are so amused. This just confirms even more your Cemetery Mary fears." Jake tossed the envelope on his desk and watched Frank's smile disintegrate. He checked the chaos in the outer office. Murphy was in his glory. Lights, camera, headlines.

Frank peered through the glass at the scene. "Isn't she the reporter who was on the news the other night interviewing the DeMarcos?"

"Looks like her."

Murphy gave a wave to Erin Starr before climbing into the elevator. Jake no sooner turned to lock his files when the reporter strolled into his office.

"You two are working the Dahlkamp homicide, right?" Her

eyes flashed hunger but it was difficult to tell if it was a story she was hungry for as she let her gaze drift over Jake's body. "Was it a mob hit? I may be new to town but I've done my homework. Chasen Heights was a bed of mob activity for fifty years."

Jake tossed file folders into the bottom drawer and locked it. "We have no comment at this time."

Her green eyes flashed at his desktop. "Any evidence you'd like to share Detective..." her gaze captured his name plate, "Mitchell?"

Frank reached a hand to her and smiled. "I'm Detective Travis and, no, we don't have anything at the moment."

"My." Erin turned her smile back to Jake, her eyes snaking over his chest, circling his face and resting on his mouth. "That's good. Your lips never moved." Her voice belonged on the other end of a 900 number men call in the middle of the night. She placed one well-rounded hip on the corner of the desk. "How about if we just talk, off the record. Say dinner?"

"Thanks, but I have plans," Frank replied, although it was clear to him the invite was meant for Jake.

Jake wanted to say, "What part of 'no comment' didn't you understand?" He grabbed the envelope and pushed past her. "It's been a long day, Miss Starr." He walked away, his thoughts on the safety deposit box and how Dahlkamp was connected to DeMarco. And, more importantly, Sam and that damn button she found.

24

S am stared at the contents in the drawer. It was so tempting. On her way home she had stopped to pick up a few items Abby needed from the store. The grocery cart had magically made its way down the cookie aisle and her hand reacted on its own, snatching the package of Salerno chocolate covered graham crackers from the shelf. Now the overwhelming guilt had settled in. She had to tell herself it was like a pacifier. It was there if she should ever need it.

The roar of a well-tuned engine echoed down the drive and through the kitchen window, Sam could see headlights illuminating the garage door as it slowly rolled open. She carefully buried the package of cookies under stacks of dishcloths and towels and kicked the drawer shut. Scooting back to the stool at the counter, Sam picked up the diary and opened her notebook.

The door by the laundry room opened and footsteps echoed on the tiled floor. Sam could mentally trace Jake's routine. He would hang up his coat in the closet by the back door. Then stash his Sig in the wall safe in the study. Next was a stop in the bedroom upstairs to change clothes, then back down to pour himself a cup of coffee. Sam smiled smugly with the knowledge that her husband was not as unpredictable as she had first thought. But then there weren't any footsteps trudging up the stairs. Several seconds later Jake appeared in the kitchen and placed a brown envelope on the counter.

"Where is everyone?" He leaned over and kissed Sam on the mouth, hovered for a few seconds, then kissed her again with a satisfying 'ummmm.'

Slowly, her eyebrows inched their way up as Jake slipped his sportscoat onto the back of the stool next to hers and grabbed a beer from the refrigerator. Sam sighed. So much for predictability.

"Abby and Alex are in the basement packing up some food boxes. Then I'm going to help them wrap some gifts for the children at Eagle Ridge. The Friends of Eagle Ridge will be taking the donations to the reservation later this week."

"Where's Pit?" Jake ran his finger around the rim of the beer can before popping the top. He took a long swig and settled against the sink.

"Come and gone. Abby left you some meatloaf."

Jake's gaze settled on the diary. "Any more lurid details from Catherine's past?"

Sam set the diary to the side and eyed the suspicious brown envelope. "We've pretty much narrowed it down to finding someone known as 'B' and Catherine's friend, Rachel Stowe."

He pushed the sleeves up on his turtleneck. She recognized this move from watching him in *The Box*. Whether he folded up the sleeves of a dress shirt or pushed up the sleeves of a turtleneck or Henley, it was a sure signal to the suspect that Jake was getting down to business and would stay cloistered in the room for as long as it took.

"How did it go with the DeMarcos?"

Sam relayed her impressions of Catherine's room, her suspicion and the confirmation that Catherine had been pregnant, the DeMarcos' reaction, and the role Forrest Eckart and Jack Olsen played in keeping Catherine's pregnancy a secret.

"You forgot the part about the lullaby," Jake said.

Sam paused for a few seconds. "Pit has a big mouth." She relented and told him every detail surrounding the lullaby, then rambled on about Pit's search through accident reports which had proven fruitless. The DeMarcos vaguely remembered Catherine claiming someone had hit their car in the parking lot at the Three Oaks Shopping Center.

There was something else in Jake's eyes that was setting off alarm bells in her head. They were intense, absorbing every word, as if they were high-powered sensors feeding computer chips rather than brain cells. She studied him with the same intensity.

"Okay, Mitchell. What's up? Why the sudden interest in a case you considered a lost cause a week ago?"

He took another long swig of beer and set the empty can in the sink. His head made a slight tilt toward the envelope. Sam hesitated, then opened it and pulled out yellowed newspaper clippings, all on the DeMarco case.

"And I'm looking at these because...?" At the bottom of the stack of clippings was the claim check. She picked it up, studied it, then jerked her gaze back to Jake and waited.

"Remember the homicide yesterday at the Miller Car Wash?"

"Dahlkamp? Robbery? Mob connection or something?"

"Something." Jake took two steps forward and pressed his hands on the island counter. He told her about the trailer in Plymouth and a short bio on Lonnie Dahlkamp. "He had major gambling debts but we didn't have any leads except a key to his safety deposit box."

Sam felt her pulse quicken. "These were in the safety deposit box?" Jake nodded. *An honest to goodness lead,* Sam thought. But then realization set it. "Let me guess." Her eyes narrowed and she shot him a look. "The case is being reopened and you're the lead detective." A smile started to form on his lips. "Come on, Jake." He reached across the counter and grabbed her wrists before she was able to jerk away.

"Hold it before you go off in a snit."

"I don't snit."

He brought her hands together, pressed them to his lips and kissed them. "Let me warm your tea."

"Wonderful," Sam mumbled as Jake nuked her tea. He then covered the dinner plate with wax paper and shoved it in the microwave. After the microwave dinged, Jake took a seat next to her and tackled the meatloaf and mashed potatoes with gusto. She never knew anyone who ate as fast as he did, except maybe Jackie.

In between bites Jake told her about Chief Murphy handing the captain an edict from Mayor Jenkins to forget about Sam chasing ghosts and make sure the execution takes place as scheduled.

"The captain doesn't want anyone in the office to know he is re-opening the DeMarco case," Jake concluded.

"Captain Robinson has scruples. That's refreshing."

"It sickened him, too, that Murphy and Jenkins are playing politics with a man's life." Jake carried his plate to the sink, rinsed it, and placed it in the dishwasher. He grabbed a second beer, popped the top, and searched the pocket of his sportscoat for his cigarettes.

"So, where does that leave me and Pit?"

He shook a cigarette from the pack and checked his pockets for matches. "Captain wants you two to keep plugging away. Report your findings to me. I in turn will keep Robinson informed."

Sam fingered the claim check. "Do you want me to take this?"

Jake shook his head. "Frank checked around and found a store named Dillon's about thirty miles south. We'll take a ride tomorrow. May not have anything to do with the DeMarco case. Dahlkamp might have sold something to a pawn shop for some pocket change. If it ends up having something to do with the case, we'll let you know." He gently tapped the tip of the cigarette on the counter as he considered that last question. "Wish you would just leave it to Pit."

"Jake." The blue in her eyes turned icy as she held his gaze.

"All right." He leaned his elbows on the counter and toyed with the matchbook. "How about if you help Pit but leave my kid at home."

There wasn't even a hint of a smile in his eyes. "How about you carry it the last four months?" Sam countered. She slowly shoved the articles and claim check back into the envelope during the long silence. Once they were safely tucked inside, she closed the flap and left it in the middle of the counter.

"There is one thing we have in common, Jake. This isn't about my needing to keep busy, or your trying to keep me from anything dangerous, or my trying to prove my uncanny talent, or your trying to disprove it."

She searched his face, but as usual, his gaze flitted from the basement door to see if Abby and Alex were returning, to beyond the sliding glass doors where the moon was peeking between naked branches, and finally back to her face.

"The truth, Jake. We all want to know the truth. No matter who it hurts, or how many skeletons we rattle out of someone's closet. Jimmy Taggart deserves it. Catherine DeMarco deserves it."

25

The next morning Jake and Frank drove thirty miles south to Dillon's Sporting Goods in a small town appropriately called Dillon Park. It was anything but a pawnshop. The year 1927 was carved on a corner stone. The cinderblock building also housed a barber shop, a small flower shop called *The Petal Pushers,* and an empty store front with soaped up windows and a *For Rent* sign on the door. An old time bell above the door clanged as the detectives entered.

The hardwood floors were worn and squeaked as the two men crossed the room. They walked past racks of camouflage pants, jackets, and hunting vests. Shelves against the wall were jammed with sleeping bags, camping and hiking gear. There was an odor of old wood and seasoned dust in the air.

The man behind the counter looked as old as the building. "You're the detectives who called earlier. I'm Morgan Dillon." He gave their badges a passing glance. His voice had an edge of sandpaper to it.

The detectives studied the glass case behind Morgan. It contained rifles, knives, bows, and arrows. The glass showcase in front of the detectives held bullets, pellets, and handguns.

"I checked my files for a copy of that receipt. I usually don't throw anything out." Morgan pulled out a dusty book and flipped through the pages. "Here." He tapped a gnarled finger on the page. "I found the item that matches the stock number."

Jake and Frank studied the picture of a pearl-handled knife.

"That's what was reported, a pearl handle, right?" Frank asked.

"Here we go." Morgan pulled out a wad of paper. He showed Jake the store copy and compared it to the copy Lonnie had in his safety deposit box. It was a match. "You've got the customer copy," Morgan said. "See, the store copy is white. Customer copy is yellow."

"Our copy doesn't show a clear date," Jake pointed out.

Morgan hobbled off to the back room. The detectives heard the hum of a copy machine and within seconds the elderly man returned. "Here you go." Morgan handed a fresh copy to Jake who glanced over it and passed it to Frank. The sales receipt was dated the day before Catherine DeMarco was murdered.

Frank pulled out the picture of Lonnie and showed it to Morgan. "Do you recognize this man? Could he have been the one who purchased the knife?"

Morgan squinted at the picture. "I never forget a face. I usually have regulars who come here, locals." After a few seconds, he nodded. "Yep, I've seen this fella before."

"He purchased the knife?" Jake asked.

"Nope." Morgan scratched his bony chin and looked up at the detectives with a wry smile on his face. "He sold it."

They left Dillon Park and headed to the Cook County Court warehouse on 31st Street in Chicago. The evidence in the Taggart case had been transferred to the warehouse after the trial.

The file clerk punched a few keys and a detailed listing appeared on the monitor. "What's the case number?" Sophie asked.

Frank replied, "1191." He lifted the lid on a candy jar and peered in. Turning a peppermint pattie over, he read the ingredients. "Corn syrup, cocoa butter, lactose, soya lecithin."

"You're spending way too much time in the gym." Jake's eyes

dragged down Frank's frame. He was wearing a dark brown suede sportscoat, pants, and matching shirt, tie, even suede shoes. "Funny you never read the ingredients of the desserts Abby makes."

"I tell myself they're all natural. Gotta be the way they taste." Frank checked his tie and pants. "You've been checking me out all morning, Jake. Don't tell me I'm starting to look good to you."

"Actually, I was thinking how much you look like a Fudgsicle."

"Fudgsicle?" Frank checked his reflection in a mirrored door.

"You look good enough to eat to me," Sophie said with a wink. She laughed boisterously, her flesh swaying under the sack dress as she sashayed into the back room.

Frank lowered his voice to a whisper. "Remind me never to wear this outfit again." He tossed the peppermint pattie back into the candy jar. "How does Sam think Lonnie fits in?"

Jake had called Sam after their visit to Dillon's Sporting Goods and relayed the information that Lonnie had worked at Dillon's for one week.

"She's got the same impression. Lonnie read about the murder and the description of the murder weapon, could I.D. the killer, and blackmailed him."

"So why bleed the blackmailer for more money after all these years?"

"Good question." Jake's phone chirped. He pulled it from his pocket and flipped it open. He listened for several seconds, then said, "No. I don't have time for that. Tell her anything." He snapped the phone shut and slipped it in his pocket.

"Let me guess. Thigh high skirt and perky breasts."

"I don't care how high her skirt goes or where the perks point. She is still the press and the last person we need to talk to. Maybe I'll have Janet give her your number."

"Thanks, but no thanks."

Sophie returned and set a box on the counter. "What do you need out of here?"

"Copy of the Evidence Log for starters," Frank said. He took the box from her. While Sophie made the copy, they sifted through the contents. "Here's the knife." Jake lifted it out of the box. It was still caked in blood, the pearl handle smudged. He turned the knife blade down and read the stock number, *"19389."*

Sam sat between Art Bigalow and Pit feeling both nervous and excited. It had been years since she had visited anyone in prison. She wondered how people who were claustrophobic handled the confinement. At least at the Sara Binyon's Retreat she knew she would be leaving. Besides, her room had been more like a hotel suite, not a prison cell.

"I'm not sure I remember what he looks like," Pit whispered. "The only image I can conjure up is a skinny, long-haired Hell's Angel with tattoos running up and down each arm."

The steel door clanged open and a guard led Jimmy Taggart into the room. He hesitated, taking time to study each of their faces, then he took a deep breath and sat down at the table. The guard handcuffed Jimmy to the chair.

If she hadn't known they were visiting Jimmy, she would never have recognized him from the photo on Rose's end table. He had added at least thirty pounds of muscle, his face had filled out, and his hair was Marine short. But there was something missing.

"Didn't think I'd ever see you again," Jimmy said to Pit.

"Well, stranger things have happened." Pit introduced Sam.

Jimmy nodded nervously toward her. "You aren't what I had expected."

Sam looked down at her stomach and wondered what part was out of place. "What?" she questioned. "Too young? Too old?" She had worn slacks with a duster coat that hit mid-calf. It was a three-piece outfit meant to cover as much skin as possible, not that a pregnant woman would get prisoners all sexed up, but she stayed on the side of caution. Abby had helped plait her hair. Her fingers reached for the medicine bundle which wasn't there, since the guards confiscated it during the search. She had refused to let them open it. They had refused to let her in without the contents being spilled out for everyone to see.

Jimmy shrugged. "No crystal ball. Mr. Bigalow told me a little about you."

"Then you know I don't use a crystal ball." Sam realized what was missing. The light in Jimmy's eyes. That devil-may-care mischievous twinkle that was so evident in the photo.

"I don't need to ask you to explain to me in your own words what happened that night," Sam started. "I've read it all in the court transcripts."

"Good, 'cause to tell you the truth, I don't see where I can add much." He leaned back, relaxed in the company of familiar faces or just glad to be out of his cell. It was difficult to tell.

"How have you been?" Pit asked.

Jimmy blinked slowly, like someone just coming out of anesthesia and trying to get his bearings. "My father called. I wished he hadn't. Just reminds me of the outside world, my mother, the funeral I couldn't attend, the heartache I put them through and especially how damn fast seventeen years flies by. I just want it all to be over." He gave a long sigh and clasped his hands together, the handcuffs jangling at the strain. "Dad said to give one last ditch effort for mom. So shoot."

In hopes of jogging his near non-existent memory of that night, Sam went into detail about what she saw the day she had picked up the button. When she finished, Jimmy just stared at her, unblinking. She wasn't sure if she lulled him to sleep or shocked him.

"Sorry. I don't mean any disrespect, ma'am, but I find it a little..." Jimmy let the word drift. "Sorry," he repeated.

"Have you ever heard the name Lonnie Dahlkamp?" Pit asked.

Jimmy narrowed his eyes in thought. "You mean the murder that was in the papers recently? No."

"Well, we now have reason to believe that his murder is some-how tied to Catherine's murder," Sam explained.

"Actually, we're trying to trace Lonnie's movements back then.

He wasn't a stellar citizen, having racked up a couple terms in jail himself." Pit pulled out a photo from an envelope and placed it on the table.

"You think he's the killer?" Jimmy studied the police department photo.

"We feel he knew something about Catherine's murder," Pit said. "And we feel the real killer silenced him. The problem will be proving it."

"Right." Jimmy chuckled but it was as lethargic as his blinking. "Exactly what is it you know?"

"I think Lonnie may have been either a witness to the murder or knew the murderer and provided him with the weapon," Sam explained. "I think he had blackmailed the murderer and then dropped out of sight, spent some time in and out of jail, then resurfaced. It wasn't until word got out in the press that I was snooping around and reevaluating the evidence that Lonnie might have contacted the murderer again. Maybe to hit him up for more hush money."

Art Bigalow had remained silent, watching Jimmy's reaction. "Of course, there was a brief interview with Catherine's parents which reminded people of the upcoming execution. Maybe this Dahlkamp guy decided to redeem himself and come clean with what he knows, but his greediness won out."

"Sam's husband is a detective with CHPD. He found newspaper clippings on the murder and a receipt in Dahlkamp's safety deposit box," Pit said. "He traced the receipt back to the murder weapon."

Sam asked, "What about Wieczynski? Does that name ring a bell?"

Jimmy shook his head. "Who is he?"

"Just someone else who might be involved," Sam replied.

Jimmy stared at his clasped hands, a flash of anger in his eyes. "So the real killer has been living and breathing in Chasen Heights for seventeen years." His attention was brought back to the table as Sam pushed a button toward him. "What's that?"

"It's off of a designer jacket," Sam replied. "Ever see it before?"

Jimmy stifled a laugh. "I never even owned designer jeans."

Sam smiled. "I didn't think so."

He stared nervously at them as the door opened and the guard announced time was up. "So, what can I do to help?"

"Glad you asked," Sam smiled. "We'd like you to go under hypnosis again. And we'd like to be there."

"So you struck out," Jake said. Sam sat in a booth across from Pit in a restaurant just one mile from the prison. It was filled with white-collar workers, some drinking their lunch. She was talking to Jake on her cell phone while her other hand held the menu. Attorney Bigalow had returned to his office.

"Jimmy feels it is useless to try to go through hypnosis again. We can't force him. He doesn't recognize Lonnie's name or photo. And I, personally, believe him."

"Well, my guess is Lonnie sold the knife to the killer, and after reading the description in the paper of the murder weapon, tied two and two together."

"How did he get the customer's copy of the receipt?"

"The killer probably didn't want to be caught with it, so he never took it with him and Lonnie put it with the store copy. Then when he realized he knew who the killer was, he took the copy for proof."

"God, all this time he knew the killer. Amazing." Sam set the menu aside and looked for their waitress.

"How was Jimmy's mood?"

"Other than counting the days, hours, and minutes? At least he doesn't have to walk the streets in this town. There's a vendor on every corner selling tee shirts with his picture and a hypodermic needle. The cute saying on them is, *The Shot Heard Round the World.*"

"Well, the clock is ticking, Sam."

"I'm aware of that. Anything on the phone records from the Harwood PD?"

"Hector and John are going through them using the Haines Reverse Directory. They'll let us know." Jake's voice took on a serious tone. "You know, desperation can make a person do desperate things. The papers tie your name to the DeMarcos. It won't take long for the killer to conclude that you might be a threat. Maybe you should let us guys handle this one."

"I do have one favor," Sam said in an attempt to change the subject. "I'd like to check out Lonnie's car. Do the crime techs still have it?"

"It's in one of the bays. I might clear it, but only if afterwards you leave the case to me and Pit."

"You'll call now? We'd like to go over after lunch."

"I'm serious, Sam."

"What's that?" Sam tapped her phone. "I'm losing you, Jake. Can't hear you." She heard Frank cackle just before she hung up.

"Were you losing him?" Pit asked.

"Of course not." When Pit gave a puzzled look, Sam explained, "He's going protective on me. He feels my life might be threatened if I continue with this case and that maybe just the three of you should work on it."

"You know..."

Sam's eyes narrowed. "Don't you start."

"Should we visit Dahlkamp's apartment or his mother's trailer?"

"Jake said there wasn't much in the apartment. And he described the trailer to me. I'll take a pass."

26

"I like a man who can control his wife." Frank studied his own reflection in Jake's mirrored sunglasses. Jake didn't smile.

"It isn't your wife who salivates at the thought of diving head first into a murder case." Jake squatted down and studied the drive on the north side of Miller Car Wash. The ground had been too dry the evening of the murder to obtain any tire or shoe prints. Jake slowly rose and turned toward the street, assessing the distance from the car wash to curious eyes.

Frank adjusted his sunglasses and stepped off the drive. "I'm sure there is a good reason why we are here again."

Jake walked the perimeter of the woods until he could see the vacuum cleaner unit. Lonnie Dahlkamp had been smart enough to park in the dark recesses of the car wash...or dumb enough.

"What did we find in the space next to Dahlkamp's car?" Jake asked.

"Nada."

"Would you park facing the woods?"

"Negative. I would have had that baby parked facing the entrance to the car wash. I want to see someone coming."

"Right." Jake continued along the outskirts of the woods, Frank trailing behind.

"And if I were the killer, I wouldn't pull up right next to him. I'd want to make sure Dahlkamp was alone, make sure there wasn't anyone else around," Frank added.

The back lot was empty. Crime scene tape and the wooden horses used to block the entrances had been removed. Jake doubted there was anything else to learn from walking the area again but it never hurt.

"Could have pulled up right next to him and made him roll down the window, then shot him. But, no." Frank thought about that and then answered his own theory. "Too much of a chance he'd miss and that wound was from close range. Besides, the shell casing was found in the car. That means he spent a little bit of time with Dahlkamp, maybe to negotiate, bicker a little."

"But he didn't even offer him a beer."

"Could have but maybe he refused, wanted to get out of there before anyone decided to take a car through the spin cycle."

Jake thought back to the size of the gym bag. "If we go on the theory that he was blackmailing someone regarding the DeMarco case, then Dahlkamp was expecting a shit load of money." He swung his gaze back to the side drive along the north side of the building. "Maybe the killer drove in with his lights off, parked on the side of the building, and walked over."

"Could have arrived early. The north side of the building is pretty much in the dark. It's away from the main entrance and too far for motorists to see from the street."

Jake nodded in agreement, visualizing the killer's car hidden in the shadows, the killer watching Dahlkamp, watching and waiting to make sure they were alone.

"Now we know the possible *how*," Jake said. "All we need is the *who*."

* * *

"You'd rather see this than the trailer?" Pit stood back, arms folded. He winced at the condition of the interior of Dahlkamp's car. "I've been away from scenes like this for too long." He unwrapped a stick of gum and shoved the wrapper in his pocket.

"I can pick up more from the car since this was the scene of the crime," Sam explained. She had felt the hairs on the back of her neck rise the moment she entered the bay. The closer she got, the more it felt like tiny electrodes darting from cell to cell.

"Just tell me you aren't going to sit inside."

"I'm not going to sit inside." Sam snapped on latex gloves as she approached the driver's side.

Suey, one of the crime techs, stood several feet away, beefy arms folded across his chest. "She's getting a feel for the auras," Suey pointed out. "She's trying to determine who's talking louder, the victim or the killer." A wide smile lit up his doughy face. "I take it you haven't had a dose of Sam Casey before."

Pit swung his gaze back to Sam, watching as she bent down and peered inside.

"What was on the menu today, Suey?" Sam asked as she studied the splatter marks.

"Pork with plum sauce." Suey's family owned The Red Dragon Restaurant which featured five entrees on their buffet table each day. Suey rarely ate anywhere else, hence his nickname.

"How can you two talk about plum sauce." Pit winced as he dragged his attention away from the driver's side window. A huge chunk had been blown out. Pieces of blood and gray matter were imbedded in the cracks.

Sam walked around to the passenger side. "What's your take on it, Suey?"

"Bunch of prints. No matches yet besides the victim's. Killer wiped the door handle clean or probably wore gloves."

"Could the killer have been in the back seat?" Pit asked.

Suey shook his head and walked over to where Sam stood.

"Angle is all wrong. The killer was definitely in the front seat."

Pit touched her arm. "Are you okay with this?"

Sam smiled at his puppy eyes and knew why girls liked to take home strays. "Are you?"

The door was open and she pressed her hand against the inside window frame while she squatted down. The dark green upholstery and carpeting were caked with dried blood. Splatter marks trailed across the dashboard, steering wheel, front and rear windshields.

Sam imagined Lonnie sitting in the car waiting innocently for his proverbial boat to come in. It was probably more money than he would ever make in a lifetime. She thought about what a man like Lonnie would be doing to while away his time. Pound out a tune on the dashboard or steering wheel?

"Was the radio playing when the body was found?" She asked Suey.

"No."

She studied the splatter marks again and could see the outline of his body. Did the killer get any blood on him? How much time had he spent in the car talking to Lonnie? Her thoughts were scattered and she barely noticed the heat coming from the vents or the bay lights dimming. Beyond the windshield was darkness and she wondered for a moment if Suey had turned the lights out.

Pit's and Suey's voices faded. From over her right shoulder a hand appeared. She thought at first that Pit was going to help her up. But the hand was holding a gun. Her body felt weightless, moving in slow motion as she backed away from the door.

'Bout time you showed up.

The disembodied words emanated from the driver's side of the car. Startled, Sam coaxed her lead feet to move but then noticed that the murder weapon had changed. It was no longer the dark metal of a pistol. It had changed to a knife, its blade dripping.

"Sam, are you okay?" Pit's voice echoed from somewhere behind her. She turned in the direction of the voice and felt Pit's arms wrap tightly around her.

"I'm okay, I'm fine."

"You don't look it." Pit led her through a doorway to Suey's office and lowered her onto a chair. "What the hell did you see?"

Sam tried to keep her hands from shaking as she tore the latex gloves off. "Let me catch my breath." Suey appeared with a cup of herbal tea and she gulped it to chase the chill from her bones. "The killer didn't get in the car," Sam said. "He opened the door and shot him. Was there anything in the report about the dome light not working?"

"There wasn't a light bulb in it," Suey said.

"So it was probably too dark for Lonnie to see the gun until it was too late," Pit speculated.

"There's more. The weapon changed from a gun to a knife. It had a pearl handle." Sam felt faint and barely reached the garbage can next to Suey's desk before she gave up her lunch.

27

A   s Jake maneuvered the turn through the gate, he noticed
     headlights growing in his rearview mirror. He pulled a bag
     of groceries out of the trunk of the Taurus just as a red
sports car maneuvered the turnaround and screeched to a halt at the
front door.

Erin Starr slid out of the driver's side, exposing a lot of leg from
under a long leather coat. Her dark hair was twisted up in a nest of curls.

"What's a girl to do to get dinner?"

You mean to get a story, Jake thought. "I didn't think you meant
tonight."

"That's okay. You show me to the kitchen and I can whip up
anything." She pulled the bag of groceries from his arms and
walked to the front door.

Jake weighed his options carefully. He had half a mind to escort
the reporter back to her car but then stared intently at the house. A
wicked half-smile played across his face as he thought of what
might lay in wait inside for the brazen reporter. With a jingle of
keys, Jake unlocked the door and ushered her in.

"My, my." Her gaze swept up the curved staircase and back
down to the stone fireplace in the sitting room, absorbing every
minute detail. "This is soooo..." she cooed, "rustic, Native
American. How masculine."

"Jacob." Abby emerged from the study and crossed the foyer. "I'll take those groceries."

"Abby, this is Erin Starr. She's a reporter with WABC news."

Abby nodded. "Miss Starr."

"Erin will be joining us for dinner."

"How nice. Why don't you make Miss Starr a drink. Dinner should be ready in a half hour."

When Abby disappeared around the corner, Erin whispered, "You even have a Native American housekeeper. How quaint." Her attention was drawn to the study where Christmas tree lights beckoned.

"My, my." Erin shrugged out of her leather coat and draped it over the back of the couch. Another fireplace crackled and sparked in the far corner near the computer.

Jake wasn't sure if her eyes sparkled admiration or dollar signs. He walked behind the bar to the refrigerator and brought out a bottle of wine.

"Love the music." A unique rendition of Christmas carols played softly in the background.

"Mannheim Steamroller."

"I've never heard of them." Erin's eyes danced down the length of his body. Visions of percale and satin seemed to dance in her eyes.

Alex strolled in from the kitchen, shirttail hanging out of his pants, collar open revealing an exquisite piece of jewelry.

He nodded his head toward the bottle. "I'll open it." His gaze rested briefly on Erin before turning to leave.

"You even have a butler," Erin cooed again.

Jake watched Alex's step falter at those words and he had to smile. Alex had never offered to open any kind of a bottle for him so curiosity over their guest obviously prompted Alex to find an excuse to enter the study.

Jake grabbed two glasses, and a bottle of beer, and walked back out to the foyer with Erin close behind.

"Never knew detectives made such good money." Her fingers

slid under the buttons of her black silk jacket. The matching skirt hit mid-thigh and she negotiated the three stairs down to the dining room with the skill of a woman born wearing three-inch heels. The jacket slowly drifted from her shoulders and Erin hung it on the back of one of the dining room chairs. The long-sleeved blouse was made of sheer chiffon. The only thing between Erin's skin and the chiffon was a camisole. Erin Starr's attributes left little to the imagination.

"I spent some time at the library going through back issues of the local papers regarding the Catherine DeMarco murder. Would be great if I could be one of the twenty-five media selected to witness Jimmy Taggart's execution."

"How do you word that on a resume?" Jake asked in all seriousness.

Alex returned with the wine bottle and cork and handed it to Jake, who filled one long-stemmed glass. Jake could swear he saw a devilish smile cross Alex's lips before he turned to leave. Something like, *Let's see you get yourself out of this one, white man.*

Erin took the glass of wine Jake offered, letting her fingers casually brush against his. "Could mean national recognition, a news anchor job. Think of the possibilities." She strolled through the living room, surveying the décor, nodding in approval, then stood in the doorway to the Florida room.

"Very nice house, indeed." Erin pulled her gaze from the surroundings and rested them on Jake. Her fingers slowly traced the thin, gold chain hanging from her neck, down to where it dipped beneath her camisole.

Jake poured his beer into a glass and watched her performance. There wasn't anything subtle about Erin Starr. Her slicked up, touch-me-not hairstyle was contradicted by the leggy, see-through outfit that said, *take me now.*

"Tell me about yourself, Miss Starr."

"Erin. Please call me Erin." She slithered over to where he

stood by the window seat. "I was born in Kansas City, have four big brothers, attended Ball State University, was a cheerleader all four years. I could really do a mean flip." She took a dainty sip of wine, leaving bright red lipstick on the rim.

"I bet you could."

"But my past is boring. I want to hear about you." Erin slowly ran her finger around the rim of the wine glass, then licked the remnants from her finger. Her eyes never left his face as her mouth appeared to suck on her finger.

Abby slipped in and lit two candles sitting atop tall patina candleholders. Jake took a step away from Erin as if she were a hot plate. He asked Abby, "Do you need help?"

"No, no. Please entertain your guest."

"I understand you worked at the *Atlanta Beacon* before coming to Chasen Heights."

"Why, Sergeant Mitchell. You've been asking around about me."

"I know you covered the killings at the abortion clinic in Atlanta. That's what first caught the attention of the station manager at WABC. You're single, twenty-eight years old, and majored in journalism, minored in biology." He didn't have to ask around. Brandon had made a point to find out everything about Erin and shared the goods earlier with the boys in the break room.

Alex stood behind the island counter watching Jake through the pass-through. "Hmmpph," he mumbled. "White men are so weak."

Abby nudged him aside. "Unlike you, who hasn't taken his eyes off Ms. Starr since she arrived." Finally, Alex shifted his gaze away from the dining room. Abby added, "She's a reporter, trying to get a story."

"She's trying to get something from Jake, but I doubt it's a story." Alex chuckled and asked, "Has Sam met her yet?"

The words no sooner left his mouth then the back door by the laundry room opened and closed silently. Abby met Sam in the hallway and filled her in on their dinner guest. Sam draped her coat on the kitchen chair and peered cautiously through the pass-through. Erin Starr had the features of a starlet and the skin of a model. What was worse, she looked great next to Jake. His face was hard to read. His brows hunkered in thought as he listened intently to whatever drivel the reporter was dishing out.

Subconsciously, Sam raked a hand through the untamed hairs that had freed themselves from her French braid. She contemplated running upstairs to take the braid out and fluff up her hair. Then she looked down at her stomach protruding like a beach ball. She considered changing into something a little dressier, more competitive, but thought, *the hell with it.* Her stomach was still queasy and all she wanted to do was climb into bed. She took a deep breath and charged into the dining room. Abby followed.

"Miss Starr," Abby said, "I'd like you to meet my daughter, Samantha."

Erin forced a smile. "Daughter?" Her head dipped back in an attempt to get their images closer together for comparison. She studied Abby's face and then Sam's, her eyes narrowed in thought as she attempted to find some resemblance. Finally her gaze rested on the medicine bundles and cheekbones. And she stared with amusement at the one earring of beads and feathers that brushed the top of Sam's shoulder. "Are you here to pick up your mother?" Her question was met with silence. "I'm sure you both can stay for dinner, seeing that you made it," she told Abby. She looked uncomfortably at Jake. "Right?"

Sam's eyes were drawn to Erin's see-through black chiffon blouse where large, erect nipples stood up like pencil erasers. She forced a smile and stuck her hand out to Erin. "Hi, I'm the pregnant wife." From somewhere behind her, Alex guffawed. A smile tugged at the corners of Jake's mouth. Erin's smile quickly faded and her eyes jerked back to Jake, who gave a disinterested shrug and wiggled his ring finger at her.

"Well, isn't my face red," Erin said.

Glancing at the pencil erasers again, Sam said, "Maybe we should bring you a sweater. You look a bit chilled."

To her benefit, Erin took the hint and slipped back into her jacket. "Thanks for the warning," Erin mouthed to Jake.

Jake said, "I thought you were an astute reporter." Erin's face flushed again.

Sam watched as Erin strolled over to Alex wielding her empty wine glass. As if the night wasn't going downhill fast enough, Alex shoved the wine bottle back at Erin saying, "Abby is NOT the housekeeper and I definitely am NOT the butler." Erin's face turned crimson.

Abby did her best to take the strain out of the evening. She steered the conversation to the Bureau of Indian Affairs and how the new Interior Secretary had disbanded it and created a new agency to handle the funds. Erin changed the subject to football.

"Huh. Ridiculous the millions they offer these kids," Alex grumbled. "They should get an education first. All this money to push some stupid ball down a field."

"I take it you don't like football." Erin turned her eyes on Jake. "You look like a man who probably played the sport."

"I don't like the obscene amounts of money paid to any athlete," Alex added.

"Their careers are short. Their bodies take a beating and a serious injury could sideline them forever." Jake pushed his empty plate aside and refilled his beer glass.

"And the career of a police officer could end any minute," Sam countered. "They should receive the millions." She stared at the lump of mashed potatoes on her plate and tried to push thoughts of Dahlkamp's car out of her head.

"And the military," Abby chimed in. "Pay them a decent salary and you wouldn't have any problem getting people to join."

"Think of the unemployed youth out of high school you could get off the street by offering them a decent salary in the Armed Forces and a paid college education when they come out. But you probably won't report that in your news program," Alex huffed.

"Maybe if the military didn't spend billions on one jet fighter, they'd have money for salaries." Erin dabbed at her mouth with the cloth napkin. Somehow she had managed a dinner and two glasses of wine without smudging her lipstick. "Football is part of the entertainment industry. Whatever the market will bear. People want to see movies and sports."

"Dessert anyone?" Abby flashed a cautious look at Alex and retreated to the kitchen.

Even the pan of brownies didn't look enticing to Sam. Abby removed her untouched plate and returned several minutes later with a bowl of chicken noodle soup. She looked up at her mother with a grateful smile. This she might be able to get down.

"You have so many interesting things happening for such a mid-sized town," Erin chatted on. "Next to Taggart's execution, I think the second most interesting trial will be your town's notorious cop killer."

Sam's spoon hovered near her mouth. *Notorious?* She lowered her spoon.

"You might have caught my taping earlier." Erin proceeded to recite her news clip: "Has an innocent man been in prison for seventeen years? If so, where is the real killer now? Sources say any effort to reopen this case is strictly a ploy by a suspended homicide detective to make yet another grandstand play for publicity."

"Who gave you the little sound bite about the suspended detective? Chief Murphy?" Jake asked.

Erin straightened. "Well, yes. I..."

"You've been here for, what? All of two months?" Jake asked.

"Yes, but I've read scores of back issues of the Post Tribune on their web site. And now Casey is trying to get the killer out of prison. I think that's news, even though the detective doesn't seem to be getting too much cooperation from the DeMarcos."

Sam's hands gripped the arms of her chair but Jake wrapped a hand firmly around her forearm.

"Sam, don't get yourself riled."

"Sam?" Erin blinked. "You're Sergeant Sam Casey?" She closed her eyes and grimaced. "Damn, am I good or what." She fumbled in her purse for her tape recorder. "I seem to always be in the right place at the right time." A recorder and notepad were slipped quickly from her purse.

"Nothing leaves this house, Erin." Jake's voice was not as threatening as his glare. He draped a protective arm across the back of Sam's chair. "I mean it. Now put the recorder away."

Erin reluctantly slid the recorder back into her purse. "I really need to know about Officer Stu Richards."

Jake stopped her. "That subject is off limits."

Abby nodded toward Alex and the two stacked up the plates and disappeared into the kitchen.

"There isn't much to tell," Sam said. "He was dead when I arrived on the scene."

"Sam, don't say another word."

"What about your gun?"

"The explosion knocked it out of my hand."

Jake played with his empty beer glass, twirling it around with the tips of his fingers as he watched Erin's hand toy with her pen.

"Listen, Erin," Jake interrupted, "all you have to do is check the medical examiner's report. You will find that Stu Richards died of a broken neck, not the gunshots."

"The Taggart case is really of more interest," Sam offered. "How about if you play along with us and we see to it that you get an exclusive in the end?"

Erin's flirtatious mask slipped away and her tone and expression turned serious. "You mean there really is something that could blow this case wide open?"

"Absolutely," Sam said.

Erin didn't hesitate long. "What do you have in mind?"

28

The next morning Captain Robinson was parked in Jake's office waiting for an update.

"Dahlkamp never made more than sixteen thousand dollars in any one year and that included his disability checks," Jake reported.

"Where did he live during his week of employment at Dillon's?" Robinson asked.

"Dillon isn't sure. The only transient hotel near Dillon Park burned down ten years ago. Best guess is Lonnie lived there."

"And you can really trust this reporter to not mention the connection between Lonnie and Catherine?" Pit asked.

"Sam's more trusting of her than I am," Jake said. "Erin promised to steer the public eye away from the Dahlkamp case. We'll have to wait and see."

"Where is Sam?" Frank asked.

"Doctor's appointment," Jake said. He flipped through his notes and continued. "According to bank records, Lonnie made a deposit of nine thousand dollars two days after the murder. Then he withdrew it all two days later, probably had a hot tip on a horse."

"Did he ever have any side jobs, maybe at Catherine's school or any of the mall stores or grocery stores?" Robinson asked.

"No," Jake replied.

"That would be going on the premise that he knew the victim," Pit said.

"But he didn't. He knew the killer," Jake replied. He checked his watch.

"What did our boys in Harwood find out?" Robinson asked.

"Very little. Dahlkamp wasn't in town long enough to garner much attention." Jake turned to Pit. "Any luck finding anyone by the name of Wieczynski?"

"An Internet search brings up fifty-eight in the States. We tried just Illinois and Indiana and struck out. But Wieczynski could have moved anywhere. Sam was going to get a listing from the IRS database of tax returns."

Jake sighed. "I can just guess how she plans to accomplish that." He traced a finger down the page of notes until he came to Rachel's name. "Rachel Stowe. Married to Phil Secrest, a podiatrist, lives in Santa Monica. She teaches art at the university. We are still waiting for a return call."

Robinson moved away from the wall, which seemed to squeak a sigh of relief. "What about your guy posted outside Mo Williams apartment?"

"We traced the Lexus that Mo was seen climbing into a few times," Frank said. "Belongs to a suspected drug dealer who DEA has its eye on. The driver isn't the drug dealer. He's Mo's cousin and runs errands for the dealer. Felicia on the other hand walks Keesha to school every day and so far there haven't been any fights or loud voices coming from the apartment."

"Hershey's a good man. I know he can't be there twenty-four-seven so I just hope to hell nothing happens in the middle of the night." The doorknob disappeared under Robinson's mitt-sized hand. "Keep me posted, guys."

Sam emerged from the elevator with Jackie in tow. They stopped for visitor badges and headed for Jake's office. Activity stopped, mouths gaped. This time it wasn't due to Sam's appearance. Jackie had a way of stopping even dust from forming. Her red dress hit mid-thigh and the calf-length green duster flowed behind her like a cape. Earrings of tiny ornaments lit up, blinking with every move of her body. A matching necklace of blinking ornaments bounced between her ample cleavage.

"I should have you accompany me every time I come here," Sam said. She had seen Jackie parking her Mercedes in the spot reserved for the press. Her friend never did like parking garages or long hikes on four-inch heels from off street parking. She usually parked wherever she damn well pleased.

Jackie took quick, short steps, as far as the hemline of her dress would allow. She pointed one long talon at Jake as she entered his office.

"Just the man I want to see." She flashed a quick smile at Frank. "Your wife is one lucky woman."

Pit just kept blinking as if in time with the ornaments. He stood but looked more like he wanted to flee. "My, my." Jackie extended a hand to Pit. "You're new." He struggled to keep his eyes from the mounds of flesh bulging from the top of her dress.

Jake asked, "Aren't you afraid of electrocuting yourself?"

"I'm hoping to. Think of all those strapping EMTs who will have to rub salve on the burn marks." She winked and joined the chorus of laughter.

Jake squeezed Sam's hand. "How did it go?"

"Everything's fine."

"What about yesterday?"

"I'm sure it was just seeing the murder scene on a full stomach. The doctor doesn't think it had anything to do with the pregnancy."

He led her to one of the chairs and made her sit down. "What's this about tapping into IRS records?"

Sam shrugged. "Would have been great if Tim wasn't at Quantico." Tim Miesner was a high school genius who volunteered his hacking talents whenever Sam needed help on a case.

"He left already?"

"He's spending his Christmas break interning there. His job is to track hackers."

"Takes one to know one I guess," Frank said.

"He'll be home for Christmas. Depending on how well it goes, they might hire him for next summer, too," Sam added.

"So much for IRS records," Pit said.

"We'll come up with something else." Sam nodded toward her friend. "Jackie wants to issue a complaint."

Jake pushed stacks of folders aside and leaned against the desk. "What's up?"

"That damn alderman in my ward had the police raid me last night. That's the fifth time this month. Everything is above board, you know that, Jake. I'm not about ready to jeopardize my business license. But that old bitty gets Reverend Suiter behind her..."

"Alderman Barbara Wheeler?"

"Yep, that's the one." Jackie talked with her hands, jabbing her talons toward the ceiling, flipping her hair, waving her arms. "Claims we're doing the devil's work, that we are fornicating behind those very walls." Words dripped from Jackie's mouth like honey and her voice and appearance had caught the attention of Captain Robinson, who had returned and was now leaning against the doorjamb.

"What ass is in charge around here, Jake? Who can I talk to?"

"You called?" Captain Robinson's resonant voice bounced off the walls.

Jackie turned toward the door. "I'm being harassed and I want a stop to it," she demanded. "My property is zoned correctly, I'm operating an establishment within the laws, and just because some old biddy has her panties in a knot over a little tit and ass is no reason to force her Christian rhetoric down our throats."

"I can understand your frustration Miss...?" Robinson held out his hand to her.

Jackie looked at it but didn't reciprocate. "Delaney, Jackie Delaney. And don't go patronizing me."

"Absolutely not." Robinson struggled to keep a straight face.

"So," Jackie folded her arms under her massive chest. "What are you going to do about it?"

"To tell you the truth, a couple of the aldermen called the mayor to complain that they believe you are employing underage youth in your establishment," Robinson said.

"What?"

"They claim the voice on the radio commercial advertising your business is a teenager."

Jackie emitted a squeal of laughter and had to brace an arm against Jake's desk.

"That isn't Maddie, is it?" Sam asked and then giggled when Jackie nodded her head vigorously, too hysterical to reply.

"Yes," Jackie repeated after she caught her breath. "That's the portly grandmother who has more chins than a Shanghai phone book." The room erupted in laughter causing heads in the outer office to turn.

"Well," Robinson said, stifling a rumble of laughter himself. "I think in order to better explain to Alderman Wheeler exactly what your business entails, I should probably have a first-hand look at your establishment and possibly meet the girls. How about seven o'clock tonight?"

"Fine." Jackie batted her hand in front of her as though warding off a case of the vapors. "I will be there to give you the tour."

Sam blew Jake a kiss. "Later." To Pit she said, "Can you stick around for the call?" Pit agreed and she dragged Jackie toward the door. "I have to eat."

Ten minutes later, Rachel Stowe returned Jake's call. "Sure, I remember Catherine. Poor kid. Haven't thought about her in years. Why the questions now?"

"We are tying up some loose ends, gathering any ammunition we might need should Jimmy Taggart file a last-minute request for a stay from the governor." Jake remembered Rachel's picture in one of the yearbooks. Where Catherine's beauty was natural, Rachel's had been noticeably artificial, from her hair color to her make-up. There were fewer coats of paint on the '57 Chevy sitting in his garage.

"Bastard," Rachel said. "He shouldn't have been allowed to live this long."

"Did Catherine ever mention to you that she was pregnant?" Jake asked.

"Pregnant? No, not at all. That was never mentioned, not even in the trial."

"Would you have any idea who the father could have been?"

Rachel thought for a moment. "Catherine was popular. That's why I liked hanging around her. Who wouldn't? You were almost guaranteed an endless stream of guys to pick from."

"Was there anyone special? Someone she might have been seeing exclusively?"

"No, well, maybe. That last few months she would still go to parties but shied away from sleeping with anyone. I accused her of getting religious on me but she would just laugh and say, 'Maybe'"

"Did she ever mention anyone by the name of Wieczynski?"

"Wieczynski? No. I would definitely have remembered a name like that."

"You testified that Jimmy Taggart was watching Catherine all night. You said he followed her into the woods. Are you sure about that? Are you sure it wasn't Catherine who followed him? Or maybe Catherine just went off by herself to be alone?" The silence stretched again. "This isn't being taped, Miss Stowe," Jake assured her. "You won't get into any trouble if your memory just happens to be a little clearer now." Jake looked over at Frank and Pit and motioned toward their notepads as though to ask if they had any more questions.

"Listen," Rachel said, her voice low, "you aren't reopening the case, are you? There isn't any way I will testify again. My husband is a respected physician and it would be too embarrassing to air my dirty laundry now."

"No. This information is strictly for our own use. Your name won't come up again," Jake said.

"Okay...okay." Rachel sighed. They heard a door close in the background and then the sounds of birds and traffic and could only assume Rachel had stepped outside of her house. "That night, well, to tell you the truth, I was a little busy myself. One minute I saw Catherine, the next minute she was gone. I'm not really sure in which order they left. I couldn't even tell you if they went in the same direction. I guess, like everyone else back then, I just wanted the bastard put behind bars. But my testimony isn't what nailed him. It was the knife and Catherine's blood on him. He dug his own grave. Thank God we finally get to see him put in it."

"What about Lonnie Dahlkamp? Do you remember anyone by that name?"

"Where are you pulling these names from?"

Jake took that as a "no."

Pit turned his notepad around and pointed at the word "charm."

Jake nodded. "Catherine was wearing a Wiccan charm. Did you and Catherine participate in any type of rituals, either in the forest preserve or elsewhere?"

"It was never anything serious. Catherine had picked up a couple books and thought it would be fun to cast a fertility spell. Well," she laughed. "I guess it worked."

"She didn't tell us much," Frank said after Jake hung up.

Pit grabbed his coat off the hook. "Actually, she said a lot. She just confirmed that a number of people stretched the truth at that trial. Between Eckart covering up the pregnancy and Rachel's comments, it makes me wonder what other facts have been kept hidden."

29

The central vacuum system provided blessed silence during Tillie's cleaning days. Tillie had been working non-stop since nine in the morning. It sometimes took close to six hours to clean if she didn't bring help along. A 4,000 square foot home wasn't easy to maintain, even for Sam and Abby. Sometimes Tillie brought her niece and sometimes a friend to help out, especially when it was time to dismantle the bookcases and dust every book. Tillie Novak had been their cleaning woman for the past ten years. She was as hyper as a twelve-year-old and had a penchant for her husband's flannel shirts.

Alex walked in through the patio doors. He shrugged out of his jacket and draped it over a kitchen chair. The television set on the counter was tuned to a news station.

"Take a coffee break, Tillie." Abby held up the coffee pot. Tillie turned off the vacuum cleaner and patted the shoulder of an elderly woman seated at the dining room table.

"*Hau Kanta,* Alex," Tillie said as she entered the kitchen.

Alex stared indignantly at Tillie while Sam and Abby enjoyed a laugh.

Tillie blinked. "What?"

"You just called him a prune," Sam said, and laughed again when she saw Alex shaking his head.

"Oh." Tillie's face flushed.

"I think you meant to say *Hau K'ola*. That is the correct phrase for *Hello, friend*," Sam said.

"Could have been worse, right?" Tillie pulled a cup from the cabinet and filled it with coffee. "Wonderful work you are doing on the nursery, Alex. You should have your own show like that Bob Vila guy."

"Yeah. I can call it *Reservation Restoration*," he deadpanned.

"I can't wait to see it." Sam wrapped an arm around Alex's waist. "I caught him and Mom watching Martha Stewart on more than one occasion, and I have a feeling it is going to look beautiful."

"And how are you doing, darlin'?" Tillie patted Sam's stomach.

"Everything is fine. I'm outgrowing my clothes every day."

"Good. Big babies are healthy babies." Tillie poked her head into the dining room and yelled, "Ma, come get some coffee."

Tillie said, "Hope you don't mind. One of the ladies at the beauty shop dropped my Ma off after her appointment. Her friend had some shopping to do so Ma didn't have a ride home."

Abby set out another cup and saucer. "It's no problem," she said. "Your mother looks very good. What is she, in her seventies?"

"Eighty-three," Tillie said with pride. "Forgetful sometimes but very independent. She can't drive anymore because of her eyes, but I think the rest of the driving public appreciates that."

"I heard that, Tillie." The elderly woman marched into the kitchen.

"And she can still dance a mean polka," Tillie added.

Mary Agnes Wolski was a spry woman dressed in a tailored suit. She smelled of hair spray and Este Lauder.

"Polka is what keeps the blood going," Mary Agnes said. "Been dancing since I was fifteen."

"Where are you going?" Tillie barked as Alex retreated to the study. "Feeling outnumbered?"

In the background, the local news station had just switched from sports to politics. A white haired man wearing horn-rimmed glasses proceeded to read an announcement:

Governor Avery Meacham today officially announced his appointee to replace State Supreme Court Justice Jasper Collins who passed away last month.

The picture of an attractive gray-haired man in a black robe appeared on the screen as the reporter continued:

Judge Andrew Wise, a district court judge in Chasen Heights, is best known for his no-nonsense approach to youth offenders and gang members. Judge Wise's appointment would be effective the first of the year. The judge was unavailable for comment but issued a statement that he was honored to serve the State of Illinois.

"Wonderful," Tillie said.

"Jake thinks he's great," Sam said.

"Maybe eventually from state to federal. Would be nice to one day have a Polish Supreme Court judge," Mary Agnes said.

Sam laughed. "His name is Wise, Mrs. Wolski. He isn't Polish."

"His father changed the family name decades ago. Didn't he, Tillie?"

"If you say so, Ma."

"Of course. My mother dated his father in high school," Mary Agnes explained. "Isn't that right, Tillie?"

"Uh huh," Tillie replied with a lift of her eyes toward the ceiling. "Whatever you say."

"You make fun of your mother. But I'm right. He is a VOY-CHIN-SKY. That's the only thing I don't like. He should be proud of his heritage."

Sam stared at the picture of Judge Wise on the television screen. "Voychinsky? How do you spell that?"

"W-I-E-C-Z-Y-N-S-K-I," Mary Agnes replied.

* * * *

Jake paced the length of the dining room table, one hand rubbing the back of his neck. Sam hadn't told him much during their phone conversation other than to say she had found Wieczynski. Within fifteen minutes all three men charged through the door.

"I can't believe it," Frank said for the second time. "There is no way Judge Wise can be involved."

Pit picked up one of the yearbooks. As if reading his mind, Frank picked up another one and started fanning through the pages.

"Here," Pit said. "Robert Wise, nickname Bobby. He was three years ahead of Catherine."

"Judge Wise has a son?" Sam asked.

Jake made a call to Rachel from the kitchen phone and placed it on the speaker.

"Yes, I knew Bobby Wise," Rachel confirmed. "But neither one of us dated him. And Catherine despised him."

"Did you know his family?" Pit asked.

"His father was a lawyer, I think."

"Would she hide her true feelings from you? After all, she never confided who 'B' was that was mentioned in her diary." Jake studied Bobby Wise's yearbook picture. Lettered in track, football, basketball. He had been on the debate team and member of the Honor Society.

"Catherine was very transparent when it came to boys. Besides, we weren't good enough for Bobby. He dated socialites and met girls at the country club or charity events. I think his family would have had a coronary if he'd started dating either one of us."

"Did you go to the same college as Bobby?" Pit asked.

"Right. Like my parents could have afforded to send me to Harvard."

Following the phone call, Jake paced behind the island counter, hands jammed in his pants pockets, his brows hunkered over.

Sam watched him from her post in front of the patio doors. Jake wasn't easy to read. Disbelief, anger, frustration, any or all of those descriptions would fit. "It does make sense. 'B' could stand for Bob or Bobby."

"Judge Wise did have a picture on his mantel of himself and his wife with a teenager," Frank added. "Gotta be their son."

"I should call Attorney Bigalow." Sam folded her arms across her stomach. "God, wait til Rose hears. Bobby probably couldn't face telling his parents he got a girl beneath his standards pregnant. There was only one way to stop her." Sam was thinking aloud, tossing out possible scenarios.

Frank asked, "How the hell do we approach Judge Wise about his son? I'd hate to do it."

Sam offered a little too quickly, "Pit and I will..."

"NO." Jake halted in mid-step and shot an icy glare that sent a chill through the whole room.

Pit stepped back and took a seat at the kitchen table. Pounding reverberated from upstairs where Alex and Abby were working in the nursery.

Sam crossed the room and stared at Jake from the opposite side of the counter. "What's with you?" she demanded. "You said it yourself. The clock is ticking."

Without moving his eyes from Sam, Jake told Frank, "First run a check on Bobby. See if he still lives in town."

Frank retreated to the dining room to call the precinct from his cell phone. Pit scooted from the table and joined Frank.

"You should treat him the way you would any relative of a suspect, Jake. No favoritism."

"This is different."

"Why? Talk to me." She saw something shut down behind his eyes. Whatever it was, it was cold and solid. "Jake." Sam reached across and placed her hands on top of his, feeling the heat radiating from his skin. He didn't shake her off but he didn't exactly reach out to her either.

"There's no Robert, Bob or Bobby in the computer database or telephone listings," Frank announced. "I doubt he still lives with his parents. What would he be? Thirty-six?"

Jake leaned his elbows on the counter and steepled his fingers. "Damn," he whispered in frustration. He took his time mulling over options, then pulled out his cell phone and dialed. Estelle, Judge Wise's secretary, told Jake when the judge would be available.

"Thirty minutes," Jake said after hanging up. "Just you and me, Frank." Sam opened her mouth to protest but the look on his face forced back the words. He checked his watch and rattled off instructions to Sam as they walked to the front door. "You don't tell anyone anything until you clear it with me, Sam."

"This is my case," she argued.

Frank climbed in on the driver's side as Jake turned to face her. "No. This is my case and I decide what information is shared."

"What's going on?"

"Leave it alone, Sam."

"Those are not the three little words I want to hear."

Jake climbed into the car, shoved his sunglasses on, and didn't even glance back as the car peeled away from the curb.

30

"Having a little blood pressure problem, Jake? Your face is a nice shade of scarlet," Frank said. They were waiting in Judge Wise's chambers with its wall of bookshelves and potted plants.

Jake stood at the window and gazed down three floors to the parking lot. He felt Frank's eyes on his back but they had been partners long enough for Frank to know when to pry and when to stay quiet. He couldn't say the same for Sam.

"It isn't going to be easy," Frank said. "Either the judge has been covering for his son all along and is willing to sit by while an innocent man is executed, or he is going to hear for the first time that his son might be a killer. Neither choice is any good."

"I know." He turned toward the wall and studied the various framed degrees and certificates.

The door to the office opened and a somber Judge Wise walked in. He blinked tired eyes and heaved a just as weary sigh. "We are beginning to see way too much of each other." He unbuttoned his robe and hung it on a hanger in the closet. "What search warrant do you need signed now?" The judge pulled out a Mont Blanc pen and sat down behind his desk, motioning the detectives to the two leather chairs in front of the desk.

"No search warrant. It's about your son," Jake said. Judge Wise set his pen down. "New evidence suggests he might have been involved in the murder seventeen years ago of Catherine DeMarco." The color drained from Wise's face.

"We'd like to talk to him," Frank said. "I'm sure you are aware that Jimmy Taggart is due to be executed in a few weeks."

"I know this isn't easy for you to talk about which is why we didn't want to speak to you at your home," Jake said.

Judge Wise leaned back in his chair. His gaze drifted to the bookcase where a framed picture nestled between reference books.

"Judge Wise, can you tell us where we can find your son?" Jake asked.

The judge remained silent, eyes focused on his desk. When he finally spoke, the words were uttered in a hoarse whisper. "My son died fifteen years ago."

"Thank you, Esther." The elderly black woman deposited the pot of coffee on the conference table. Judge Wise waited for her to close the door. Then he explained to the detectives, "Bobby died in a plane crash during a routine training flight. He was a son any parent would be proud of." His smile showed genuine affection but his eyes couldn't mask the pain. "He was never in trouble, a straight A student. Almost too good to be true. And, I can assure you, he respected women."

"I thought he attended Harvard?" Frank asked.

"He was registered for Harvard at the time his acceptance to the Air Force Academy came through."

Jake asked, "Did he know Catherine DeMarco?"

"Bobby dated a lot of girls, none serious. Said he wasn't ready to settle down and wasn't looking for Ms. Right. But a girl three years younger than him? No."

"But it's possible you didn't know every girl your son dated,"

Frank said. "What about Rachel Stowe? She was a friend of Catherine's and around your son's age."

The muscles in Judge Wise's face tensed and he slowly turned his chair to face the bookcase where the framed picture of his son and wife was displayed.

"Frank." Jake gave a nod of his head toward the door.

"Sure that's a good idea?" Frank whispered. After a few seconds, Frank shrugged and walked out.

Jake walked over to the table, poured two cups of black coffee and placed one on the judge's desk. He cradled his own in his hands as he sat down in front of the desk and waited. The judge pulled his gaze from the picture and turned back to the desk. He grasped the cup of coffee and took time to drink half of it before speaking.

There was fatigue in his voice and he looked emotionally exhausted. "To my knowledge, Bobby did not date much less know Catherine DeMarco. I lived with that boy all of his life. Don't you think I would have known there was something not right with him? Don't you think I would have suspected that he possessed the kind of rage that her murderer had?" His fist slammed against the table in a burst of frustration. "NO, not my son." An uneasy silence drifted through the room. Wise ran his finger along the design on the coffee mug and stared at the contents.

Jake gave him some time and focused on his next question. It would be difficult to get an answer but it still had to be asked.

"Can you recall where Bobby was seventeen years ago, the night of July nineteenth?"

Judge Wise flashed a weary smile. "You must be kidding. I don't even know where I was." He paused, the smile fading. "How did my son's name come up now after all this time?"

Jake didn't want to bring Sam or Pit into this. Instead he explained about Lonnie's murder and the papers in his safety deposit box.

"That still doesn't explain how that ties to my son."

"Information we discovered mentions the name Wieczynski. That was your family name, wasn't it?"

"It hasn't been used in years. And Bobby certainly never used it." Wise finally took a long swallow of coffee and studied Jake over the rim of his cup. "I suppose you aren't going to tell me your source."

"You know I can't. It's an ongoing investigation. Unfortunately, one that the chief and the mayor don't want us to open," Jake added. "But it will be political suicide if an innocent man is executed."

"Well, if the murders are connected, your source better come up with more evidence because my son certainly couldn't have killed Lonnie Dahlkamp."

"There may have been more than one person involved in Catherine's murder. Lonnie has been blackmailing someone, which is why I want to keep this as discreet as possible. There's no need to have any of this leak out to the press until we have all of our facts straight."

"I appreciate that. I can't have my wife reading about your suspicions in the paper. And I'm sorry to sound like a parent in major denial, but I'll say it again...my son had nothing to do with the murder of Catherine DeMarco."

Judge Wise waited for the door to close, then sank back in his chair and whispered to the empty room, "Damn, why? After all this time?"

"Where is Tim when I need him?" Sam pounded the keyboard. "He would have hacked into the Harvard registration files by now."

"I doubt they have all their files on computer." Pit was relaxing on the couch, hands clasped behind his head. "Do you do this often?"

"Do what?" she asked, her back to him as she focused on the monitor.

"Circumvent legal routes?"

She paused, then leered over her shoulder at him. "You are sounding too much like Jake. Has he been filling your head with rumors?"

Pit smiled. "No. I'm just observant."

"He has our hands tied. Doesn't that frustrate you?" Sam exited the Harvard web site and accessed one of the search engines.

Pit walked out of the room and returned a minute later, one of the yearbooks in his hands. "Where's your phone book?"

Sam nodded to the wall of bookshelves. "Second shelf from the bottom, right-hand side."

He retrieved the phone book and took a seat on the couch.

"He probably never finished college," Sam mumbled. "Probably been sailing around the world on a schooner, stopping to build huts in Third World countries."

She could hear Pit behind her leafing through pages, punching numbers on the phone, asking to speak to people she had never heard of. Sam stopped typing and turned to face him.

"Yes," Pit spoke into the phone. "I'm Lance Blade. I'm on the reunion committee for Chasen High and I'm trying to locate Martin Caroley." He listened for a few seconds. "Do you have a forwarding address?"

Sam moved over to the couch and studied the yearbook. Pit had made checkmarks by some of the pictures. The one similarity was that they were all on the football team. Pit hung up the phone and wrote Alaska next to Caroley's picture.

"They all were on the football team with him?" Sam asked.

"Not everyone moves away from their home town. I didn't."

"Clever. There's hope for you yet." Sam smiled. If they couldn't talk to Judge Wise, then they would just find someone who knew Bobby. "Who's Lance Blade?"

He flashed the yearbook at her. "Classmate."

They worked through the next hour, going down the list of students who were in the same clubs and sports as Bobby Wise.

"Sticking to guys, you chauvinist?"

"They stay in touch more. Girls come and go."

"You are a chauvinist."

"Proud of it." He broke out in a wide grin.

Sam remembered seeing a similar easy smile and twinkle in the photograph on Pit's bookcase. His daughter had the same devilish twinkle, as if she knew with her father she could get away with anything.

"Why don't we play the odds?" Sam turned the pages in the yearbook and locating the last checkmark alphabetically. "Murphy's Law says it will be the last name you try." Her finger traced through the pictures. "Try Danny Valukis."

Pit fanned the pages of the phone book. "Son of a gun. We have one Daniel Valukis." He dialed the number and gave the same reunion committee spiel. "Is this Mrs. Valukis? Oh, his mother. Really." Pit's gaze shifted to Sam and he shrugged. "Do you know when Danny will be home?" Pit listened for a while, pulling the phone a couple inches from his ear. "I'm sorry to hear that. Yes, that's a shame." He slumped back against the cushions, his right hand motioning to Sam like gums flapping. Danny's mother was obviously talking his ear off.

Sam continued thumbing through the yearbook and stopped at Bobby's picture. She wondered what he looked like today. Was his hair receding? Had his muscular build given way to beer and gravitational pull? If he was married, was he faithful to his wife? Did he have any children?

"Yes, I would like to talk to Danny. I was hoping he could help me find someone else from our class...Bobby Wise." Slowly, Pit straightened, his eyes flicking quickly to Sam. Pit gave Carmen Valukis his cell phone number and ended the call abruptly, a stunned look on his face.

"What?" Sam turned to face him, her arm on the back cushion.

"Bobby died fifteen years ago."

Sam remained silent, wondering if Jake had been told the same news. "How?" she finally asked.

"He didn't make it to Harvard. He was accepted in the Air Force Academy and died in a training flight."

Sam reached for the phone. "I should tell Jake."

Pit grabbed her arm. "I think by now Jake already knows."

"You're right."

"Any reason why Judge Wise seems to be some sacred cow to Jake?"

She thought about that for a few seconds but her mind was a blank. It was hard to admit to a stranger that your husband was a stranger. She shook her head no.

Pit checked his watch and stood. "Danny might be an interesting character, though. Seems he served three years for sexual assault."

31

Jake climbed into the Taurus and slammed the door. Frank slid in behind the wheel. He was in no hurry to put the key in the ignition.

"What do you think?" Frank asked.

Jake stared at the court building. A bus maneuvered the turn-around and came to a stop. People exited, rushing toward the courthouse while the sun slid behind a cloud.

"With Bobby dead it's going to make our job a bitch. I believe Judge Wise. If Bobby was involved with Catherine, he wasn't aware of it." Jake pulled a cigarette from his pocket, lit it, and rolled the window down. He inhaled long and deep, blowing the smoke out toward the open window.

"I don't know what's going on in your head, Jake. But if you can step back a minute and think like an FBI agent, what would your next step be? Even if Judge Wise's son is dead, someone killed Lonnie Dahlkamp."

Jake watched people rushing from the bus. He knew Frank was right. His personal feelings shouldn't get in the way of a murder investigation.

"First, I would verify that Bobby Wise is actually dead. Get a copy of his prints. See if any match the prints taken from Lonnie's car. Check Judge Wise's bank records for any large withdrawals seventeen years ago. I doubt Bobby would have had that kind of money so he would have had to get it from his parents, with or without their knowledge."

"What about phone records from seventeen years ago?"

"I doubt they'd have it. Phone companies have changed numerous times since then."

"I'm talking about recently," Frank said, meeting Jake's eyes. "Daddy might have had to clean up his son's mess."

Jake let out a rush of air and sank back against the seat. "I really hate to do that, Frank." He sucked hard on the cigarette, watching the tip glow red.

"It will be easier if Judge Wise just signs the subpoena for these records. Then we don't have to involve the State's Attorney and another judge," Frank said.

"How are we going to identify him?" Sam looked around the restaurant. Danny had returned Pit's phone call and was more than eager to meet up with Lance Blade. They had agreed to meet at Finnegan's near the shopping center. Pit was beginning to wonder what kind of trouble Danny and Lance had gotten into in their youth.

Pit pulled a sheet of paper from the folder and handed it to Sam. She smiled. "Of course. You pulled his rap sheet." The face staring back at her looked like every mother's nightmare. Danny Valukis exuded sexuality from his bedroom eyes to full lips. There was a dimple in his chin that made you come this close to saying Danny was cute.

"Ted Bundy had eyes like those," Pit said.

A figure appeared in the doorway. Pit compared it to the police photo. Other than a little wear and tear, Danny looked the same.

"There's our guy. Let's just hope Lance Blade has changed a lot since his yearbook picture." Pit slid out of the booth and gave a wave. Danny's eyes narrowed as though trying to place him. Then he saw Sam sitting in the booth and his reaction changed.

Pit may have had the same dark hair as Lance Blade, but there were no other similarities. Lance had been on the wrestling team in high school. Pit could possibly bench press a twelve-pack.

"How are you doing, Danny?" Pit grabbed his hand and pumped it. "This is my wife, Melanie." He steered Danny into the booth before the memory could click in, and slid in next to him.

His sweater was cashmere and the jewelry flashed gold. The long, curly hair Danny had sported for his police photo had been replaced with short, straight hair.

"You aren't Lance." His eyes did a slow roll over Sam's face, down to her breasts, and back up. "And I'm hoping you ain't the missus." One corner of his mouth smiled.

"Isn't that what got you into jail in the first place?" Sam asked.

His head swiveled back to Pit. "What is this?"

"We're investigating a murder," Pit said.

"Cops?" Danny tried to push his way out of the booth.

"No," Pit replied, tossing him a business card. A waitress appeared with a coffeepot and three cups. Once she left, Pit said, "Tell us about Bobby Wise."

"Bobby?" He slid a mug of hot coffee over and settled back. "He's dead. What is there to know?" Danny ripped open three bags of sugar and dumped them into his cup of coffee.

"How about I change the question a little," Pit said. "What do you know about Bobby and Catherine DeMarco?"

Danny pulled a pack of cigarettes from his pocket.

"This is the non-smoking section," Sam said.

Danny tossed the pack on the table. "They didn't date." He toyed with the pack, spinning it, turning it around. "Why all the interest?" Suddenly, his eyes lit up. "Ahh, of course. You're the cop trying to get Jimmy Taggart out of prison." He plopped back against the booth and laughed. "Good luck."

"Why do you say that?"

"They've got a solid case."

"Back to Catherine DeMarco," Pit ordered.

Danny's thick shoulders shrugged. "Bobby had plans, big plans. Serious relationships couldn't get in the way. He was focused like that."

Sam tried again. "But you couldn't have known every girl he dated. What if she were pregnant?"

"Pregnant?" Danny toyed with the cigarettes again. "That never came out in the trial." His fingers danced around the package. "Bobby didn't even know her. He was in college before she got through playing with dolls."

"Only three years," Pit reminded him.

Sam watched him run his hands through his hair, his eyes suddenly everywhere but on her. Her mind was quick to translate his actions. She leaned closer, waiting to lock eyes.

"You dated her, didn't you, Danny?"

Andrew didn't look up when he heard Ellie's wheelchair. As usual, she was dressed as if she were attending a gala party. He didn't mind. She seemed to dress to detract from the appearance of the wheelchair.

"I didn't hear you come in, Andrew."

He sat on the couch, elbows resting on his knees, hands clasped in a tight fist under his chin, while he stared thoughtlessly into the burning embers.

"How was your day, Ellie?"

"Ran the quarter mile, climbed the garbage dump on 111th Street, sprinted through every store in the mall."

Andrew blinked heavily but his weariness was more mental than physical.

"My jokes used to cheer you up." She ran her hand down the back of his head just as Marjorie walked in.

"Anything I can get you, ma'am?"

"How about two glasses of white wine." Ellie looked at her husband's despondent face. "No, make that two brandies."

They sat in silence until Marjorie returned with their drinks. She sipped hers and watched as Andrew studied the contents of his glass. Andrew had always used Ellie as a sounding board. And, although Jake had said something about protecting her from publicity in her fragile state, Andrew knew she was stronger than either of them.

"Okay, Andrew. Spill it. What has you so preoccupied that you didn't even notice this raving beauty wheel herself into the room?"

Andrew took both of their glasses and set them down on the end table. He took her hands in his and told her about Jake's suspicion that Bobby may have had something to do with Catherine DeMarco's death.

"That's impossible," Ellie said.

"That's what I told him."

"This has something to do with that private detective who is trying to free Jimmy Taggart, doesn't it."

Andrew nodded. "Probably."

"Are you aware that the detective working with Pit Goddard on this case is Sergeant Mitchell's wife?"

Andrew looked up, startled. "No, I had no idea."

"Chief Murphy's wife mentioned it to me. But I thought the papers said that Mr. Dahlkamp's death had nothing to do with Catherine DeMarco. That his was a syndicate hit or something."

"They planted that story so the press wouldn't tip their hand."

"I see. So their claim that Taggart is still their man was false."

"Apparently."

They remained quiet for a while, studying the fire, gazing up at the picture of their son on the mantel. Ellie flipped up the foot rests on her wheelchair and hoisted herself onto the couch. Andrew knew not to assist her. She prided herself in being able to fend for herself.

She kissed Andrew on the cheek and wrapped a consoling arm around his shoulder. "Everything will be fine, Andrew. I know it. Sergeant Mitchell is good. You've said so yourself. He'll get to the bottom of this."

Andrew patted her hand and envied her optimism. He continued to gaze into the fireplace, lost in thought.

32

Jake walked past the dark study and into the kitchen. He didn't expect anyone to be up at eleven-fifteen in the evening. He peeled out of his clothes and took a quick shower in the gym. After pulling on a clean pair of jeans, sweatshirt, socks and shoes, he trudged back to the kitchen. A pint of coffee was on the sink. He filled a cup and, while the microwave did its magic, he slipped into a fleece-lined jacket, and shoved a pack of cigarettes and matches into his pockets. He found Alex outside sitting on one of the benches filling a pipe. Lying at his feet was Poco, Alex's Irish Setter.

"You're up late," Jake said as he slid the door shut. He side-stepped Poco who lifted her head lazily from her paws.

"Still seems early to me." Alex touched the match to the tobacco and a puff of smoke circled above the pipe. "Too many holiday lights to turn off. Takes an extra hour just to make sure all the candles are blown out." Alex took another puff, his profile sharp and angular.

Jake lit a cigarette and stuffed the smoking match in a flower pot filled with sand and cigarette butts. Without the interference from the kitchen and deck lights, the night sky was a blaze of stars. Orion's distinct shape was visible over Lake Michigan. They sat on a wooden bench in silence, enjoying the crisp night air, smoke and coffee. Jake took a long drag as if warming himself from the inside out. He kept his eyes on the stars as he asked, "Were you ever in trouble, Alex?"

A puff of smoke billowed skyward. "You mean besides being born?"

A smile formed at the corners of Jake's mouth. "As a kid," he clarified.

"You mean like when I stole money from parking meters, vandalized parked cars, and siphoned gas?"

"I guess that qualifies." Jake smiled again as he brought the cup of coffee to his lips.

"It was more fun to hang out with my buddies than go home."

"What did your parents say?"

"My *Ina,* she say, *Iglu mat'o.* I was angry like a bear, all the time. Didn't like school, didn't like to be home. Too small of a house. Too many kids."

Jake didn't know much about Alex other than he had to wait for him to offer information. If you came out and asked, he would clam up. Sam would say he reminded her of someone else. The silence stretched. Jake lit another cigarette. Alex stoked his pipe.

"I almost killed a man once." Jake glanced over at Alex but the Indian had no immediate reaction. Didn't even turn his head to look at Jake.

"How old were you?"

"Fifteen." He waited for that comment to sink in, then added, "It was my father."

The two men sat, bent over, forearms on their knees. It was the longest conversation they'd had since they met.

Alex finally said, "That explains it."

Jake jerked his gaze back to Alex. He wasn't exactly sure what he meant by the comment. Alex had seen the scars on Jake's back. He had heard of his reaction to homicide cases where husbands had battered their wives or kids. And there was the fact that Jake sometimes had the warmth of a breeze off the Arctic Ocean.

"There's only so much anyone can take year after year. I hit my limit. First time I was big enough, I struck back. My father pressed charges to teach me a lesson."

Something darted across the walkway toward the garage. Eyes glowed yellow from behind the underbrush and soon the animal moved back into the safety and shadows of the gardens.

Jake continued. "I had a court-appointed attorney who created a youth program at his own expense. Sent me to a cattle ranch in Colorado to work for the summer." Alex continued to stare into the darkened yard, offering no comment. "The lawyer took me under his wing, had Family Services visit my home to check on things. Pissed the hell out of my father. When I didn't want to go home after school, the lawyer let me do my homework in his office." Jake took one last puff and shoved the cigarette butt into the mound of sand. "That lawyer is a judge now."

"Huh." Alex finally turned his head to face him. "That definitely explains it."

Sam leaned her head against the wall. She was sitting by the open balcony doors in the bedroom. The voices below had carried in the still night air, bringing tears to the corners of her eyes. She should be glad Jake was confiding in someone. It just hurt that it wasn't her. She grabbed the edge of the chaise and struggled to her feet. That was when she felt something and grabbed her stomach.

Jake crept around in the dark bedroom, stripping out of his clothes and slipping into his gym shorts. He closed the bathroom door before turning on the light so he wouldn't awaken Sam. After washing up, he turned the light off before opening the door and waited for his eyes to adjust. He noticed the balcony door was open several inches and wondered if their voices had carried. Was Sam awake while he was on the patio talking to Alex? He looked over at her still body and wondered if she had heard any part of their conversation. He sighed heavily and slid the door closed. As soon as he climbed into bed, Sam stirred.

"Jake?"

His chest tightened and he felt her roll over on her back. "I really don't feel like talking, Sam. Not tonight."

"Give me your hand," she whispered.

He looked over at her in the darkness as she reached for his right hand. She fumbled with a button on her nightshirt and placed his hand on her naked stomach. There was a slight flutter and he started to jerk away but Sam laughed softly.

"Do you feel it?"

He did. There was something rippling just below the surface, like the soft lapping of a wave. He had been a witness to death too many times during his career. But he had never been this close to life in the making. He flattened his hand against her stomach and felt the flutter through all five fingers. After several minutes, the fluttering diminished. Jake gathered her in his arms and pulled her close. Nothing surprised him more than how damn fortunate his life was now.

33

"Let me get this straight." Jake motioned for Frank to close the door behind him. He had Sam on the speaker phone. When he had left the house early this morning, Sam had snuggled deep into the covers and mumbled something about having some interesting news and that he should call her later.

"This Danny Valukis was also dating Catherine DeMarco?" Jake asked. Captain Robinson was leaning against the glass partition. His fingers splayed the blinds as he checked for potential interruptions in the shape of Chief Murphy. "Does he have an alibi for the night Dahlkamp was murdered?"

"He was home in bed. Says his mother will verify that."

"Mamas have been alibis for more suspects than I care to count," Robinson huffed. He moved away from the glass. His deep voice could carry through walls so he parked himself in the chair next to Frank. "What's your feel on him, Sam?"

"He did three years for a he said/she said charge several years ago. Doesn't have a history of violence and his name certainly doesn't begin with a 'B'."

"We can't really count on the 'B' referring to a name, people," Robinson pointed out. "Could be boy, bastard, buddy, even body beautiful. Don't know what terms went through that young girl's mind. For all we know, Valukis could be the body beautiful. Did he ever frequent Briar Woods?"

"Yes," Sam replied.

"There you go. I wouldn't exactly call him a time-waster." Robinson shifted his mass of muscle in the uncomfortable wooden chair. "What did you find in the police reports?"

Jake flipped through the pages of a report on Danny Valukis that Frank had just printed off the computer. "Kept his nose clean since his release. Just a couple speeding tickets and misdemeanors in his youth."

Robinson wrestled his body from the form-fitting chair and stood. "Might be worth talking to his mother to verify his whereabouts." He nodded his mammoth head toward them. "Jake and Frank will handle that, Sam. If this Romeo character is home when you question his mother," he told Jake, "ask him when's the last time he was at Dillon's Sporting Goods."

Jake said his good-byes and hung up the phone.

Robinson asked, "Any other suspects?"

Jake caught Frank's gaze for several beats. "What?" Robinson asked. The look on their faces prompted him to sit back down. "I have a feeling I'm not going to like this."

Jake grabbed his empty cup. "I need some fuel before I start." He wondered how Robinson would take the news about Bobby Wise...a viable candidate for the mysterious 'B.'

"Where are we going?" Pit stared out of the passenger window of Sam's Jeep.

"I thought we'd have a little tea with Judge Wise's wife."

Pit swiveled his head toward her. "You are kidding." Sam just smiled. "You've got balls, lady. Does Jake know?"

"We're going to ask her about her son's friends. Namely, Danny Valukis." Pit let out a soft moan. "What?"

"Jake is going to hang me from that willow tree in back of your garage."

"Jake's a pussy cat."

"Right. The face of an angel."

Sam could feel Pit's eyes on her and heard him patting his pockets for his cigarettes. He moved his fingers to the window frame and started his incessant tapping.

"Can I ask you something?"

Sam flicked her gaze to him and then back to the road. "You want to know about Stu Richards."

"Yeah. Unless you don't want to talk about it."

There had been a long time after the incident when she couldn't talk about it. Couldn't remember. But it had all come flooding back at Sara Binyon's when she had spent hours talking with her therapist.

"Guess it starts back farther than seven months ago."

"With your father?"

"Yes. It's true what they say about repressed memory. At least when you are five years old and see something so horrific it makes you catatonic. But I pulled through with no memory of how my father and his wife died."

She drove past the shopping center and toward the older section of town where some of the more elite homes were built. It amazed her how she could read the question on people's faces, but they were too polite to ask how Abby came to be her mother and not Melinda, and how all of them had lived under the same roof.

"Anyway, my father's death involved a car bomb and a cover-up. Fast forward to present day and his killer appears out of nowhere while I was investigating a body that had been hidden in concrete for eons."

"You certainly don't lead a dull life."

"Tell me about it. Anyway, this guy was hired by one of our very powerful politicians to squelch the facts of my father's death and how my father was connected to the dead body, but, of course, I'm not going to stop investigating. So the hired goon lures me to a warehouse. I find Stu Richard's body, a beat cop who obviously was in the wrong place at the wrong time. No gun shot wounds but very dead. The goon blows up the patrol car. I lose my gun in the confusion."

"And the guy uses your gun to make it look like the cop's death was caused by a bullet to the back."

"Right. And the brass, namely Dennis Murphy, is having a field day holding up my hearing as an example of what happens to a dirty cop."

There was silence from the passenger side of the Jeep and Sam risked a glance at Pit, trying to decipher his reaction.

"That sounds like it's going to be hard to beat the rap without an eyewitness."

"Especially since the state rep allegedly had the hired goon killed." That was all she had thought of since being released from Sara Binyon's. She wasn't any closer now to proving her innocence.

"Now your turn," she told him.

He looked at her quizzically. She pulled the visor down to shield the glare from the sun. Pit shifted in his seat, and when he wasn't quick to respond, she didn't think he wanted to talk about it.

"His name was Jules Browne. Known as JuJu to his friends. Dispatch received an *Officer Down* call following a silent alarm from the 7-Eleven over on Baylor."

Sam stole another glance at Pit. His hands were playing with his jacket pocket and she was tempted to pull over and let him have a cigarette. He looked less at ease talking about his shooting than she had been.

"Was it a robbery?" she asked, trying to keep him talking.

"Clerk was killed and the officer who had responded was shot. His partner had called it in and me and my partner were the closest unit. Prescott, that was the responding officer, said the two suspects were cornered in an alley behind the convenience store." Pit unzipped his jacket and fidgeted with the temperature controls on the console.

Sam never doubted she had adjustment problems of her own but Pit looked ready to hyperventilate.

"Was the alley dark?"

"Very," Pit replied. "Not even a strip of moon light. It was a Tuesday night, fifty-two degrees. Time was two-fourteen in the morning. Slowest night for calls."

A train rumbled across the tracks ahead and Sam pulled to a stop. She pressed a button and the passenger window rolled down several inches.

"Did you want a cigarette?"

Pit forced a smile. "Thanks." He shook out a cigarette and struck a match. The flame caught and Pit inhaled deeply. "Guess I thought it would be easier to talk about since it's been so long."

"Maybe you didn't talk about it often enough. Between my therapist, Abby, and Jake, I haven't had much chance to keep the Stu Richards case or my father's death bottled up."

Smoke chased the currents, swirling through the open window only to dissipate in the crisp air. Pit wiped moisture from his hair-line and leaned back against the headrest.

"I don't think a night goes by that I don't see that kid in the alley. All I saw was the flash from the gunfire. Bullets were flying past my head and I just returned fire. Had no choice." He sucked hard on the cigarette and tapped the ash outside the window. "Didn't know how old he was until they pulled his rap sheet."

"What about the wounded cop?"

"Died in surgery."

"Which gun fired the fatal shot?"

Pit flipped the cigarette butt out and closed the window. Several car lengths ahead the gates raised and traffic slowly moved. "Juju's," he finally replied.

Sam didn't feel she had to say much more. If Pit repeated it often enough it might start to sink in that Pit reacted in self defense. JuJu may have been a kid, but he had been a dangerous kid who hadn't hesitated to kill a cop.

She drove the Jeep down a long drive and applied the brakes. The Wise home was one of the more prestigious estates in Chasen Heights.

"You did call, right?"

Sam pressed the accelerator and continued down the drive. "Of course. Besides, how can anyone refuse a pregnant woman."

34

C armen Valukis opened the door to her penthouse condo. The exclusive gated community was nestled between the expressway and shopping center, and overlooked the Three Oaks Golf Course.

A cigarette flopped in the corner of her mouth as she spoke around it. "Hope to god you didn't pull up in a squad car, Detectives." She stepped aside and checked the hallway before ushering them in. "Damn nosy neighbors. Never know when they are lurking around corners."

"We won't take up too much of your time." Jake pulled off his sunglasses but wanted to put them back on. The sunlight blazed through the wall of windows making the colors in the furniture and drapes appear fluorescent. The wall-to-wall carpeting was a bright strawberry red. Barrel chairs colored in solid lime and lemon yellow nestled up to a stark white couch.

Frank leaned into him and whispered, "I feel like we just crawled into a tube of Life-Savers."

Carmen didn't sit on her couch, she draped it, flaring her arms out so her chiffon coverlet flared behind her. Her slacks were the same bright orange color as the toss pillows. She pulled her legs up to sit cross-legged, as if she were at a slumber party.

"What's up, boys." She pulled a cigarette out of a silver case and lit it against the cigarette in her mouth. "What did my no-good son do this time?" Carmen pointed at another ashtray on the coffee table. "Don't be shy."

Frank made a subtle attempt to wave the air in front of his face. Jake lit up. "What makes you think Danny might be in trouble?" Frank asked.

"Wishful thinking." She threw back her head and laughed, a ring-studded hand pressed against the folds in her neck. "The three years he was in prison were the best years of my life, next to his father kicking the bucket five years ago. Died the Errol Flynn way." She sucked on her cigarette, and as an afterthought added, "but it wasn't with me." She ran her fingers through her flaming red hair. Dark eyebrows looked out of place and drawn unevenly. "Danny would suck every dime out of me and not work a day in his life if he could. No ambition whatsoever. Just like his old man."

The detectives studied the expensive furniture, statues, and wall hangings.

"I owned two trucking companies," Carmen explained, as if reading their thoughts. "Not my husband...me. Worked sixty-hour weeks. Jack was a truck driver. He loved over-the-road trips. Think he had a girl in every port, so to speak." She looked at the two men and jammed the cigarette butt into the ashtray. "But enough about me." She turned all serious on them, leaned back, hands resting on her knees, palms up. She closed her eyes and took several deep breaths. Then her eyes popped open as she announced, "I'm ready."

Jake looked over at Frank who was running his thumb and forefinger along the sides of his mouth, smoothing his beard, hiding his amusement.

Frank strolled over to the window, which looked out onto the fairway. His fingers traced a crack in the pane. It looked like a bullet hole had been covered with electrical tape.

"I'm still waiting for our maintenance guy to replace that damn window," Carmen said. "It's from a golf ball. Get them all the time. Drives the insurance company crazy."

"Was your son home last Tuesday evening?" Jake asked.

"Jeez, Louise. How would I know?" Carmen leaned over and picked up the *TV Guide.*

"Specifically between the hours of eleven at night until maybe three in the morning." Frank returned to the barrel chair.

"There was a Sci-fi movie marathon that night. We watched it together."

"Are you sure he stayed up after you went to bed?" Jake asked.

"I usually stay up until three o'clock. I'm a night owl." She looked from one to the other. "Why do you ask?"

"To your knowledge, did he know a Lonnie Dahlkamp?"

Carmen opened the silver case and pulled out another cigarette. She tapped it on the lid and slid the cigarette into her mouth. Jake leaned over and struck a match.

"Thanks," she said, releasing a plume of smoke. "I read about that murder." Carmen picked a fleck of tobacco from her lip and dropped it in the ashtray. "One thing about my son. He's a chicken shit. Can talk big but never follows through." She leaned back against the cushions and eyed her visitors. Her voice toned down a few notches and her eyes revealed the pain of a mother. "Is this what the future holds?" she asked quietly. "Every crime in this town will bring the police to my doorstep just because he did a little time?"

"I hope not, Mrs. Valukis," Frank said. "Even if Danny hadn't been in prison, we would still be here." Carmen straightened, the cigarette pinched between her fingers. "We have been working on a case and, unfortunately, can't discuss the details at this time. But if you could tell us if Danny has ever been to Dillon Sporting Goods in Dillon Park, that could help to exclude him."

"I haven't even heard of that store. I doubt Danny has."

"This would have been seventeen years, ago," Frank clarified.

Carmen shook her head slowly. She pressed well-manicured fingers to the corners of her eyes.

"So, not only will he be a suspect for crimes happening in the future, but now you are delving into crimes from years ago. What did he do? Rob a store?" She sucked long and hard on her cigarette, pillows of smoke drifting toward the ceiling fan. "Have you asked Danny these questions?" When the detectives remained quiet she laughed. "Course not. You're going to have my answers before talking with him."

"Do I need a lawyer?" The figure in the doorway was dressed nouveau prep. He had a cocky lift to his mouth, a poor James Dean or Elvis impression. Danny tossed his jacket over the back of a chair, a lit cigarette in his hand. Without moving his eyes from the detectives, he barked, "I'm hungry, Ma."

Carmen dutifully unwrapped herself from the couch and trotted off to the kitchen.

Danny's smile broadened as he straddled the arm of the couch and propped one foot on the coffee table. "Funny, I'm questioned by two P.I.s last night and today you two show up. I'm so damn popular." His gaze flicked from Frank to Jake and back.

"Dillon's Sporting Goods. Ever hear of it?" Jake asked.

"Nope." Danny took a long drag and blew a series of smoke rings.

"Damn," Frank deadpanned. "It's amazing what they teach in prison these days."

Danny eyed him through the smoke and smiled back but his smile didn't reach his eyes.

"What about Lonnie Dahlkamp?" Jake continued.

"I read the papers." Danny slid off the arm and onto the couch, slouching down and propping both legs on the coffee table.

"We can subpoena your phone records," Frank said.

"Subpoena to your heart's content."

Jake stubbed his cigarette out in the ashtray and stood. "You had some drug problems in high school. Was Dahlkamp your supplier?" He threaded his way between the coffee table and chair. With hands shoved into his pockets, he casually wandered around the living room.

"Never heard of him until his murder was splashed across the headlines last week. I am curious, though." Danny crossed his ankles, looking too damn comfortable and in control. "The dicks last night were asking about Bobby Wise and Catherine DeMarco. Today you're asking about Lonnie Dahlkamp. You trying to tie all this up into one pretty package?"

Jake could tell Danny wasn't stupid. He also had a feeling the guy was enjoying his notoriety. All this attention in two days was feeding his ego.

"The police department isn't working on the DeMarco case. Right now, we're focused on the Dahlkamp murder."

Carmen returned carrying a tray. She was serving her son as if he were royalty. Jake expected her to bow before setting the tray in front of him.

"You didn't put the mayo on the same side as the mustard, did you?" Danny removed his feet from the table and she set the tray in front of him.

"Of course not." Carmen flared out a linen napkin and placed it on his lap.

Frank stifled a laugh. "What?" he blurted. "You're not going to tuck that fancy napkin under his chin?" Carmen and Danny both looked up, a display of indignation on their faces. Frank thought of asking if she was going to feed him but thought better of it.

"Did Bobby know Lonnie?" Jake asked.

"Again, I told the dicks last night, no. He didn't hang around with lowlifes."

Jake wanted to say, "but he hung around with you," but with Carmen there he decided to swallow the insult.

"And he considered Catherine DeMarco lowlife," Frank said.

Danny shrugged, jammed a corner of the sandwich in his mouth and chewed loudly, smacking his lips.

"She was great to look at. Damn, she had a nice set of tits."

"Danny, show the girl a little respect." Carmen resumed her cross-legged position on the couch next to her son.

"Whaaat? It's the truth. She was a great piece of ass."

"My son, the sex addict. Every mother would be proud." Carmen flicked the lighter in front of her cigarette and puffed away. "That's what got you in trouble since you were a kid. Couldn't keep it in your pants."

Danny flashed his cocky smile. "What can I say? When you've got it, use it."

Jake kept his eyes on Danny and strolled over to the couch, casually gazing at the paintings on the wall.

Frank leaned forward, taking his time turning the pages of his notepad. He made deliberate motions of pulling the pen from his pocket and tapping it on the pages.

"Where did you usually take the young women when you exposed your...uhhh...best feature?" Frank looked across the coffee table at Danny and smiled. "Ever go to Briar Woods?"

Danny's chewing slowed to a gentle gnashing and he set the sandwich back on the plate.

Jake walked up behind Danny, pressed his hands on the back of the couch and leaned in close. "Where were you the night Catherine DeMarco was murdered?" Jake didn't choose his words as carefully as Frank had. The one thought going through his head was what an egomaniac would do if a girl turned him down.

"I don't remember."

"But Briar Woods is where you met Catherine, right?" Jake asked.

Carmen turned her head sharply toward her son. Her arm was quick and Danny didn't see her hand until it whipped across his shoulder.

"Answer the detective, Danny."

"Jezzus, Ma. All right." He rubbed his shoulder and a shade of pink rushed up from his neck. "Yeah, okay? She was there a number of times. All it took was a couple beers and she'd be dancing on the picnic tables stripping." He rotated his shoulder as though Carmen's light touch had done some major damage. "But I wasn't there the night she died. No way."

"You don't remember where you were but you remember you weren't in Briar Woods," Frank said, doing little to hide the doubt in his voice.

"That's right."

35

S am studied the picture on the fireplace mantel of Bobby Wise
in his Air Force uniform. He was standing behind his mother,
his hands gripping her wheelchair. Judge Wise stood next to
him, one hand clasped on his son's shoulder.

Judge Wise wasn't bad looking. There had to be something in
the water that was a fountain of youth for the men in this town. Her
godfather, the late Chief Connelley, had the same distinguished
gray hair, athletic build, and country club tan. And so did her father.

"Nice looking family," Pit said from behind her.

Sam moved away from the fireplace, taking in the expensive
décor, the subtle accents, and wondering if the paintings on the wall
were authentic. Either Eleanor Wise had a flare for design or hired
the best decorators money could buy.

"Excuse me." The words were spoken with a heavy accent.

They turned to see a moon-faced woman dressed in a black and
white uniform. What looked like a black lace doily rested on a nest
of coarse gray curls. Her skin was the color of mocha and her
accent from a country somewhere south of the border.

"Tea is being served in the atrium." She turned and led them
down a wide hallway.

"Damn," Pit whispered. "I thought your house was big."

"Mine is a slum compared to this part of town."

They followed the maid through another foyer void of furniture. Their footsteps echoed on the marble floor. Sam imagined waiters meandering through large gatherings waiting to be led to the formal dining room.

"I'm losing my bearings," Pit whispered.

All of the hallways and doorways were exceptionally wide to accommodate Eleanor Wise's wheelchair. Sam couldn't begin to imagine exactly how many doorways that included or what the cost could have been.

They knew they had reached the atrium when they saw a beam of sunlight streaming from the ceiling. Potted trees reached up to the domed glass roof. They followed an actual yellow brick walkway toward a large bay window. A glass top table was set with silver carafes and at the head of the table was Eleanor Wise. Her auburn hair was pulled back in a French twist.

"Pardon me if I don't get up." She let out a throaty laugh and waved a jeweled hand at the maid. "Marjorie, do hurry our guests along. Everything is getting cool."

"Yes, ma'am." Marjorie motioned them to the seats closest to Eleanor. Pit and Sam faced each other over an elaborate display of fruit and homemade scones.

"We appreciate your taking time to meet with us, Mrs. Wise," Sam said.

"No formalities, please. Call me Ellie."

While they continued with the introductions and niceties, Marjorie tended to everyone's needs and then stood to one side, which made Sam nervous. She wondered if the maid had orders to pick up any crumbs they might drop.

Refined was the word that came to mind when Sam looked at Ellie. No matter what her handicap, she doubted Mrs. Andrew Wise missed a spa appointment or facial. She wasn't afraid to laugh like some older women who tried to remain stoic for fear a smile would reveal too many wrinkles.

"When are you due, dear?" She asked Sam.

"April."

"You must be starved. Come, come. Eat up."

"Everything smells wonderful." Pit loaded his plate and added cream to his coffee.

"This is my favorite part of the room, isn't it Marjorie?"

"Si, Senora Wise."

Sam admired the flowering plants, hibiscus and delicate bonsai trees. In one corner of the room a waterfall flowed into a pool of koi and comets.

"This whole room spells Nature. The sound of the falls, smell of the earth, the flowers." Ellie inhaled long and deep. "Oh, I'm so sorry. I bet you wanted juice."

"No, no. Tea is fine, really." Sam wondered if Ellie dressed specifically for the atrium. Her dress was an earth green with a bright splattering of roses, lilies, and birds.

Ellie made idle chat between dainty bites of a blueberry scone. "Andrew tells me your husband is one fine policeman, Sam."

"Yes, he's good at what he does."

"Chasen Heights is lucky to have someone of his caliber. His partner, too."

Sam was starting to feel guilty. If Ellie was putting on a good front, how badly was she going to fall apart when they started their questioning? She stared across the table again at Pit who was busy licking his fingers and wiping his mouth. He finally looked at her and read the panic in her eyes.

Pit cleared his throat and wiped his mouth again. "You do know why we're here, don't you Mrs. Wise?"

"Ellie, and I don't want to have to remind you again." The deep, throaty laugh erupted again. "I'm sure you are not here to ask for a donation from my Duncan Foundation." She looked at Marjorie and nodded. The maid moved quickly to fill Ellie's coffee cup.

Sam wondered if they had certain signals. One nod for coffee. Two to bring in dessert. Three to show them the door.

Sam asked, "The Duncan Foundation?"

Ellie held her teacup with both hands, each pinkie raised as though lowering one would unbalance the cup. "It's a foundation my grandmother started years ago. We provide scholarships and grants to the underprivileged. But enough about that." She set her teacup down and clasped her hands in her lap. "Now, how can I help you?"

"I'm sure you know we are working on Jimmy Taggart's case," Pit started. Ellie just smiled. "And we know whatever is said in this room will stay in this room." Pit looked at Marjorie.

Ellie did another signal toward her maid and Marjorie left the room.

"We are looking into the boys Catherine DeMarco dated in high school," Sam said. "We wondered if your son or any of his friends had known her."

"Of course not." Ellie's voice was firm and her smile had thinned out.

"We are hoping you can help us out with names of students Bobby hung around with."

"We had a very tight circle of friends. I assure you, outside of school he didn't associate with anyone except our friends' sons. And, of course, with my standing in the community, you can understand my not being eager to divulge any of those names."

"What about Danny Valukis?" Pit asked.

Ellie sighed and flicked her eyes skyward. "Let me amend that." She sighed again. "I guess there can be some thorns in a rose garden and Daniel Valukis was one of them."

"Did Bobby ever mention Danny in relation to Catherine?" Sam asked.

Ellie shook her head. "I don't know what Bobby saw in that hoodlum. He didn't come from good breeding and he was a terrible influence. I'm just glad Bobby had his head on straight. Daniel amused him, but he frustrated him, too. Had no ambition, no direction in life and a man of few morals."

"Did your son ever discuss Danny's relationship to Catherine?" Pit asked.

Ellie waved her hand impatiently. "Please. Daniel's conquests are the least of my concerns. He rarely set foot in this house and when he did he never brought a girlfriend nor did I engage in any conversations of a personal nature. Personally, I wouldn't have been surprised if Daniel pursued the girl, any girl for that matter."

Sam tried another approach. "From what little you did know of Danny, did you feel he was capable of murder?"

Ellie's face showed little reaction. Her wrist flicked, a subtle movement that could just have easily been shooing a pesky fly. Marjorie responded to Ellie's hand signal with amazing speed for someone who had been sent out of the room.

Ellie settled her gaze on Sam. "My husband has reviewed those files and I trust his judgment. They have the killer. Justice will be served." She pressed a button and her wheelchair moved away from the table. "Please finish eating. I'm tired now and need to rest." She mastered the buttons on her control panel and wheeled herself down the yellow brick road with Marjorie trailing behind.

Jake passed a report across the desk to Captain Robinson. "The Pentagon faxed us reports on Bobby Wise's death. They confirmed dental records, DNA, you name it. And there were witnesses that Judge Wise's son climbed into the aircraft. They have tapes of his voice to the air traffic controller. There is no doubt that Bobby Wise is dead."

Robinson studied the reports carefully, his chair creaking as he propped his elbows on the desk. "These look pretty conclusive to me. However, somebody did kill Dahlkamp. Think we need to pressure Danny Valukis? He and Bobby could have been in on it together."

"I don't know," Jake admitted. "Danny may be a jerk but he's also a coward."

"Not to mention a mama's boy," Frank added. "Course the way his mother was waiting on him hand and foot, it wouldn't surprise me any if she hired some goon to make Danny's problems go away. She had the money for it."

"He could be a coward now but you don't know how he was seventeen years ago," Robinson said. "Keep a tail on him."

Jake remained quiet, studying the plaques on the wall and the family pictures on the credenza. When Murphy was captain, he had considered it beneath himself to brainstorm with his detectives. It was as though it might bring him down to their level and he felt destined for bigger and better. Captain Robinson's next question whipped his attention back to the case.

"And what about Judge Wise?" Robinson asked softly. "Would he pay enough to make his son's indiscretions go away?"

Jake pondered that question but remained quiet. There was something about the degrees and certificates on the walls in Judge Wise's office that bothered him.

Robinson said, "Better pump this into overdrive. What about phone records?"

"Dead end on Dahlkamp. Hector hasn't come up with anything from the pay phones. Dahlkamp could have popped into any store or gas station and used one of those phones," Frank replied.

"Then I'd suggest you get Wise to sign those subpoenas for his bank statements and telephone. We need answers." When Robinson didn't receive a response, he looked at Jake and said, "Have a problem with that?" His chair moaned as he shifted. After a few seconds of silence, Robinson said, "I didn't expect this from you, Jake. Wise has the means to hire someone."

Frank jumped in. "We really doubt Dahlkamp would have Judge Wise's home phone."

"Has Judge Wise changed his home phone number in seventeen years?"

That was one of the first details Jake had checked. "He's changed his number twice but it's never been unlisted. Wise has always made himself accessible," Jake said.

"What about a gun?" Robinson challenged.

"Didn't have a reason to ask before," Jake admitted.

"You do now."

Jake remembered the look on Judge Wise's face when he had insinuated that his son might be a suspect. To even consider the judge as a suspect now went against everything he thought of the man. "I have to go with my gut on this one, Captain. I don't feel Judge Wise is capable of murder."

Robinson studied the reports on his desk and the notes from the investigation. "Have any other ideas, guys?" His broad head moved from side to side, his experienced eyes taking in every lift of their eyebrows, every skeptical frown. With a lift of his own eyebrows, he let his gaze pause on Jake's face.

Jake was staring at the wall over Robinson's shoulder, not really focusing on anything in particular. Just thinking and building up a counter-attack against the naggings buzzing around in his head.

"I hear it cooking, Mitchell," Robinson said.

Jake jerked his gaze away from the wall and straightened. "Just thinking about opportunists like Dahlkamp. They work on impulse. No long-range thinking there. Which is why people like him make mistakes."

Robinson's shoulders shrugged like huge boulders being unearthed. "And your point?"

"I think the timing is all wrong. Sam's original trip to the DeMarcos was strictly in our local papers. Erin Starr's attempted interview with the DeMarcos was the same day Dahlkamp was murdered. It may be worth checking newspaper articles prior to Dahlkamp's murder. I think something else brought him into town on the spur of the moment."

36

Sam was jarred awake by a phone call at seven-thirty the next morning. At eight o'clock she was opening the front door to a man wearing dark sunglasses with a suit to match. She couldn't keep from smiling as she thought of the movie, *Men in Black*. She ushered him into the house.

"Agent David Brackin. Sorry to call on you so early, Sergeant." He showed her his I.D. and she took her time examining it.

He was a large man, almost as tall as Jake but with an additional thirty pounds of muscle. He had a broad face and tight smile, if you could call it a smile. Sam thought if he ever lost his job with the FBI he could see if Buckingham Palace needed another guard.

"No problem. I had to get up sometime." Although seven-thirty in the morning would not have been her first choice.

As she closed the front door, Sam noticed the dark sedan at the curb was still running, a clone of Agent Brackin sitting behind the wheel.

"Did you want the driver to come in?"

"I only have about fifteen minutes. Have to catch a plane." Brackin checked his watch and poked at dials. Sam wondered if he were setting a timer.

He held up a video case. "I need to play this for you."

Sam wished she weren't meeting with this guy alone and wanted to call Jake who was already at the precinct. What on earth could the FBI want with her? Were there some old videotapes of her prior fishing expeditions through politicians' houses that have now surfaced?

She led him into the study and pointed toward the VCR. "Can you give me a hint what this is about?"

Agent Brackin popped the tape from its case and inserted it in the recorder. Without turning back to her, he replied, "Stu Richards."

"You better take this one, too, Pit," Jake said. He didn't want anyone else in the precinct working on the DeMarco case or chance the press or Chief Murphy's moles seeing any of the paperwork. It could get into the wrong hands.

Pit thumbed through one of the reports before placing it in a box. "How did Chief Murphy find out you were working the case? I thought you kept things pretty low key."

"So did we," Jake replied.

"Don't forget the phone records from the Harwood PD." Frank held up a log. "They've been over them with a fine tooth comb but you are welcome to look at them with a fresh eye."

Pit placed the lid on the file box and set the box on a chair. "What does Chief Murphy have against Sam?"

The outer office was coming alive as the day shift staff streamed from the elevators and break room. Frank closed the door to muffle the noise.

Jake checked his watch and sat down. Exhaustion had hit him early and he opened the desk drawer for a bottle of vitamins, shook one out and washed it down with coffee. "Before, when Sam's godfather was chief of police, word was Murphy wanted to find any way possible to embarrass the man who got the promotion he wanted. Now that Chief Connelley is dead, you would think he'd give it up. But he doesn't. Connelley had taken Sam under his wing. Anything tied to Connelley seems to be a threat to Murphy."

"Seems pretty juvenile to me." Pit jammed the last folder into the box.

"Records Department should be open now," Frank said as he made a move toward the door.

"We're checking the newspapers for something that might have brought Dahlkamp out of hibernation," Jake explained to Pit.

"Why not use the computer?" Pit asked as he hefted the file box.

"I want to see a full page, not scroll until I get calluses on my fingers." Jake's jacket pocket shrilled. He pulled the phone out and listened to Sam's rapid words. "Hold on. Catch your breath, Sam." Jake listened for several minutes and slowly stood.

"Where is she?" Jake asked.

Abby wiped the last of the crumbs from the counter where the package of chocolate covered graham crackers still lay. She looked up at him with a sigh.

"I don't know what happened. Her visitor left and she charged in here and went straight for the cookies. Obviously something is terribly wrong. She wouldn't tell me." She slid the leftover cookies into a plastic storage bag. "We probably shouldn't have restricted her cravings so much."

"Bet it was the lime Jell-O," Alex said. "It was really ugly. She looked like a cave woman guarding her kill the way she hovered over that package."

"I think it was a little more serious than lack of desserts. Is she still in the study?" Jake asked.

"Yes." Abby handed him two Tums. "She's going to need these."

* * * *

Jake pressed a button to replay the tape Agent Brackin had left with Sam. The image on the large screen TV brought to life an evening Sam had not been able to describe in detail to Jake. He had remained standing throughout the first run and now through the second.

Sam was pacing behind him, a thumbnail planted firmly between her teeth. She had given out information piecemeal and Jake was waiting for the other shoe to drop.

The videotape showed the murder of Patrolman Stu Richards by a hulk of a bruiser. Cain Valenzio had been hired by State Representative Preston Hilliard to kill a laundry list of people over a number of years, starting with Sam's father, an investigative reporter, over twenty years ago. Cain's brute strength had snapped Stu Richards' neck with the ease of turning a loose screw. The tape showed the patrol car exploding, Sam's attempts to escape, the loss of her gun, and Cain Valenzio using her gun to shoot the patrolman in the back.

"How many copies of this tape are floating around?" Jake asked as he ejected the tape and shoved it back in the cardboard sleeve.

"The Bureau has one, I have one, and one was given to Chief Connelley the following day."

Jake looked puzzled. "But Chief Connelley was killed that morning."

"Right." Sam forced a smile, her hand rubbing across her stomach as if to ease the heartburn. "Agent Brackin said Chief Connelley even signed a receipt for it."

"Come here." Jake motioned her to the high-backed chair and he took a seat on the coffee table in front of her. She avoided his eyes, choosing instead to glare at sunlight streaming through the tall windows while her mind conjured up methods of retribution. "I see revenge and excitement written all over your face, Sam."

She pulled her legs up and hugged her knees. "I think what you are seeing is nausea. I feel so sick."

"Probably five too many cookies." He fingered a mass of hair away from her face. "I think we both know who might have signed for that tape."

"Murphy," Sam said. "He was cleaning out Chief Connelley's office even before the burning wreck had been extinguished."

"Or Connelley's secretary could have signed for it."

"And Murphy took it from her and probably destroyed it." The words were blurted from behind gritted teeth and Sam started to knot Jake's fingers.

Jake pressed her hands together. "Can you take a deep breath and let me make one phone call?" She shook her head and he pried his fingers from hers.

Abby walked in carrying a cup of herbal tea while Jake retrieved his phone from the sportscoat draped on the staircase banister. He returned to the study as he dialed. Abby's answer to everything seemed to always be hot tea but he was grateful she was able to keep Sam calm. The only thing keeping Sam from acting impulsively was that she wasn't sure which to do first: Charge into Murphy's office throwing out accusations or call a press conference.

Jake hung up the phone and Sam's eyes followed him as he returned to his seat on the coffee table.

"Mary said Murphy was there that day but she's not sure if there was a delivery, and who would have signed for it." Mary was Chief Connelley's former secretary and now the department's Community Liaison.

"Just as well." Sam sank back against the cushions. "Murphy would claim Mary was just being loyal to my godfather."

"Not necessarily. Mary is sure Murphy signed Connelley's name to a number of documents so she is going to wait until Murphy's secretary goes to lunch and then search for a couple of them."

"What will that prove?"

"By the time my FBI contacts are done examining them, we'll know if Murphy forged Connelley's name. So conjure up a little patience and think about how you want to handle it if Murphy did indeed forge that signature. You might even be able to engage the help of your newfound friend. Erin seems like someone who loves to go for the jugular."

Sam thought about that for a moment. Sending a copy of the videotape to Channel 7 News was ranking right up there as her favorite option. But how many people does Murphy have in his corner? Mayor Jenkins for one. His people could put a spin on it and make it sound as though Jake's FBI connections concocted the film.

"Sam?" Jake placed a hand on each of her legs and gently squeezed. "You *are* going to stay put and let me handle this, right?"

"Sure."

"Promise?"

"Promise."

"Let me see your hands." Her fingers weren't crossed. He checked her feet and her ankles weren't crossed. Jake retrieved the two Tums from his shirt pocket and placed them in her hand.

"Why is it I feel like Poco when she's been given a treat for obeying the order to *stay?*"

Jake's face turned serious as he sandwiched her hands between his. "No matter how much you may criticize Murphy for his tactics, when you think about it, Sam, you've been guilty of the same things."

The burning in her stomach intensified and she found it difficult to swallow the last of the antacid pills. She lifted one eyebrow as if to question, "What do you mean?"

"Chief Connelley encouraged you to engage in your break-ins, reveling in all the dirt you dug up, dirt he would use in the same unethical way Murphy did and still does. You saw nothing wrong in what you did because you were going after who you considered to be the bad guys."

"And what's wrong with that? Sometimes you have to play by their rules. That's what DEA does."

"That's their job, not yours."

Sam stiffened and leaned away from him, pulling her hands from his grasp. Abby had once said what she admired most about Jake was his integrity. Now she wondered how far he could have been pushed.

"What would you have done?" Sam asked. "If you had been the captain?"

He took little time analyzing the question. "If I had been your superior? For the first offense, you would have been suspended for a week. The second time?" He paused and there wasn't a hint of a gleam in his eyes. His look was hard and his words firm. "I would have fired your ass, no matter how cute it was."

Sam felt a verbal knife plunge into her chest. Abby had been the only one to effect that feeling of guilt. With Abby, Sam would take immediate steps to make amends. But with Jake, her first reaction was to strike back.

"Tell me honestly, Jake, since that seems to be your strong trait. If you had the chance to kidnap Keesha Moore and place her in a loving home a thousand miles away, you wouldn't do it? Even if it meant her safety?"

"No," he replied without hesitation. "There are legal ways, through the courts, to place Keesha in a safe home, if the courts deem it necessary."

"That's the point, Jake. By the time it's necessary for the courts to step in, it may be too late."

"Vigilanteeism is only honorable in the movies."

"You made up that word."

"I have another." Jake let his eyes scan down to her stomach, then slowly flick back to her face as he said, "Role model."

37

Sam watched Jake walk out of the room. No apology that he might have hurt her feelings. Jake rarely, if ever, apologized when stating something he felt needed to be said. He just left her with those final words and a searing pain that was more than just heartburn.

She sought refuge in a feel-good spot of the house. Usually that would be her bedroom, on the chaise in front of the balcony which overlooked the gardens. But the gardens were void of color this time of year. Once she reached the open door to the nursery, though, the scene caught her breath. Stepping over the threshold she was transformed into a veritable nature walk. The walls had been painted a soft blue with just a hint of cloud pillows. A variety of animals were stenciled on the walls, standing among tall reeds of grass and flowers. On two of the walls a three-foot-high, white picket fence had been nailed to give the illusion the animals were peering at sightseers at a zoo or on a safari. Looking up, she saw a ceiling of stars, but these weren't painted on. They had been glued, some in constellation designs. Sam guessed once the lights were turned out, the stars would glow in the dark.

"Oh my god," she whispered as her hands crept up to her mouth.

"I take it you approve?" Abby said from the doorway.

"It's absolutely beautiful."

"Here is where the crib will be." Abby walked over to a corner where a large oak tree had been painted. "We'll angle the crib in the corner so tiny hands can't reach the walls."

Branches spread out from the tree trunk, across the walls and a portion of the ceiling. A real birdhouse was suspended from the ceiling, appearing to hang from a branch of the tree.

"And look." Abby flitted across the room, her face beaming with excitement. She pulled open what looked like a fence post, revealing a large closet with double clothes poles and shelving. "Alex built drawers for toys and games."

Sam picked up one of the bean-stuffed animals from the cluster and moved away from the closet. Abby pulled her toward the large window seat.

"And then we made a toy box out of the window seat." Abby opened the cushioned bench and the faint whiff of cedar burst into the room.

Sam gazed at the climbing rose bush stenciled on the wall next to the window. A colorful butterfly with silk wings rested on a rose petal. Curious, Sam pulled on the butterfly and it came away from the wall.

"It's a magnet. Alex used nail heads so the bug magnets stay on the wall."

Sam noticed the butterflies, ladybugs, and dragonflies were out of reach of little hands, even if the child stood on the window seat. She could feel Abby's eyes on her and saw her hands clasped tightly together as if waiting for final approval.

Sam sank slowly onto the window seat and clutched the stuffed bear. "I've never seen anything so beautiful." Fabric rustled as Abby sat down and placed her hand on Sam's head.

"Samantha, are you feeling all right?"

Stuffed animal and head nodded vigorously. "I'm just happy." She pushed back Jake's comments and tried to focus on the room.

If she were too transparent, Abby would pull every painful word from her.

"Are you sure it isn't something else?" Abby's fingers wrapped around her wrists and pulled the stuffed animal from Sam's face.

"I just..." she took a deep, steady breath, and fought the tears that were welling. "Do you think I'll make a good mother?"

"But of course." Abby smiled with a confidence Sam only wished she could feel.

The pain in her chest had not eased. Sam hadn't realized that Jake didn't respect her as a cop, that he considered her dishonest, just like the common criminals he pursues every day.

"How can you be so sure?" She stared intently at her mother, hoping for some reaffirming statement to take away the sting of Jake's words.

"Because." Abby cupped Sam's face in her hands and softly laughed, clearly amused. "You had me for a role model."

38

J ake had a newspaper spread open on his desk. Frank was seated at the table facing the wall sifting through another stack of papers.

"That doesn't make any sense," Frank said after Jake had told him about the videotape. "You know the Board of Police and Fire Commissioners is going to want to talk to the agent who was the eyewitness."

"They will have to settle for a signed affidavit. Brackin said the agent is on another undercover assignment. Can't have his identity disclosed. It was just by sheer luck the guy was in town and caught the news about Sam. He was surprised his report and the tape hadn't been disclosed."

"So the agency had the warehouse district under surveillance for a major drug shipment, using a video-cam to watch for some gang lord. Instead, he catches the murder of Stu Richards on tape."

"And the DEA agent is the one who made the 911 call."

"That was the anonymous phone call." Frank swiveled his chair around to face Jake. "Damn. What's Sam going to do?"

"She doesn't know yet."

"Huh. Better question: What are you going to do? Sam would be coming back here, right?"

"Don't know that either," Jake replied with a shrug. "We'll

worry about that when the results of the handwriting analysis come back."

Frank glanced at the stack of papers and let out a long sigh. "Hate to tell you this but there ain't no reason I can see that prompted Dahlkamp's urge to merge with us city folk. Do we know if he even read our Chasen Heights paper?"

The two men stared at each other for several beats. Frank pulled out his cell phone and flipped through pages in his notebook. "Hey, Sparky." Frank had a difficult time not thinking about the story she had told when they were in Dahlkamp's trailer and he started chuckling before she replied. "Listen, did Einstein subscribe to the *Chasen Heights Post Tribune?* ... How often does that come out?" Frank jotted down notes, thanked Sparky, and hung up.

"Sparky said the only paper his mother received was the *Plymouth Weekly.* It covers local events and garage sales. And it's a freebie."

The desk phone rang and Jake answered, "Homicide, Mitchell." He listened for several seconds to Agent Brackin's report on the handwriting analysis. "Are you willing to bring that report with you and testify at the hearing?" Jake thanked Agent Brackin and hung up. He couldn't keep from smiling as he told Frank, "Murphy forged Connelley's signature."

Judge Wise found himself spending far too much time staring at his son's picture. Even his current court cases have suffered from the lack of his full attention. Hopefully, the upcoming conference trip would prove to be a welcome diversion. He didn't hear the soft drone of Ellie's wheelchair until she appeared in the doorway.

"You're home earlier than usual, Andrew." Ellie maneuvered the wheelchair into the study and stopped several feet from her husband. "Maybe we can finally have dinner at a normal hour."

"I'm really not that hungry."

She followed his gaze to the family photo on the fireplace mantel. Judge Wise leaned down and kissed the top of Ellie's head.

"Maybe later." He moved to the couch and gradually lowered himself as if every movement produced unrelenting pain.

"You know what?" The wheelchair hummed softly as Ellie steered it toward the couch. "You have not been to the club in ages. What you need is a long massage and a soak in the whirlpool. Then I'll have Marjorie prepare something light for you to snack on when you return."

Ellie was right. It had been too long since he had enjoyed the amenities of the club. A massage was probably the only thing that would ease the tightness in his muscles.

"You don't mind? I'll probably be gone for several hours."

"Of course not. You work way too hard, Andrew. You need some time to yourself."

Sam drove down Sibley Boulevard toward Lonnie's apartment. Pit had begged off on Abby's invitation to stay for dinner, choosing instead to stay home and finish going through the phone records. Jake had called earlier to say he would be late and not to hold up dinner. Sam hadn't bothered to call him and tell him where she was going. She didn't think he would be too angry. What could be dangerous about an empty apartment? She found a parking space right in front of Tombstone Liquors.

J.D. closed the door to the upstairs apartment and stood guard. Sam stared at the frail man and wondered if he was going to stand there the whole time.

"I'll be fine," Sam said.

"Don't think it's safe to leave a woman here alone," J.D. said.

Sam wondered if Jake had contacted every establishment in Chasen Heights and forwarded her picture with a note to "be on the lookout."

The first thing she noticed when entering was the smell. Damp and musty, like walking into a cabin that had been closed up for the winter. She glanced at Lonnie's unmade bed where a suitcase lay open. Her search through drawers and the closet gathered little insight into the hapless life of Lonnie Dahlkamp.

She returned to the living room to find J.D. barking at someone on his cell phone. Peering out of the window, she noticed a pay phone at the curb on the east end. The Harwood Police Department had already obtained listings of calls made from pay phones up and down Sibley and State Line. Even if Pit found something in those reports, it would be difficult to tell who had placed the call. The Harwood PD had reached the same dead end with calls placed from J.D.'s liquor store.

Sam studied the little man as he ended his call and snapped the phone shut. "Did Lonnie ever borrow your cell phone?" she asked.

J.D. stared at the phone as if looking for Lonnie's fingerprints. "Could of. I leave it on the counter." He paused and scratched his fingers through his thinning hair, leaving strands standing at attention. "Matter of fact, there was one day I couldn't find it for about an hour. And then, before I knew it, there it was next to the cash register where I always leave it."

Sam pulled out a notepad and pen. "Can I have the number?" She wrote down the number and called Jake.

"Have another number for you to work on." She told Jake she was at Lonnie's apartment.

"And where's Pit?"

"Working on more important things. J.D is here with me. I'm fine, Jake."

"Sam."

"I didn't pick the lock, if that's what you think."

"I didn't say..."

"I'll be home soon."

"Just let me know if you need anything else," J.D. said as he held the door open. A low watt bulb gave off just enough light to see the stairs. He struggled to close the door and finally succeeded on the third attempt. It rattled the frame and was followed by the sound of breaking glass.

"What was that?" Sam was going to suggest they check the apartment in case something fell over but J.D. tore down the stairs grumbling. Sam struggled to keep up but she was more concerned with seeing the stairs over her stomach than speed.

"Damn those punks. Seems a week doesn't go by that the neighborhood kids don't toss a rock through one of my windows." He stood on the sidewalk, eyes glaring at the storefront in search of cracks and holes in the glass.

"Everything looks in one piece to me."

"Well, something broke." J.D. turned around and gawked at something over Sam's shoulder.

She followed his gaze. Traffic was light. Several cars were parked at the convenience store across the street. But only a few souls were braving the sidewalks on this side of town after dark.

A clatter brought Sam's attention to the sidewalk where a chunk of glass lost its struggle to stay intact. The rear window of her Jeep was shattered.

"Well," J.D. said as he scratched the stubble on his chin. "Looks like your Jeep saved my windows. Lucky for me those hoodlums can't aim straight."

"Yeah." Sam wondered how this would play with Jake. She can't even make a simple trip to an empty apartment without something going wrong. "Lucky for you."

39

Jake stared at his empty coffee cup. There was a time he could practically main line coffee and not feel any aftereffects, but that was before he met Sam. Seeing the shattered back window in the Jeep when he walked into the garage this morning left an uneasy feeling.

He opened the bottom desk drawer and pulled out a bottle of water and unscrewed the cap. Through the plate glass window Jake could see a sea of slow-moving bodies, the dreary weather spreading a feeling of lethargy throughout the office. Jake tried to blame his own languid mood on the weather and nothing more. But he and Sam hadn't said more than ten sentences to each other since his harsh words to her yesterday. She was already asleep when he crawled into bed last night and still asleep when he dressed for work.

Adding to his mood was the lack of anything newsworthy in the papers to prompt Dahlkamp to visit Chasen Heights. Frank was now leaning toward drugs or gambling. Jake still wasn't convinced. There weren't any drugs listed in the tox report following Dahlkamp's autopsy.

The phone jarred him out of his doldrums. He punched the speaker phone. "Mitchell."

"Yo, bro."

Jake peered through the plate glass window at Frank who was leaning back in his seat, feet on the desk.

"Can certainly tell when Robinson is out of the office."

"Need a breather. What can I say?" Frank leaned back farther, clamped one hand behind his head, phone pressed to his ear. "Got an idea."

"Enlighten me." Jake took a long pull off the water bottle, then stood and stretched.

"Television."

Jake waited for more, checked his watch to see how much longer until lunchtime. "Still not enlightened."

Frank's attention was drawn toward the entrance. He pulled his feet off the desk. "I asked for tapes from Channel Two, Five, and Seven news programs prior to Dahlkamp's arrival in town." Frank stared more intently toward the elevators, a quizzical look etching across his forehead. Several of the clerical staff and detectives also stopped what they were doing to stare in the same direction.

"Best suggestion I've heard yet. How soon can we get copies?"

"You have a visitor," Frank said as he stood. "This one you're going to love."

"If it's Erin, get rid of her." He punched the speaker phone off and walked to the doorway. Standing at Sergeant Scofield's desk was Alex who was studying the visitor's badge as though indignant he was being labeled. He clamped it on the collar of his blue jean jacket and picked up his hat, running the brim between his fingers.

This was a first. Alex had never visited Jake at the office before, and he wasn't carrying a doggie bag, although a large Christmas canister, probably filled with Abby's cookies, was sitting on Scofield's desk.

"Everything okay?" Jake asked as he approached.

"Not sure."

Jake led him to his office and closed the door. He motioned for

Alex to have a seat but he declined. Through the plate glass window Jake could see everyone's attention riveted on his visitor. At first glance, few people could tell Sam's heritage. Other than Abby, the precinct had never been visited by a Native American, let alone one decked out in ornate jewelry and looking like a twin brother of Senator Ben Nighthorse Campbell.

"Had the glass replaced in the Jeep."

"Thanks." Jake waited. There was obviously another reason for his trip. If it was a problem at home, either he or Abby could have called. Since Alex chose to remain standing, Jake did the same. He crossed his arms and waited.

"I cleaned the glass out of the Jeep first. Used a vacuum."

Jake pressed a thumb and forefinger to his lips to keep the smile from forming. Whatever it was Alex wanted to tell him, it was something Alex didn't want Abby to hear, because if she already knew, she would have been on the phone in a heartbeat.

"I looked around for the rock. It might have damaged something inside the Jeep that would need fixing."

Jake wondered exactly how much damage a rock could do. Upholstery could easily be fixed but wasn't worth a trip to the precinct. Alex was dragging this out as only Alex could do. His subtle *I told you so's* usually sparked a smug smile but Alex wasn't smiling. Instead his eyebrows had formed a V above his dark eyes.

"What's going on, Alex?"

"When I was vacuuming the floor in the back, I glanced up and noticed some damage to the passenger side headrest." Alex dug around in his denim shirt pocket and pulled out an object which he placed in Jake's hand. It was a bullet.

Sam pressed the STOP button on the VCR and waited.

"This is going to be explosive." Erin had been taking notes feverishly while the tape played. "Can I get a copy of this tape?"

"I do have to warn you, though," Sam said. "The mayor can make the television executives jump through hoops. You could be fired if the station gets a lot of heat."

"Let them fire me." Erin smiled, a devilish smile that confirmed what Jake had said...that Erin was one who delights in going for the jugular. And she was one who saw herself as an on location reporter, her goal probably to work for CNN. "Getting fired and the reasons for being fired make for a good story and garners attention."

"I already called Agent Brackin's office and they will make an extra copy of the tape for you."

"And you are sure I can't interview the eyewitness?" Erin slipped into her coat and patted the pockets for her keys. Even with little make-up and her hair gathered in a ponytail, Erin Starr looked camera-ready. "Maybe I can convince him to let me do a telephone interview and have his voice distorted." Sam led her to the door as Erin considered her options. "Maybe I can just type up a list of questions and let him provide typed responsives and I'll read them on the air."

Erin was still talking to herself as she climbed into her red sportscar. Sam noticed Jake's department vehicle parked by the garage and heard the back door close. She closed the front door, crossed through the study to the kitchen to find Jake searching through cabinets.

"Abby thought for a moment you and Frank went out to lunch."

"Got tied up." Jake set a butter dish on the counter. The dome lid rested on top concealing the contents. "Saw the familiar red sports car."

"You were right. Erin jumped at the chance to make this a major breaking news broadcast."

"Good. Just hope she times it right."

"I told her I'd let her know when my hearing is scheduled." She stared curiously at the butter dish. "There are sloppy joes in the pot on the stove."

"In a minute." He nudged the domed dish closer to her. "Have something for you."

She studied his face and wondered if she should brace herself for another lecture. The ceramic butter dish was decorated in Kokopelli designs but Sam doubted it was butter Jake wanted her to see.

"Okay," she said finally. "I'll give you two for circuses but a nine for presentation."

Jake lifted the lid and exposed the nine-millimeter bullet.

Sam tugged her hair behind her ears and forced a smile. "Hate to see what side dishes you're going to serve with that."

No reaction. Not a hint of a smile or a sparkle in Jake's eyes. After several uncomfortable seconds he said, "Alex found this in the headrest of your Jeep."

"Oh." She winced, waiting for the barrage of rhetoric. Instead Jake picked up the bullet and rotated it slowly as if wanting her to see the markings.

"I took it to Ballistics," he said, placing the bullet back on the dish. "Know what they found?"

The chill leaped from vertebrae to vertebrae and Sam had a sneaking suspicion where this conversation was headed.

"It came from the same gun that killed Dahlkamp."

Sam swallowed hard, her mind racing to last night, where she was when she heard the glass breaking. Probably when J.D. pulled the apartment door shut it masked the sound of the gun. Almost immediately they had heard glass breaking. Neither one had even suspected a gun had been fired.

"Oh." This time the word came out in a frail squeak.

"Know what that tells me?" Jake reached across with both hands and grabbed fistfuls of her hair. His eyes scanned her face as he gently pulled her closer. "It tells me," he kissed her forehead, "that the killer," then each cheek, "is desperate." He finished with a kiss on her mouth. "What do you think?"

She leaned in for more, her lips hovering dangerously close. "That tells me," she whispered back, "that someone only wanted to warn me. After all, the killer obviously followed me, watched me enter the apartment, and knew I wasn't in the Jeep when he fired at the window."

"You didn't notice you were being followed?"

"Actually, no. Guess Benny is right. The baby is sucking out my brain cells."

Jake straightened and moved to the stove, turned the heat on under the pot of sloppy joes. Sam gave the butter dish a quarter turn and studied the bullet.

Jake said, "I called Carmen Valukis and asked where Danny was last night."

"What did she say?"

"He started a new job as a bartender at the Ritz Carlton."

"Was he there?"

"According to the manager, yes. And according to our tail on him, yes."

"Bet your tail didn't check the back exit to the place. And I bet no one checked to see if Carmen was home last night."

"Carmen would be afraid of breaking a nail."

"She could have hired someone."

Jake spooned the hamburger mixture onto two buns and set the plate on the counter. In between bites he said, "Funny how we went from having a guilty man behind bars to a laundry list of suspects."

Sam watched him finish each one off in three bites. "Get anywhere with the newspapers?"

Jake shook his head and checked his watch. "Frank is having videotapes from the news programs delivered to the office. He thinks Dahlkamp might have been influenced by something on the news."

* * * *

After Jake left, Sam grabbed a cup of tea and returned to the dining room. Poco was dozing outside on the patio. Every now and then the Irish Setter's tail came to life, flipping up like a warning to invading insects.

The sun had succeeded in pushing the clouds aside and Sam welcomed the warmth. It radiated through the windows and helped to ease the chill she had felt after seeing the bullet.

She spent the next two hours pouring over Catherine's diary, starting from the first mention of 'B.' It amazed her how careful Catherine had been to not give too many details about the man in her life or her physical condition. After a while the words seemed to blend together and the warmth from the sun sapped Sam's energy.

Leaning back Sam told herself she would just close her eyes for a second. She wasn't sure how long she slept but remembered running through a forest, pursued by a knife-wielding attacker.

She woke with a start and felt a breeze on her face. Slowly she looked down at her lap. The pages of the diary were fanning first one way and then another. Glancing up, she saw that the ceiling fan was off. She knew neither the patio doors nor kitchen window were open. So what caused the breeze? Returning her attention to the diary, Sam watched one final page flip over slowly as though unseen fingers were leisurely turning the pages. She studied the page even though she had read it countless times before.

> *I called. She answered the phone again. But I didn't care this time. I left a message for him to meet me at Briar Woods and that I have something I had to tell him. Something that would change his life.*

"Wait a minute." Sam rushed to the dining room and flipped through the papers on the table. All the times she had read that passage, she had assumed Bobby's girlfriend had been intercepting Catherine's calls. But now she realized that might not have been the case.

Sam moved from one pile of papers to the next until she found what she needed...the obituary on Bobby Wise that had appeared in the *Post Tribune* fifteen years ago. "Oh my god." The obituary referred to Bobby as Robert Andrew Wise, Jr.

40

"Jake, did you hear me?" Frank asked. "Do you think there's a connection?" He had just played a tape from Channel 7 news three days prior to Dahlkamp's murder. It was the first time rumors were reported that Judge Wise might be the governor's choice for the Illinois State Supreme Court. The same rumors had been reported in the papers around the same time.

"Pretty sound assumption." Robinson was leaning his body against the windowsill in Jake's office. "Good chance Judge Wise saw his son's involvement as bad timing and so he took care of it."

Jake leaned back in his chair and washed his face with his hands. No matter how much he wanted to deny Judge Wise's involvement, something he saw in the judge's office was flashing like a strobe light. His fingers played through the papers in the file folder until he found Bobby's military records.

"There is another alternative and it's been staring me in the face all this time. Damn." He flung the page across the desk at Frank. "They had listed Bobby as Robert Andrew Wise, Jr. And the certificates on the walls in Judge Wise's office use his full name. Can't tell you how many times I looked at them and didn't make the connection."

Frank picked up the page and studied it. "So we may have been looking at the wrong Bobby all along." They were silent for several seconds as they digested the latest revelation.

"Judge Wise had an affair with a sixteen-year-old girl." Robinson shook his head. "Who would have thought."

The phone rang and Jake punched the speaker button.

"There's more than one Bobby," Sam announced.

"You're a little late," Robinson bellowed from his perch.

Sam told them about the obituary and Jake filled her in on the news report they had watched and the certificate Jake had seen on the judge's office wall...his law degree that stated his full name as Robert Andrew Wise.

"Why didn't he ever use the name Robert?" Sam asked.

"Force of habit, probably. I've only known him as Andrew," Jake replied. "And maybe Bobby didn't like the junior denotation."

"This puts a whole different spin on things," Frank interjected.

Jake didn't like the spin it was taking. He refused to believe Judge Wise of adultery let alone murder. This was one instance where he wished they were wrong.

"...is all that we can go on." Frank waited for Jake's response. "You haven't heard a word I've said." Jake was staring blankly at the file folder and slowly shifted his gaze to Frank. Frank repeated, "I took the liberty of checking when Judge Wise exchanged his attorney briefcase to a judicial robe. It was just after Catherine's murder."

"Maybe Pit and I should talk to Judge Wise," Sam offered but Jake was shaking his head even before the last of her sentence was heard through the speaker.

"I want Jake on this one, Sam." Robinson pushed away from the sill, the movement and his bulk scaring Tonto and Cochise off the sill outside of the window. "It could be worse than Judge Wise covering up his affair. He could very well be our primary suspect in two murders."

Jake rubbed the back of his neck as he paced. He felt Frank's eyes on him, flicking back and forth like a metronome. They were back in Judge Wise's office waiting for a court recess.

"You are going to wear out a path on that expensive rug," Frank said.

Jake hadn't said much on the ride over and Frank's attempt at humor had done little to change his mood. "I should have noticed it sooner, Frank." He faced the wall of certificates and pointed at the law degree from Valparaiso University. It couldn't be much plainer than that and Jake was now worried that his judgment had been blinded by his faith in Judge Wise. "No wonder Catherine was so careful with what she wrote."

"Well," Frank said, trying to fill the silence, "at least we know now that Bobby Wise was not the 'B' Catherine referred to in her diary."

"Finally, you're talking sense," Judge Wise remarked as he entered. After closing the door, he hung up his robe in the closet and settled into the chair behind his desk. "You have twenty minutes of my undivided attention, hopefully for the last time."

Jake pulled a chair away from the table and turned it to face the judge's desk. He sat slowly and leaned his elbows on his knees, hands clasped. The image of Catherine's bloodied body flashed before his eyes but he still couldn't bring himself to believe that a man he highly respected was capable of such a monstrous act.

Slowly, Jake raised his head and looked directly at the judge. "When did you first start dating Catherine DeMarco?"

The judge's face turned ashen as he slowly sank back in his chair. "Damn," he whispered. For several seconds Judge Wise just stared at the desktop, closing his eyes briefly and shaking his head. "They say your sins will come back to haunt you." His hand shook as he poured a glass of water from the carafe on his desk.

"We know Catherine was involved in a fender bender in a shopping center parking lot," Frank explained. "It was her parents' car and the other driver didn't bother to leave a note on the windshield. Was this when the two of you met?"

"An eyewitness wrote down the license plate number. Catherine thought she needed an attorney and picked my name out of a phone book. The license plate number proved bogus." His gaze turned wistful as he mentally turned back the clock. "Damn, she was beautiful."

"And underage," Frank added.

Judge Wise rubbed his eyes and studied the wood grain on his desk, his face tense. "She told me she was a college student. I even dropped her off at Northern Illinois University a couple times. So you can imagine my shock when I found out she was only sixteen."

"That's when you broke it off?" Frank asked. He cast a quick glance at Jake who stared back with fingers steepled.

"I love my wife," Wise assured them. "But our marriage was not based on passion. I'm human, folks. Just flesh and blood like anyone else. But I assure you." He looked into their faces and leaned forward as though making closing arguments. "I did not kill Catherine." He paused between each word. "I never got the message that day to meet her and I was shocked to hear of her death the next day."

"Did you have any suspicions seventeen years ago of who might have killed her?" Frank asked.

"You've seen the evidence against Jimmy Taggart. I believed then and I still do now. Jimmy Taggart was the killer."

Jake asked, "Why didn't you mention it to us earlier when we were accusing your son of a relationship with Catherine?"

"What man is going to admit to an affair?"

Jake stared at the judge and tried to erase the image of him with a sixteen year old girl. He saw movement from the corner of his eye as Frank settled back and clasped his hands across his stomach.

"Jake," Wise said, "you are staring at me as though I were the suspect."

He tried to keep his voice calm, but the image of the Jeep's shattered back window came to mind. "The one constant thread in this investigation is your election to this position around the time of Catherine's death. Your involvement with a minor would have ended your career. Dahlkamp sold the murder weapon to Catherine's killer. Dahlkamp shows up in town. News about your affair following the recent announcement of your appointment to the State Supreme Court would also have ended your career. But then Dahlkamp is killed." Jake was an expert at deciphering reactions. He could see the facts of the case slowly register on the judge's face and was certain the shock was genuine. "This has become personal, Judge Wise. Someone took a shot at my wife last night."

"What?" The judge slowly straightened.

"Someone followed her from our house to Lonnie Dahlkamp's apartment." Jake watched him closely. "Where were you last night around six o'clock?"

"You can't possibly..." But the look on Jake's face stopped him. Judge Wise sighed and shook his head. "I went to the club. Hector was working the desk. I arrived around six and left at nine o'clock. Swam a few laps, had a massage. A number of people can verify that. I have nothing to hide. This has to be some bizarre set of circumstances."

"What about blackmail, Judge Wise," Frank asked. "We can help if anyone..."

He shook his head. "No, no. Nothing like that."

"What about suspects, prisoners, someone who might have made some idle threats seventeen years ago and was released recently," Frank pressed.

Judge Wise shook his head as he pushed away from his desk and stood. He walked over to the window and leaned against the frame, arms crossed. "As a lawyer, the case against Taggart was airtight. As a judge, I've seen a lot of men like Dahlkamp mixed up with the wrong people and killed just to make an example." He turned away from the window and pressed his hands on top of the desk. "An appointment to the State Supreme Court is an honor, but my life isn't going to end if I lose it. And I certainly wouldn't kill over it." He checked his watch. "I really have to get back to court, gentlemen." Judge Wise moved toward the door.

"Did you know Catherine had been pregnant?" Jake said.

Judge Wise's face paled as his hand gripped the doorknob. He whispered, "No." Slowly he returned to his desk, looking more like a frail invalid than the athletic, energetic man they were used to seeing.

Frank tried another tactic. "You and your son were close, weren't you?" The judge nodded. "Would you do anything to get him out of a jam?"

"What are you saying?"

"Act of passion, things got out of hand and he killed her. He came to you to help the matter disappear."

"And what?" Judge Wise glared at Frank. "I waited in the bushes for Taggart to pass out so I could plant the knife on him? And then what? Dahlkamp saw me and blackmailed me?"

"Dahlkamp sold the killer the knife," Frank replied, trying to keep his voice calm.

The gravity of the situation finally sunk in and Judge Wise slowly lowered himself into his chair. "My god, if I were talking to a suspect, I would tell him he needed an attorney." He looked directly at Jake. "Do I need one?" He looked at the detectives for a response but neither one spoke. The twenty-minute limit had come and gone but the judge wasn't making a move to return to the courtroom. He leaned forward in his chair and said, "I want to cooperate fully. What can I do to help myself out of this mess?"

"Sign a subpoena so we can access your phone records," Jake started, "and then request bank statements on all your accounts for the week before and after Catherine was killed. We aren't trying to find evidence against you, Judge Wise. We just want to erase any doubts of your involvement."

"Okay."

"Also," Frank added, "we would like the name of your secretary seventeen years ago."

"I only have one request," Judge Wise said with a note of supplication in his voice. "I do not want the press to get hold of this. And it's not because of my appointment to the State Supreme Court. I just need to find the right time to tell Ellie what's going on."

Jake waited for Judge Wise to finish calling the bank and signing the paperwork for the phone records. Then he asked him, "Do you own a gun?"

41

Jake no sooner climbed into the car then his cell phone chirped. "Well, Sergeant Mitchell. We need a little talk. Like why you're visiting Judge Wise so much and what's going on with the case."

"Having me tailed now, Miss Starr?"

"So now it's Miss Starr and not Erin."

Jake heaved a sigh and cared less if she heard it. He wasn't in the mood for clever repartee. "I told you I would give you an exclusive after we have confirmed all of the information."

"Sure, when everything is finalized and my competitors have the same details. I need something now. You people don't understand. I have bosses to answer to, just like everyone else. If I don't keep the spotlight on this, they'll move me to another story line."

Jake studied the parking lot as Frank steered the Taurus away from the courthouse. Exactly where was the reporter hiding? In a van? Her car? Or had she been lurking in the hallway outside the judge's chambers?

"Then interview the warden, or Taggart, or the Harwood police," Jake suggested. "Or why don't you work on that little matter concerning Sam's hearing."

"I suppose I could let the bosses in on that gem. I haven't shown them the videotape yet."

"There you go. Now get to work." Jake hung up before she could respond. He asked Frank, "Where are we headed?"

"Bank first. Then the phone company."

They rode in silence for several blocks. Jake stared through the passenger side window at the strip malls and fast food restaurants, at new constructions and boarded up buildings.

"What do you think about Judge Wise's story?" Frank asked.

Jake thought back to the man who had helped him during his teen years. Wise had the uncanny ability to spot a problem child and know which ones were salvageable, which ones needed professional help. It was inconceivable to Jake that the judge would not be able to spot problems with his own son.

"He was guilty of adultery, but not much more than that." Jake glanced over at his partner whose elbow was propped on the doorframe, fingers smoothing the soul patch under his bottom lip. "I have to admit, though, there was very little I knew about his personal life. I hadn't even known he had a son."

"You obviously saw just one side of him." Frank paused, as though letting that remark sink in. Then he added, "Try this theory: They were both doing the girl, Junior bought the knife, followed her to the preserve, observed her carrying on with a drunken Taggart, killed her and left the knife by Taggart's unsuspecting sleeping body. Dahlkamp puts two and two together, blackmails Senior. And now tries it again following the publicity regarding Judge Wise's appointment. Neat and tidy."

"I just can't see Judge Wise participating in any of it."

"I'm sure you couldn't see him having an affair with a sixteen-year-old either. And I'm sure he knows the right people to hire. Desperate times require desperate acts. What other explanation is there?"

"And that same hired gun is going to be available to Wise now? Don't forget, it's Sam's belief the same person killed both Catherine and Dahlkamp. And that certainly excludes Taggart."

Frank steered the car into the bank parking lot. "This may take a while. Care to get something to eat first?"

"You underestimate Wise's influence. They probably have the printouts ready and waiting. Let's get all the reports to Sam and Pit."

Frank no sooner put the car in park then his phone chirped. "Hey, Hershey. What's the scoop?" Frank's smile faded as he listened to the frantic message from their snitch.

"Anything yet?" Sam asked. Pit sat across from her pouring over bank statements. Jake had called earlier and asked Pit to pick up the reports from the bank and telephone company. He and Frank had an emergency.

"You ask me that every ten minutes." Pit stood and stretched. "I haven't found any large withdrawals that couldn't be accounted for. I've gone over these lists twice. Judge Wise also had a number of savings accounts."

"I'll trade you. I've come up with the same dead end with Judge Wise's phone records." She shoved the stack across the table and pulled his listing toward her. Folding the sleeves of Jake's flannel shirt over her forearm, she watched Pit staring out of the window. The clouds hung dark and heavy in the sky. Naked limbs swayed in the breeze. If she hadn't heard the weather reports predicting sixty degree temperatures, she would almost expect those clouds to start dumping snow.

Sam asked, "When is the last time you were in Phoenix?"

Pit turned from the window. "Not since the funeral."

"Bet it's nice at Christmastime."

Their eyes met and Sam held his gaze. She might have stepped over the line but she was a firm believer that people sometimes needed to be shoved in the right direction.

"Someone has to make the first step," she added.

Pit's phone rang and he dug through his jacket hanging on the chair.

"Yes?" After several minutes of listening, Pit covered the mouthpiece. "Attorney Bigalow received a call from that reporter.

She wants to interview Taggart."

Sam held her hand out to take the phone. They needed to appease Erin Starr who was getting more impatient each day. She told Bigalow, "Restrict Erin to questions about Taggart's possible release and what he plans to do. I'm sure he'd agree to that. She should not ask him how he feels about his execution, as I'm sure that was the first question on her list. Oh, and Art, tell her to dress conservatively. She's going to a prison, not a bar." She handed the phone back to Pit. "I'm sure Erin Starr will brighten his day."

They poured over their lists until Abby and Alex joined them.

Sam told Pit about the nursery. "I swear Alex is becoming a Martha Stewart clone." She winked at Alex and watched in amusement as color rose to his cheeks. "I'll have to show you the nursery later."

Abby studied the stacks of reports sitting on both sides of the table. "You seem frustrated."

Sam filled her in on Jake's visit to Judge Wise. "I guess all we can do is keep scouring the bank statements for a huge cash withdrawal, but so far we are coming up empty. Judge Wise claims he wasn't involved."

"You don't believe him?" Abby asked.

Sam thought about that for a moment, thought about someone taking a shot at her Jeep. "Funny thing is, I have my doubts that he was involved in either killing."

"Hmmm." Abby pulled out a chair and sat down. "What was the first piece of information you ever received regarding this case?"

Sam thought back to her walk through the woods and the construction site. "The button," she replied.

"Then that is what you should return to," Abby said, making it sound so simple.

42

She looked like a broken doll lying at the bottom of the stairs, face down, her slender legs twisted as if someone had given her hips a quarter turn. Hair plaited and tied with colored ribbons haloed around her head. Leaning on its side next to the body was a bright red skateboard.

Jake sifted through the photos looking for anything that could turn this suspicious accident into a homicide investigation. Benny shook his head in disgust as his crew brought the gurney to the top of the second floor landing.

"These are the days I hate my job." Benny rose from the floor and walked over to Jake.

"Tell me something good," Jake said. He had remained silent on the drive over and his eyes had searched the crowd for Mo Williams when they entered the building. He couldn't trust himself to be near him right now so Frank offered to interview Mo and Felicia while Jake interviewed the few neighbors who had been home during the accident.

"Wish I could tell you something conclusive," Benny said. "Good-size bump on the back of her head. Probably a fractured skull caused by the fall, internal bleeding, brain swelling. Probably died instantly."

"From the fall," Jake echoed, not keeping the doubt from rolling off his tongue.

Benny stepped aside so his assistants could remove the body. "We'll have to wait to see what the techs and the autopsy discover."

"I want to check out the apartment." Jake stared at the girl when they rolled her over. A long gouge marred her face just below the cheekbone to the corner of her mouth. Jake remembered her shy smile and his anger swelled, filling every nerve ending in a frantic search for an outlet. Glancing quickly at the skateboard, he failed to see any blood and wondered if the fall could cause such a gouge.

Once the body bag was zipped, Jake kept to the railing of the broad stairway and took every other stair to the third floor. Uniformed officers pushed back the neighbors milling around the corridor. The apartment was quiet and Frank was standing just inside the door. It closed with a click and neither Mo nor Felicia looked up from the couch.

"Mo was allegedly in the kitchen," Frank whispered. "Keesha wanted to go outside with her skateboard. Felicia said it was too cold but that she could play in the hallway."

Jake's eyes quickly scanned the room. Laundry had been dumped on one chair. Dolls cluttered a table. A girl's jacket lay across the back of the couch.

"What did the neighbors say?" Frank asked.

"The three neighbors who were home didn't hear anything prior to Keesha falling down the stairs," Jake whispered. "No one was in the hallway. No one witnessed the fall. No one heard any yelling but since the last incident the neighbors say there is always loud music coming from this apartment." He looked over at Felicia who was sitting next to Mo. Her face was tear-streaked, eyes staring into space. But her body language was all wrong. No matter how many times Mo tried to console her with an arm around her shoulder or a tug on her limp body, she refused to lean against him and just rocked back and forth, her fingers knotted tightly. "I don't want to talk to them here. Get them downtown. I want the crime techs to go over this apartment."

Felicia looked up suddenly, as if someone had called her name. "I have to make arrangements." She stood abruptly, stepping away from Mo. "I don't have money for a funeral."

"You don't need to do that just yet," Frank said calmly. "They have to do an autopsy."

"Autopsy? They gonna cut up my little girl?"

"I'll talk to Social Services about the funeral." Frank looked around the room for coats. "We need to talk to both of you downtown. Would you get your coats, please?"

Mo shot up from the couch and glared at the detectives, his bony finger jamming at the air between them. "Don't go startin' this police harassment shit again. We don't speak to you without our lawyer."

Jake had tried deep breathing, tried focusing on the Dahlkamp case, but the only scene that kept replaying in his head was the image of Keesha Moore lying at the bottom of the stairs. And then there were Sam's words about whisking Keesha a thousand miles away to a loving home. He had said he wouldn't do it, that it was better to let the courts decide. What he couldn't understand is why, after what had happened, he still didn't think he would have changed his response. Cases like these weighed too heavily on him. He hated to distance himself but, if Captain Robinson hadn't suggested he go home and cool off, Jake wasn't sure he would have been able to control himself around Mo Williams.

"I heard the news."

The words barely sifted through his subconscious but he recognized the soft, concerned voice. Jake glanced up to see Abby standing on the other side of the island counter. He blinked wearily and shook his head.

"I'm so sorry. I know there wasn't anything you could have done. At least nothing you could have done and lived with yourself," she added.

Jake wished he had gone to the gym and poked at the punching bag for an hour. He had chosen, instead, to sit here consumed in anger. He settled his gaze on Abby's face and envied her calm demeanor. In the short time he had known her, she had never raised her voice, never seemed angered or distraught. Right now he was just so damned tired he couldn't think straight.

Abby poured two cups of coffee and set one in front of him. She studied him with a smile and clasped his fist between her hands.

"You are wondering why is it the unjust rarely get their just desserts?"

"It's a question most cops ask themselves."

"Ummm, most people ask themselves. Most people magnify their failures and don't look at the sum of their accomplishments. You have not failed Keesha yet."

"Not sure about that. No witnesses, mother who collaborates her boyfriend's story. Even if we had found blood in the apartment it could be argued in court that Keesha cut her finger a year ago. Every damn piece of evidence we found is circumstantial. It would take a miracle to nail this guy."

Abby glanced at a spot over his right shoulder and smiled. "Sometimes miracles are just a heartbeat away."

Jake slowly turned and looked through the pass-through where Sam was standing at the dining room table. He looked back at Abby who patted his hand and left him with his thoughts and lukewarm coffee.

Sam was treading softly. After hearing the news on the radio about Keesha Moore, she was giving Jake some space. She found it strange that he wasn't with Frank interviewing Mo Williams, but given Jake's mood, it was probably best he wasn't anywhere near the precinct.

She walked into the kitchen, opened the freezer and pulled out a carton of Edy's Grand Light. She grabbed a spoon and dug into the caramel praline. Out of the corner of her eye she saw Jake outside on the patio. Cigarette clamped between his teeth, smoke trailing out as he sat, forearms on his thighs.

She wondered if he was thinking about their conversation and if she were cruel enough to tell him, "If you had done it my way." But she couldn't. He was doing a pretty good job of beating himself up. He didn't need her help. Suddenly she didn't have a taste for ice cream. She tossed the spoon in the dishwasher and returned the container to the freezer just as Jake walked in, slammed the door closed, flipped the lock and charged past her to the back door. He returned several seconds later and held up her blanket coat.

"Take a ride with me."

Sam looked at the coat as if deciding what to do. She asked, "To the ends of the earth?" Her humor brought little response other than the shake of her coat as though they were wasting time. "Just in case I need to pack a lunch." Her continued quips elicited little more than a squeeze of her shoulders as Jake gathered her in the coat.

They rode in silence. The route he was taking didn't head in the direction of the precinct or Izzy's. They were driving in the opposite direction, past the shopping district and elaborately decorated homes. She had never outgrown her love of driving through streets admiring Christmas decorations. Some homes resembled gingerbread houses. And there were a few streets where neighbors participated in transforming their blocks into Santa's village. But even animated lawn decorations failed to turn Jake's head.

They drove past eerie forest preserves where the cold air trapped by thick underbrush collided with warm ground. It created a mist identical to what she had seen in the clearing. She shuddered and huddled inside of her coat. Jake stared straight ahead, elbow on the doorframe.

He turned the Jeep east and Sam willed herself to keep her mouth shut. Shoving her hands deep into the pockets of her coat, she kept her attention on burned out street lights, houses with strings of holiday lights drifting from gutters, and cars jammed bumper to bumper along the curb. It seemed there were bars on every corner and she soon realized they were in the old downtown district of Chasen Heights.

Jake pulled the Jeep to a stop in front of an apartment building across from a cigar store. Near the store, figures moved deeper into the shadows and a man in a tattered coat walked a dog that looked just as tattered. Jake turned the key and the engine kicked off. For the first time since they left the house, he looked at her.

"I would like you to take a look at something."

Sam didn't know what to say. He had never asked for her help before, at least not this kind of help. And all she could do was nod in response.

He held the front door open and a mixture of food aromas quickly assaulted them. Spicy, greasy, sweet and sour. Sam could almost tell what nationalities lived in the building just by the odors. As they climbed the first set of stairs the scent of wet diapers, garbage, and cigarette smoke battled for supremacy. Jake steered her to the second floor landing and stopped. She turned to him and held up her hand.

"It's best if you don't give me any details yet."

"Okay."

The walls of the stairways were marred from years of abuse. It was difficult to tell the color of the carpeting. It looked like beach sand muddied with dirt and stained with past winters' salt.

Sam remembered that they had sectioned this old retail store into one, two, and three bedroom apartments with wide stairways strategically placed in the middle of each floor. She remembered reading that the elevators had sustained so much vandalism during the years the Minas building was closed that they eventually had to be removed. And since every building with more than three floors was required to have working elevators, the new landlords just lopped off the top floors.

Sam trudged up to the third floor feeling the effects of carrying the extra weight and wondering how people made endless trips with groceries. She hit the top step and waited, shrugging out of her sweater coat as a blast of heat from the ceiling vents pounded her head. She thought it unusual for an apartment building to have heat vents in the hallways.

Folding her coat over her arm she turned to find Jake standing at the bottom of the stairs, one foot on the second stair, one hand jammed inside his pants pocket.

"Maybe this wasn't such a good idea," he mumbled under his breath, but Sam was able to make out the words and decipher the disappointment in every syllable.

He was staring so intently at the stairs that Sam slowly descended, stopping just above him. She followed his gaze to a gouge in the wall flecked with red. Then she remembered the radio reports. Keesha had been found at the bottom of the stairs.

"This was where...?"

"Yeah," Jake said. "This is where she died."

Puzzled, Sam sat on the third step and pondered why she hadn't felt anything when she walked up the stairs, no chills, no whispers, no pull of the hairs at the nape of her neck, no image of a young body lying twisted and lifeless. Sam touched the gouge in the wall as if expecting the blood to still be wet.

"That's paint from the skateboard," Jake said. His voice was low as though not wanting to arouse the residents of the building. "She allegedly was riding the skateboard too close to the stairway. A neighbor heard the clatter and found Keesha lying on her side at the bottom of these stairs."

"Anyone hear arguing from Keesha's apartment?"

Jake shook his head no.

She let her gaze drift slowly down each of the stairs, trying to see the image of a small body tumbling. But it had been hours since that 911 call and maybe the crime scene had been too contaminated by cops and neighbors. Or there could be another explanation.

Sam wrapped her hands around his wrist and he helped her to her feet. Her hands slipped down to his and she squeezed.

"This may be where they found her body," she told him, "but it isn't where she died." He looked at her sharply. "I'd like to see the apartment."

Sam waited on the third floor while Jake walked down to the landlord's apartment to retrieve the keys. She studied the wide hallway and walked the length past six apartment doors. Turning, she tried to see the hallway from the eyes of a six-year-old. It was a tempting makeshift runway any child would love to use to catapult his or her body and skateboard.

Jake trudged up the stairs and she joined him at the apartment door closest to the stairs. They entered and he flipped on a wall switch. The heat was overwhelming. Jake located the thermostat to jack it down a few notches. Sam handed Jake her coat and turned to study the living room. The furniture was frayed and mismatched, lost in a sea of hardwood floors and scattered rugs. A small television set teetered on a snack tray and toys and clothes were scattered around the room. Dolls, stuffed animals, and jigsaw puzzles covered the coffee table.

Sam lifted the corner of a sheet that covered the couch. The center cushion had several burn spots. She slowly circled a barrel chair where a nest of clothes was piled. Sorting through the clothes, she picked up a pair of child's slacks, then a shirt. After setting them aside, Sam shifted the dolls around on the coffee table. But nothing gave off a sign and she resisted looking at Jake's face for fear of seeing disappointment.

There didn't seem to be anything out of the ordinary and Sam finally forced her attention to Jake. He was leaning against the door, arms folded.

"I take it the techs went through the apartment with a fine tooth comb?" she asked.

Jake shrugged. "What was there to find? The body wasn't found here. It wasn't like she was shot and they could look for a gun. There isn't even a baseball bat in the apartment." He didn't hide the frustration or fatigue in his voice and Sam knew he had to really be desperate to ask for her help. He walked through another doorway into the kitchen and flipped on a wall switch.

She moved slowly between the couch and coffee table, pausing to pick up a stuffed dog. It was a black poodle with long ears and a red bow around its neck. The fabric was so soft and the features lifelike that Sam could understand how a little girl could take a liking to it.

But I want a dog. Sam heard a little girl's voice whisper. She halted and clutched the dog to her chest. Jake must have sensed her reaction because he stepped away from the kitchen.

"What is it?"

Sam studied the dog as if waiting for it to speak. "Keesha wanted a real dog but this was the best her mother could do. Her mother told her they couldn't have a dog in the apartment."

She walked past him and entered the kitchen. Dishes, cereal boxes, dirty cups and glasses were scattered on the counter. More dishes were in the sink and draining in a rack. Stained placemats dotted the kitchen table. Another doorway led to a hallway and Jake flipped a wall switch.

"Which room is Keesha's?" she asked.

"First one on the left."

Sam paused in the doorway, her fingers fumbling for the light switch. Mini-blinds had been pulled open, obviously by little hands that couldn't pull them evenly as one end dipped ten inches lower than the other. The twin bed didn't have a headboard and the white paint on the three-drawer dresser was chipped and scuffed.

The hair on the back of her head did a little dance and she didn't step any further into the room.

"Is this where Anton died?" Sam wasn't sure if she was getting mixed signals but it had been too long since Anton's death. The oldest death so far that she had been successful with was from twenty-five years ago. But the body had been encased in concrete and the aura strong, as though the victim had just died.

"No. He was in the living room. That's why the sheet was on the couch. Most of the damage was to him. His clothes had caught fire."

Sam turned to leave and placed one hand on the doorjamb.

I don't want to go out. Sam heard the girl's pleas clearly. And then she saw Keesha, standing in the doorway to her bedroom, clutching the black poodle she would rather play with than go outside.

She didn't see Mo but she heard his voice and then she heard Keesha's voice again.

I hate you. You killed my brother. The words were spit out with vile and hate. In the background loud hip hop music blared from another room down the hall.

Mo suddenly struck out and backhanded Keesha. Her fragile body slammed against the doorjamb and blood trickled from a rip across her perfect face. Something flew from Keesha's mouth and danced across the hallway. Then Sam saw that frail, limp body glide along the doorjamb to the floor.

"Sam?" Jake had his hand wound tightly around her forearm. His eyes were etched in worry but also curiosity.

"This is where she died, Jake. He hit her, backhanded her." Sam used her right hand to demonstrate. "Does he wear a ring? It was his ring that tore her face. And..." she searched the hallway carpet. "Was she missing a part of a tooth? I saw it fly out of her mouth."

"Yes, but we didn't find anything on the stairs." Jake squatted down for a closer inspection. "Crime techs vacuumed the stairs."

"It hit in this area." Sam pointed to a section near the baseboard.

He pressed his fingers between the baseboard and carpet. Sitting back on his heels, Jake pulled out his cell phone and called Frank. He relayed Sam's findings and told Frank about the ring. "He's ours for twenty-four hours. Get that ring over to the lab. With a little luck we'll find skin samples."

"Did the autopsy discover Keesha's tooth in her stomach?" Sam asked.

Jake shook his head no as he told Frank, "I'm on my way in."

Sam talked Jake into letting her tag along since the precinct was on the way home. It wasn't until they were several blocks from Keesha's apartment that Sam realized she still had the poodle.

43

"You can't hold my client on such flimsy evidence."
Jake despised the woman sitting next to Mo. He had to deal with Connie Lemmack on more than one occasion and she seemed to pull the most ironic legalese out of her briefcase of tricks, anything to get her clients off. Barely out of law school, she dressed drab and plain as if that would make juries and judges take her more seriously. And she always spoke in a loud voice. *Pushy broad* was a term used quite often behind her back, but it only made her smile.

"Twenty-four hours. You know the law, Miss Lemmack," Jake said. He stood against the far wall so he could watch Mo's body language.

"So what if there might be skin from the deceased on his ring," she barked.

"Yeah, that could have happened any time," Mo jumped in.

"I told you, don't say anything." Her voice was stern and she glared at Mo over her wire-rimmed glasses.

Frank thumbed through the autopsy and crime scene reports. He was deliberate in his movements and sat directly across from Mo and his attorney. Frank let his finger trace his beard and soul patch and every few seconds he let out an inquisitive, "hmmmm."

"One thing I don't understand, Mo." Frank flipped back a few pages. "According to the medical examiner, Keesha's tooth cracked during the, uh, incident, yet we didn't find any part of her tooth on the stairs nor had she swallowed it."

Mo lifted his bony shoulders and sat up when his attorney raised a warning finger. He then whispered something to her.

"Somebody might have picked it up, one of the residents," Miss Lemmack responded. "Really, Detectives, this is harassment. You don't have anything to charge my client with. The tooth was so small it's probably imbedded in the bottom of someone's shoe." She raked wisps of untamed hair behind ears that were too large and misshapen. Most women would have made every effort to conceal ears this unattractive. Pulling a report from her briefcase, the attorney smiled smugly at Jake. "I would just love to get you on the stand, Sergeant. According to your history, you are a prime candidate for planting evidence."

Jake pushed away from the wall and glared at the papers in her hands. His knuckles whitened as he gripped the back of the chair next to Frank.

"I would let that jury know how, when you worked for the Bureau, you refused to guard someone under the witness protection program."

Mo leaned back against his chair and broke out in a broad smile.

Jake knew eventually if someone dug deep enough they would find out why he left the FBI. She paused as if expecting him to elaborate. He waited her out.

"Seems the Bureau needed to bust a Russian mob dealing drugs in D.C. for years." Attorney Lemmeck didn't bother to hide the smugness in her voice. "And here was an informant awaiting trial for sexually abusing six children and allegedly killing two, who had all kinds of information that could hand these Russians over on a silver platter. His information was so conclusive the Bureau was willing to make sure credit was given for time served and charges dismissed." Her voice had a certain tone that seemed to question why the Bureau took so long to make this necessary deal.

This angered Jake even more. He remained silent, choosing instead to drill a cold stare between her eyes.

"And gee, let's see." She dug through several more pages. "And at fifteen your father had you arrested for assault."

"Hot damn!" Mo exclaimed as he applauded. "And they gave you a badge?"

"Those were sealed records, Counselor." Frank jumped in.

"I could have a field day with you on the stand." Connie Lemmack set the reports down and folded her hands on top of them.

Jake braced his hands on the table and leaned forward. He felt the muscles in his neck tighten and it was an effort to keep from glancing at Mo because he wasn't sure what he would do if that smug smile was still plastered on his face.

"Twenty-four hours. Deal with it." Jake stormed out of the room.

Sam stood when Jake entered his office. "Didn't go well?"

"Lawyers like her shouldn't be allowed to practice."

"What about the tooth?"

"She says anyone could have picked it up or stepped on it. I didn't want to mention that it might have been knocked out in the apartment and not on the stairs, because she'd want to know how I came up with such a theory."

Hard to prove, Sam knew. And it would be tough to find a judge who would consider her theory.

"What if you used luminol? It would show where the tooth hit the wall and landed. There had to have been some blood."

"The blood could have been from any time, Sam. Mo could claim Keesha cut her finger or scraped a knee."

"But they can find her skin and blood on Mo's ring."

"Mo's attorney could argue that Keesha had access to the ring. Our only ace in the hole is if the ring picked up any mucous lining or fluids from Keesha's mouth. Maybe then Benny can prove the skin and fluid sample on the ring are a match to the wound on Keesha's face. But we have to wait two weeks for the DNA results. I would just hate to give this guy a chance to walk." He leaned against the doorjamb and stared toward the elevator and Scofield's desk. Between the two was a waiting room where Felicia Moore was sitting, arms crossed, face down. "She's our only hope, but she won't give him up."

Sam followed his gaze. Felicia was petite, delicate, just like Keesha. And she was, or had been, a mother. Sam wondered how anyone could sit by when someone is injuring a child, especially if that child is your own.

"Can I try something?" Sam fumbled through the pockets of her coat hanging on the back of the door and pulled out the stuffed poodle.

Frank approached from the direction of the interrogation room. The knot of his tie was loosened and his shirt wrinkled. "Our boy has been put to bed for the night but the legal witch is sticking around to make sure he gets his hot chocolate and a nice blankie." Frank looked quizzically at the stuffed animal. "Hi, Sam. Was your blanket in the wash?"

"I was just going to have a mother-to-mother talk with Miss Moore, if it's okay with you guys."

Frank shrugged. Jake said, "Can't hurt."

The night desk sergeant gave her a passing glance as she walked into the waiting room. It was the size of a doctor's examining room with two small couches and three chairs. The table in the center of the room had been cleared of the day's newspapers.

Sam sat down in one of the chairs, leaving an empty one between her and Felicia. The young woman kept her eyes focused on the floor. The thin sweater she wore didn't appear warm enough to stave off the night air. Dark, coarse hair had untangled itself from the knot at the top of her head. Felicia's skin was the same deep tan color, smooth and clear, as her daughter's. Sam wished she had called Jackie and let her have a ten-minute go at Felicia. For now, all Sam could think of was, "what would Abby say?"

"Oh, he's kicking!" Sam pressed her hand against her stomach. "This is the first week I could feel the baby." She could see Felicia's eyes slowly move to Sam's stomach. "Four more months," she added.

From the corner of her eye Sam saw Frank and Jake make their way to the desk sergeant. The walls in the waiting room were thin for a reason.

"Do you have any children?" Sam asked.

Felicia's eyes moved back to the spot on the floor and a flash of anger danced across her face. Sam sensed Felicia wanted to say something, probably tell her to shut up.

"This is my first," Sam prattled. "I'm so nervous. I just want everything to be right, you know? I want to keep my child as safe and secure as possible." She giggled. "Listen to me, chatting away like I know what I'm talking about." Still no response from Felicia and Sam considered another approach. It was taking a chance admitting that she was in Felicia's apartment but the landlord had signed a Consent to Search form, so everything had been within the law.

Felicia shuffled in her seat and for a second Sam thought she was going to get up and walk out. Sam placed the black poodle on her stomach and held it with both hands.

"I was in your apartment today."

Felicia's eyes drifted to the dog and she suddenly straightened, her head turned to face Sam.

"Since I was little I've had this strange ability to sense the dead. I see things, sometimes hear them speak."

Felicia's eyes widened like orbs and her lips parted but it was as though the words wouldn't come out.

"I saw when he hit her, Felicia. He hit her in the doorway to her bedroom. I saw that little body fall against the doorjamb. Keesha lay so still and just kept staring up at you."

Sam watched the tears start, the left eye first, just a lazy trickle down Felicia's cheek, followed by the right eye.

Slowly, Felicia wrapped her arms tightly around her chest and murmured, "You saw her?"

Sam nodded. "She is...was beautiful. Looks...looked just like you." Another tear dropped onto Felicia's right cheek. "You pulled Mo away and ran to her." Sam stroked the velvety fur of the poodle and traced its thread mouth with her finger. "She was holding this poodle. Wanted to stay inside to play with it, but Mo wanted her to go outside." She turned toward Felicia and tried to conjure up the images she had seen when she was in the apartment, tried to remember what she had heard Keesha mumble before she died. "Keesha asked, 'Why Momma?'"

Felicia's bottom lip quivered and the tears flowed freely, dripping on her arms. She didn't bother to wipe them away.

"But she wasn't asking, 'Why did it happen?' She was asking, 'Why did you LET it happen?'"

Felicia choked back a sob and Sam tried to keep her own tears at bay. She slowly pressed the poodle into Felicia's hands and walked out.

A low moan seemed to rise from the very bowels of the building, increasing in volume, and erupting into a soulful wail. It ripped through the silence in the office, drawing out the few people who were in the break room, forcing the desk sergeant from his chair. It tore at Sam's heart to cause someone so much pain but it was a pain Felicia had to feel to put away the person responsible. The wailing continued and Sam finally looked back to see Jake and Frank enter the waiting room followed by Felicia screaming, "HE KILLED THEM. HE KILLED MY BABIES."

Sam didn't know what woke her. All she knew was that the clock radio read two o'clock in the morning and Jake's side of the bed was cold and empty.

She slipped into her robe and staggered toward the hall. Lights in the baseboards lit up the hallway like a miniature runway. She leaned on the railing and listened for movement downstairs. It was silent. As she passed the nursery, she noticed the door was open and Jake was stretched out on the window seat gazing up at the ceiling.

"Hey." Sam scanned the ceiling and smiled. The stars glowed and sparkled, just like a night sky.

Jake held his hand out to her and whispered, "Come here."

She crossed the empty room. "How long have you been sitting here?" Jake was still dressed in his work clothes.

"Awhile." He pulled her onto the window seat and she sat between his legs, her back against his chest.

She felt his arms tighten around her and his chin touch the top of her head. "They did a beautiful job, didn't they?"

"Didn't know Alex was so talented."

"He may grumble a lot but he loves doing these little projects."

They sat in the dark in silence listening to each other breathe and studying the placement of the stars. She could feel the steady rise and fall of his chest. How much more relaxed he was now compared to when she had seen him at the precinct. Maybe it was the room. There was something peaceful and serene about staring at the night sky. That was probably Abby's logic behind her theme for the nursery...Nature and the stars.

"Can you identify the constellations?" Jake asked.

Sam pointed at the familiar three stars in the belt and said, "Orion."

"That's the only one you know."

"Not true. I also know the Big and Little Dipper."

Jake placed his hand on top of hers and moved it to the left. "See the bright star to the bottom left of Orion? That's Sirius, the Dog Star. It's in the Canis Major constellation and is the brightest star in our galaxy, just a mere eight-point-eight light years away. Abby and Alex only used the winter constellations."

"Wonder why that is."

"Probably because the summer constellations can be viewed outside in the warm weather."

Sam could imagine him sitting in this very seat, content, their son or daughter nestled in his lap, and Jake pointing out the same constellations. She should be asking him about Mo and Felicia and what had happened after she left the precinct but she didn't want to spoil the moment. Something rare was happening...Jake was cracking open that elusive door to his private life.

"I thought you majored in criminology."

"I've always been a Carl Sagan fan. Used to sneak off to the Planetarium every chance I got."

"Did you own a telescope?"

"Bought a pretty good one when I was in college but sold it when I started working for the FBI."

Sam was wide awake now. There was something tempting about a dark room, a star-filled sky, albeit ceiling, and the scent of lingering aftershave. It wouldn't take much to turn this astronomy lesson into anatomy. But she was finding this crack in the door more enticing than romance.

"Do you have a favorite constellation?" she asked. She felt him shrug.

"Actually," he replied, "I have a favorite galaxy...Andromeda. It's spiral-shaped and one-hundred-thousand light years across. Do you know what Andromeda means?"

Sam was too mesmerized to speak so she just shook her head no.

"Chained Maiden."

"Hmmmm. No wonder you like it."

She heard him chuckle and as he proceeded to tell her the Greek legend of Andromeda and Perseus, Sam delighted in the fact that she not only learned a little more about her husband, but she also knew what they could buy him for Christmas.

44

Abby hummed as she watered the plants in the window box. The flowers seemed to perk up immediately just from her touch. A speck of dust dared to mar the gleaming chrome on the faucet and she swiped at it with the hem of her apron.

"Where is Sam?" Alex asked as he set several small boxes wrapped in festive paper on the island counter.

"She and that nice Mr. Goddard had an appointment." She splashed water on Jake's poinsettia plant, which she had managed to resuscitate. The joyful humming continued as she carried the wrapped boxes and set them on the kitchen table.

"Sam seemed rather cheerful this morning." His eyes followed her movements around the room. "As do you."

"She received a call from a member of the Board of Police and Fire Commissioners. They have scheduled her hearing."

"I'm sure seeing a copy of that video put a fire up their butts."

"But more importantly she was able to help Jacob with his case last night, the one with the little girl who died in a fall. She was riding so high from the outcome that she couldn't even concentrate on her other case. We actually think Jacob might be seeing some credibility in her work."

"Hmmpph," Alex mumbled. "Didn't know hell froze over already."

"Jacob has his own methods." Abby pulled ribbon and bows out of a bag and sat down at the table. "You can't fault him for that." She busied herself adding the finishing touches on the presents all the while aware that Alex was watching her. "Out with it, Alex. You obviously have something on your mind."

He poured himself a cup of coffee and joined her at the table. "You are the master of manipulation, Abigail."

She forced back a smile as she trimmed the ribbon with scissors and moved to the next package. "Whatever are you talking about?"

"First you make a subtle suggestion to Jake that he ask for Sam's help. Now you see her reaction, how wonderful it feels to help him on a case."

The scissors snipped away at another long tendril of red ribbon. "Why shouldn't she feel good? It was quite an accomplishment and, even more importantly, a tiny step toward her husband understanding our ways."

"I see exactly what you are doing. And your daughter would see through it, too, if she weren't so absorbed in these cases, her baby, and her new husband. Admit it."

Abby affixed a red bow to each of the boxes and set the festive packages aside. A twinkle lit up her dark eyes as she leveled her gaze at her friend.

"I will admit that I think it's wonderful Samantha can see how much good she can do from the sidelines, that she doesn't need to work at a place that only serves to frustrate her."

"Uh huh." He washed a hand slowly across his mouth, his eyes narrowed as though pondering a complex problem. "And I'm sure the fact that you and Jake don't want her to go back to work plays no part in your conspiracy."

Abby laughed softly and reached across the table to pat his hand. "Don't be so melodramatic, Alex. Samantha can make up her own mind."

"You mean she has to *think* she's making up her own mind."

She smiled again, aware that her friend knew her far too well. Sam was too absorbed to notice the signs of Abby's manipulations. And she would never take an order from her mother or Jake that she quit work, something Jake had wanted her to do. Abby had suggested to Jake that would not be the best approach. Jake wanted Sam safe. But Abby had her own reasons.

"The fondest memories I have of Samantha when she was a baby was seeing her reactions to all that was new to her, and witnessing all the changes. That first awkward step, the first tooth that falls out, the look of sheer delight when she saw a butterfly for the first time or smelled a flower." Abby folded her hands prayer style and pressed her chin to the fingertips. Her smile was euphoric as though witnessing those wonders for the first time.

"Melinda loved Samantha as though she were her own daughter but she missed out on all of it, as did her father. They were just too busy. I don't want that to happen to my daughter. These are rare moments. You don't get to press a rewind button. I think helping Jacob from time to time will satisfy her inquisitive and intuitive nature."

Dorothy Sobek lead Sam and Pit into a sunroom filled with wicker furniture, a Kimball piano and a variety of potted ferns on tall pedestals. Dorothy motioned them to the couch and she sat on the cushioned recliner. She tucked her feet under her petite frame as her long fingers, which Sam guessed could still type one-hundred-words-a-minute, pressed the fabric of her twill pants.

"Do you remember the Catherine DeMarco case?" Sam asked.

"The one that's been rehashed in the papers lately? Yes, yes I certainly do."

"Did you meet Catherine in Attorney Wise's office about six months prior to her murder?"

Dorothy pushed off with one foot and the cushioned glider

started a slow rock. "Yes. She had had a minor accident and thought she needed a lawyer."

"How did Judge Wise feel about her? I mean, did he feel she had a valid case?" Pit asked.

"Of course. Andy thought every client had a valid case."

Andy? Sam thought. "How long did you work for him?"

"About nine years. Wonderful man. I really hated to leave. But my mother's illness, she had cancer, you know, made it impossible for me to work full time."

Sam asked, "Did Catherine call the office often?"

"Every client called a lot. They all thought their case was the ONLY one Andy was working on." Dorothy stopped rocking and studied Sam. "You don't think Andy had anything to do with that poor girl, do you?"

Sam shrugged. "If he did, would it surprise you?"

Dorothy gasped. "Absolutely. He was a devoted family man. And besides, Catherine was only eighteen." She thought about that for a moment. "Well, at least at the time she had a drivers license and even a student I.D. card for Northern Illinois so we all assumed she was a college student, until it was revealed in the papers that she was only sixteen years old."

"How did you feel about Catherine?" Sam felt this one needed elaborating. "Did you sense any hostility on her part?"

"I felt as if she were my own daughter. She came in here so timid and shy." Dorothy smiled. "What was there not to like about that girl? She was beautiful, funny, a breath of sunshine."

Pit asked, "In your mother and daughter relationship with Catherine, did she ever confide in you about boys, dating, typical teenage stuff?"

Dorothy shook her head. "Nothing like that."

Sam was disappointed that Dorothy wasn't the epitome of a nosy secretary. They weren't learning anything from her. Either she was completely in the dark or was trying to paint her former boss in the best light.

Pit reached across the wicker table and handed Dorothy a business card, asking that she call if she thought of anything else.

Sam and Pit spent the rest of the afternoon reviewing bank statements and phone records. The Harwood PD had run into a snag with J.D.'s cell phone records. This one would probably be the briefest report yet it was taking them the longest to obtain. Hector had promised that he would get them to Pit first thing in the morning.

By eleven o-clock, Sam gave up trying to wait up for Jake. Her thoughts wandered from Catherine to Judge Wise to her hearing. She wasn't sure what time she finally fell asleep but she was jarred awake by the click of the closet door.

"Sorry," Jake whispered.

She swiped her forearm across her face to sweep the errant strands of hair back, then peered at the clock radio. It was midnight.

"Just getting home or you stayed up to watch CNN?"

"Guilty of the latter," Jake replied as he climbed under the covers, gently moving her aside but she quickly returned like a tide on a beach, slipping an arm across his chest. His fingers combed through her hair while he asked about the scribbled note on the kitchen counter.

She told him about her talk with Commissioner Falco and how the Board reluctantly agreed to schedule a hearing date.

"Guess sending him a copy of the videotape worked."

"At first it didn't seem to have much weight. It was when I told him about Murphy forging Chief Connelley's name and losing the original videotape that he agreed to call an emergency session."

"I hope you didn't mention that Erin had a copy."

"No. She's my ace in the hole." Sam felt a ripple of movement in her stomach and shifted her position. Then she told him about her talk with Dorothy Sobek. "I was hoping you'd call about Felicia."

"Frank and I were tied up most of the day with paperwork and the arraignment. Felicia's lie detector test was flawless and the fact that Mo refused to take one doesn't reflect too well. Then we got another break."

"What was that?" Sam did a slow stretch, like a cat, moving one extremity at a time, and then yawned.

"Felicia told us Mo had tossed the broken tooth in the toy box in Keesha's room and that's where we found it."

Jake's words started to fade in and out. He jumped to the Taggart case and the barricades that kept piling up with every turn of events. She snuggled closer and the last words she remembered hearing were, "We may have to rethink Taggart's innocence. He could be the proverbial wolf in sheep's clothing."

45

olf in sheep's clothing. Sam's dreams were a menagerie of jungle animals behind picket fences, and Catherine DeMarco behind a backdrop of Jake's words. *Wolf in sheep's clothing.* She wasn't sure if those words had floated in and out throughout the night or pushed their way to the surface at the break of dawn. The last image was of sponge-painted animals. Peering between the legs of a giraffe was a wolf which slowly morphed into a sheep. Out of the tall blades of grass appeared a hand, sheathed in a latex glove and wielding a knife.

Sam's eyes snapped open and she propped herself up on one elbow, fighting off the sleep and grasping desperately to those last images of her dream. She looked around the bedroom for Jake. The bathroom door was open. The time on the clock radio read nine o'clock. She didn't know how she used to be able to get up at six when she was working.

Her legs felt like heavy weights as she untangled them from the covers. She just wished whatever the dreams were trying to tell her they they would be a little more explicit or give her a few more seconds before jarring her awake.

After a quick shower, she slipped into a roomy pantsuit and hurried downstairs to find Pit in the dining room slugging through bank statements and waiting word from Hector on J.D.'s cell phone report.

"About time."

"I needed my beauty sleep." She pulled her hair back and snapped on a banana clip. "Where did Abby go?"

"Shopping, that's all she said."

Sam poured a bowl of Cheerios and milk and carried it to the table. She curled one leg under her and reached for one of the stacks of papers.

"Uh uh." Pit pulled the stack from her. "Those are done. Finished them last night while you were out ghost hunting." He clamped a pencil between his teeth and flipped open the top page of another report.

"Heard about that, huh?" Her spoon dabbed at the round O's and she watched as they floated right back to the surface.

"Hmmm." Pit pulled the pencil from his mouth and placed an "X" at the top of the page. "I think Frank is still talking to himself. Jake is trying to tone things down a bit. But the night shift desk sergeant has a big mouth and Mo's attorney caught wind of your talk with Felicia."

Sam shrugged and watched Pit's pencil zig across the page and move onto the next. He had a routine going so who was she to stop him.

"I'm sure she'll have me testify and claim I unduly influenced her client and that Felicia was emotionally fragile and prone to suggestion. I've heard it all before."

The gate alarm sounded and Pit called out as Sam headed for the security monitor. "That could be the cell phone reports. Hector said the phone company would send them by messenger."

Sam retrieved the package and was ripping it open as she returned to the dining room. "Not very thick," she noticed.

"There should only be three days' worth of data. No use sloshing through useless paper." Pit took the report and read the handwritten memo from the phone company. "Great. They didn't have time to run it through the Haines Reverse Directory. Now we have to do it all by hand." He glanced at the bowl of cereal. "Are you sure that's going to fill both of you up?"

"For now," Sam said with a shrug.

Pit fumbled in his jacket pocket for the cell phone. There was a growing spark in his eyes and enthusiasm in his movements. Sam believed there was a reason for their lives crossing, especially at that fateful moment when Pit was thinking of taking his own life. That made her feel good. And thinking of Felicia made her feel even better. Now she just had to cross her fingers that Felicia didn't claim amnesia when it came time to testify.

Pit called J.D. and was able to exclude seven of the twelve calls made from his phone during the three days specified.

"Five isn't bad," he said after hanging up. While Sam finished eating, Pit called each of the numbers. They were quick calls, most not even requiring him to do more than listen to who answered. Sam carried her empty bowl to the sink and was just returning to the dining room when Pit hung up from a call. His puppy eyes frowned as he pensively tapped the phone against his chin.

"Found something?" Sam said.

"Yeah." He set the cell phone down and stared across the table at her. For some reason Sam had a feeling she wasn't going to like his news. "I think we might have discovered Judge Wise's secret stash."

Sam wandered aimlessly from cabinet to cabinet. She was hungry but didn't have a taste for anything in particular. Pit had convinced her it would be best if he broke the news to Jake. Pit figured the only reason Judge Wise was so forthcoming with his records was that he was confident they wouldn't discover the other account. The recording Pit had heard when he dialed the number was, *Welcome to the Duncan Foundation.* What better account to suck bribery money from than a charitable organization. Pit doubted Mrs. Wise ever questioned her husband's withdrawals.

Sam tried to busy herself folding clothes and eating, but she couldn't stay focused. Instead, she went for a drive and let the Jeep pick its own destination. Within fifteen minutes she was parked in the back lot of *Jackie's Boutique.*

"What a surprise, Sam." Jackie led Sam to her office of pink and mauve hues and parked her in one of the plush chairs in front of the desk.

A pleasant aroma of potpourrie and incense filtered through the office. Sam studied the charm hanging from her friend's necklace. "Is that a Cimaruta?" she asked, peering over the desk.

Jackie's manicured fingers nervously patted the charm. "This old thing?"

Sam aimed a look of suspicion at her friend. "You went back to *Bell, Book and Candle,* didn't you?"

"Well, I did need a few new candles." Jackie repositioned the chain above her low cut sweater. "You gotta admit. It is unique."

Seeing the Cimaruta reminded Sam of Catherine. For some reason Judge Wise withdrawing funds from the Duncan Foundation just didn't have a satisfying ring to it. She was missing a piece to the puzzle and she couldn't figure out what it was. But she put thoughts of the DeMarco case temporarily on hold and focused instead on her hearing before the Board of Police and Fire Commissioners. Sam heard tap-tapping and looked over to see Jackie's long talons doing a dance on the desk.

"Okay, out with it."

"I have a dilemma," Sam admitted, but couldn't help smiling at the prospect of finally having her long-awaited hearing.

"You don't look like you have a dilemma. You are beaming from ear to ear." Jackie settled back in her throne-type chair. "Tell Jackie."

Sam told her friend about the videotape and the rescheduled hearing.

"That's wonderful. Hope you nail Murphy's ass to the wall. When will you be able to get back to work?"

"This will be a great victory," Sam mused, "but I'm not sure I want to go back to work."

Jackie's eyebrows arched. "You? Not a cop? No more fun escapades with you?"

"We don't have to stop those," Sam replied with a smile. She turned serious as she considered her options. "I don't want to force either Jake or Frank out of their jobs. And knowing Murphy, he'll reluctantly reinstate me but he can have me directing traffic, if he wanted to really be the bastard we all know he is."

"Not if you hold that threat over his head to go to the papers and television stations about his forgery."

Sam shook her head. "Too late. Channel Seven received a copy of the tape from the FBI. If Murphy even suspects I helped Erin get the copy, he'll make Jake's life miserable."

"All right then." Jackie kicked off her shoes and shifted in her chair. "Tell me, what in your mind would be a perfect Sam Casey World?"

"Perfect world," she repeated as her fingers toyed with the embroidered design on her maternity top. "I really like working on my own, being able to pick and choose whatever cases I want."

"You mean whatever case the dead want you to work on." Jackie shivered when she mentioned the word *dead.*

"For the first time I think Jake believed I could really be helpful. The hug of thanks he gave me after Felicia's admission felt," she drew her arms around herself and beamed, "let's just say it felt almost as good as sex."

"Ummmm, that good?" Jackie giggled, that wicked laugh that usually left people smiling, and Sam was no different. "Lamon could just consider you a consultant. He doesn't have to get approval from Murphy, right?"

"Lamon?" Sam cocked her head and studied Jackie. Sam had

been so busy with her own news that she failed to see that her always bubbly friend was especially bubbly today. "When did you start referring to Captain Robinson as Lamon?"

Jackie fidgeted with the chain around her neck and struggled to keep a coy smile from forming. "We went out to dinner. That's it. Don't make a big deal out of it."

"Dinner?" Sam was glad her friend had someone in her life but Jackie had a habit of picking the wrong man.

Jackie must have read the word *caution* stamped all over Sam's face. "My eyes are wide open this time, sugar. He's a widower, kids are out of college, one is a teacher and the other a forest ranger."

"I just don't want to see you get hurt." Sam didn't add "again," but Jackie knew that's what she meant.

"I'll be fine. You just concentrate on that baby."

"I will." Sam reached into her pocket and pulled out the button she had found at the construction site. "But first I need to get my head out of the clouds and concentrate on my original case." She held the brass button up to the wedge of sunlight filtering through the blinds. "Just wish it could talk."

Jackie leaned forward and glared at the object. "My lordy. I haven't seen one of those in years." As soon as Jackie started explaining the button, Sam saw the missing piece of the puzzle slipping into place.

46

"Where is the judge today?" Pit asked.

Jake stared at the withdrawal amount on the bank statement. "He's supposed to be leaving for Cincinnati. Probably on his way to the airport now." Once Pit had confirmed the call from J.D.'s phone to the Duncan Foundation, it didn't take long to obtain bank statements, seeing they already had a signed subpoena from Judge Wise. Seventeen years ago a cash withdrawal had been made in the amount of ten thousand dollars. The undisputed proof was sitting in front of him yet Jake had a hard time believing it.

He sank into his chair and swiveled it toward the windows. It was getting dark too damn early this time of year. He stared down at the lit candy canes decorating the street lights. This was not how he wanted to start the holiday season...arresting a man who had been a major influence in his life.

Captain Robinson appeared in the doorway. "What's the verdict, gentlemen?" He closed the door and Frank told him the news.

Robinson pressed his frame against the closed door and caught Jake's eye. "You've got to bring him in, Jake."

"I know." Any gratification he had felt after Mo's arraignment had slowly seeped out since Pit's arrival. Jake looked at Frank.

"His flight leaves in two hours out of Midway," Frank said.

* * * *

Sam had a hunch and made a quick call to Dorothy Sobek. "I just have a few quick questions." Sam wanted nothing more than to call Art Bigalow and tell him the latest turn of events, but first she needed proof. "Did you know that Catherine was pregnant?"

"My goodness! No. I thought the trial revealed that she was an innocent child raped by a brutal man."

Now Sam knew Dorothy wasn't the one who had heard Catherine's message of, *The rabbit died.* "Who watched the phones when you were on vacation?" Sam was firing questions at her and hoped she was rattling the poor woman.

"A temporary. I used an excellent service that specialized in legal secretaries."

"Other than you, these were the only people who answered your phones?"

Dorothy was silent for a few seconds, ratcheting down the tempo of Sam's barrage of questions.

"No," Dorothy finally replied, "come to think of it, there was someone else."

"I don't understand." Judge Wise stood in front of the airline counter, suitcase in one hand, carry-on bag in the other. "I thought you didn't have a problem with my going out of town for a couple days. My flight leaves in one hour."

Jake grabbed the suitcase, Frank the carry-on. "Something has come up that we need to bring to your attention. We can't let you leave just yet."

Judge Wise reached into his pocket for his airline ticket and waved it at the detectives. "I'm at the end of my patience. You better have a damn good reason for this."

"We do, sir," Frank said.

"Do you have your car?" Jake asked.

"I came in a limo." He followed them out to the Taurus which was parked at the curb with Pit in the passenger seat. "Exactly where are you taking me?" the judge asked.

Jake opened the car door for him as he said, "Your house."

It was a somber drive back to the Wise residence. The long drive to the front turnaround was dark as was most of the house. Sam arrived immediately after and parked behind Frank's car. They unloaded the suitcases and Wise led them up the walk.

"This is insane," Wise said as he unlocked the front door. "I can't believe I let you bring me back here." They dropped his bags in front of a closet door.

They followed Judge Wise through the spacious kitchen with its white cabinets and black-and-white-checkered floor to the darkened family room. He checked his watch. "Ellie might be in the atrium." He disappeared down a hallway only to return several seconds later. "That's strange, she's not there."

"Could she be shopping with the maid?" Pit asked.

"Maybe." They trailed after him down a long corridor to a paneled study. Judge Wise nodded toward the crackling blaze in the fireplace, which provided the only light in the room. "Someone must be home. They wouldn't leave a fire burning."

Pit pointed at a dirt-caked black plastic garbage bag, torn, it's contents spilling out onto the floor. "What's this?" A trail of dirt led from the French doors.

Sam threaded her way around the maze of furniture grouped in front of the fireplace to the French doors. She peeled back a corner of the wood blinds and peered out. In the shadows about fifty feet from the house, a figure was raking the ground.

"Out there," Sam whispered. Jake approached in time to see the figure rushing toward the door.

"What is it?" Judge Wise made a move toward them.

"Step back," Jake whispered.

A few seconds later, the figure rushed in, closed the French doors, and ran to the bag on the floor. Frank hit the light switch.

Judge Wise gasped. "My god, Ellie!" Eleanor Wise stood on two very strong legs. She clasped a hand to her throat and straightened. "Andrew!" She looked at the detectives. "You're home." She glanced at the garbage bag and back to her husband's face.

A look of shock froze on the judge's face as he studied his wife's legs. He made a feeble grasp for the armrest and slumped down in a wingback chair. "You can walk? It's all been a lie?"

Ellie's bottom lip quivered but with squared shoulders and back straight, she lowered herself onto the couch. "I couldn't let her ruin your life, Andrew. You would never have been elected judge if the public knew of your tawdry affair."

Jake crouched down and poked through the articles on the floor with the tip of a pen. Pit and Frank circled him as he sifted through the stained trench coat, dark pants, and a navy and white tweed suit jacket which was missing one button.

"Frank." That's all Jake had to say to prompt Frank to read Eleanor Wise her rights. Judge Wise made no attempt to call a family attorney much less defend his wife. He just kept staring at the clothing on the floor, his face reflecting the horror and realization.

"You thought your husband's relationship with Catherine DeMarco was getting too serious but you knew your husband would never divorce a crippled wife. It wouldn't look good in the papers. So you staged your accident, didn't you, Mrs. Wise?" Sam asked.

"I think it even helped him get elected. People felt sorry for me. I think I handled my handicap rather well, don't you?"

"Lonnie recognized you when you went into the store. He knew you weren't handicapped and he had read the description of the murder weapon in the papers," Jake said.

Ellie stared into the fire and the light gave a maniacal gleam to her eyes. "He had the nerve to try to blackmail me twice. Everyone knew Andrew was being considered for the State Supreme Court."

She looked at her husband with admiration. "You would have made a wonderful Supreme Court justice."

Puzzled, Judge Wise said, "I don't understand. Doctor Egan never said anything. And what about the trips to the specialist?"

Ellie shrugged, leaned back and crossed her legs. She spoke with the ease of someone sharing secrets with a friend over tea. "I actually had a bruised tailbone and let me tell you, it was painful. Doctor Egan wouldn't know a bruise from a fracture. Everyone knew the poor man only had a couple months to live. But the specialist in Evanston was fictitious. Marjorie and I would spend the day shopping in Chicago. You were too busy to even ask."

The judge looked at Sam and suddenly remembered her encounter at the liquor store. "You were willing to kill Sergeant Casey?"

Ellie shook her head. "I only wanted to scare her off of the case." She turned to Sam and said, "That is the truth, dear."

The fire crackled and danced as her confession was met with silence. Sam tried to calm the pang of sympathy that was pushing to the surface by focusing on Catherine DeMarco and the utter rage that had torn her body apart.

Pit asked, "Mrs. Wise, I'm curious why you kept the clothes."

Ellie sighed as if fatigued from discussing a subject she found extremely dated and boring. "I couldn't exactly light a fire in July and I didn't want my maid to see them so to ask her to dispose of them was impossible. Andrew was out of town so it was much simpler for me to handle it myself."

Frank turned away from her and pulled Pit aside. "See if you can find a brown paper lawn and leaf bag to put these clothes in. You might find something in the garage."

"Why dig the clothes up now?" Jake asked. The way he figured it, there wasn't any evidence to link Ellie to Dahlkamp's murder and the withdrawal of money from the Duncan Foundation could not be traced directly to Dahlkamp as the recipient. The only thing Ellie was guilty of was lying about her handicap. If she had never dug up the clothing, they wouldn't have had any physical evidence.

"The pond," Judge Wise said in a tired voice. "Of course. I just arranged to have a three-tier pond installed next week right in the spot where the..." He tried to avert his eyes from the pile of clothes by staring at the woman with whom he had spent most of his life, but that view was even more painful. "My god, Ellie. Two people. I don't understand."

"I had to look out for your future, Andrew. The blackmail. It would have never ended. He would have kept it up. I HAD to do something. Don't you see?" Her eyes drifted to each of their faces. "Doesn't anyone see?" Her pleas were met with more silence. "Well." The word was emitted in a huff, as though she were the only sane one in the room who understood something so transparent. Ellie slowly rose from the couch and told the detectives, "If you can give me a few minutes to freshen up, I'll get my purse and be with you." She paused briefly and mumbled, "I'll have to leave a note for Marjorie to cancel my Garden Club meeting tomorrow."

Pit returned with the paper bag and rubber gloves. He opened the large bag and set it on end. Frank snapped on the gloves then lifted each piece and carefully dropped it in the bag.

"How? I don't understand," Judge Wise said.

"We didn't find any large withdrawals seventeen years ago in your personal checking account," Pit started. "So we checked the bank to see if there were any other accounts with your name on them. You and your wife had an account from which you made all of your charitable donations."

Judge Wise nodded. "The Duncan Foundation."

"Your wife made a ten-thousand-dollar withdrawal one day after Catherine's murder," Jake added.

"It turns out that Catherine had told someone she was pregnant after all," Sam said. "She had left a message at your office to tell you *the rabbit died.*" Dorothy told me there were days when your wife would fill in for her during lunch hour. And I have a friend who recognized the *MB* on the button I found. Her mother used to wear clothes designed by Millicent Bradley. I incorrectly assumed it was a man's clothing designer."

"Oh, god," Wise rubbed his eyes and turned away from them.

"Lonnie used his landlord's cell phone the day of his murder," Jake said. "We obtained a copy of the phone records and discovered he had called the Duncan Foundation. That phone number hasn't changed in seventeen years."

"No one noticed that her legs had no symptoms of atrophy?" Frank asked. "Matter of fact, how did she drive?"

"Her personal trainer helped her exercise religiously three days a week in a swimming pool. At least, that's where Ellie told me she was going. And her own car is equipped for her to operate everything by hand."

"Is Marjorie a legal alien, Judge?" Pit asked. "I can't see how she could not have known Ellie's secret, but to stay in this country she might have been convinced to keep her mouth shut."

"Ellie assured me she was but obviously even that is a lie. Marjorie is from Paraguay. I just," he shrugged hopelessly, "I just assumed Ellie was getting better. Then our son died and her health took a tailspin. The specialist thought her continued paralysis may have been trauma-induced." His eyes moved to the picture of his son on the fireplace mantel. "Every time I suggested changing doctors or trying acupuncture, she'd withdraw, stay in bed for days. After a while, I gave up pressuring her." He looked up at them, but averted their eyes as his face flushed. "Ellie was a very giving person, but she never was much for physical closeness. We don't have separate bedrooms; we have separate wings."

Frank looked in the direction Ellie had disappeared, puzzled as a thought popped into his head. "Judge Wise, you said you don't own a gun. Where did your wife get the gun to kill..." He didn't finish his thought. The detectives fled down the hallway, but they didn't get far before the explosion echoed through the house.

47

"Seems like such a hollow victory." Sam raised her glass of orange juice in a toast. They were gathered in the kitchen the following morning. It had been a long night and none of them had slept well.

"We saw Judge Wise's news conference," Abby said. "He really looked despondent. How terrible to have to admit an affair and his wife's guilt in the murder of two people. And then deal with his wife's suicide."

"Do they know for sure?" Alex asked.

Jake said, "Ballistics confirmed it was the same gun used to kill Lonnie Dahlkamp. The blood on the clothing matches Catherine's blood type. DNA tests will give us the positive I.D."

Abby shook her head. "That poor man."

"Even with all he's going through," Jake said, "he felt he needed to make amends to Jimmy. He's giving a check for twelve-million dollars to Attorney Bigalow. One-third would be for Bigalow, the rest would go to Jimmy. The check would come from the Duncan Foundation. He feels it only right after what Jimmy has been through."

"That was a nice gesture. Attorney Bigalow certainly lost out on a lot of business because of his involvement," Sam said.

"How did you ever zero in on Mrs. Wise?" Alex asked Sam.

"It was the dreams. The killer had worn clear, plastic gloves. It wasn't until Jackie told me about the button that I realized the killer had long, painted nails."

Abby cleared the counter of dishes and cups. The entire mood of everyone in the house could be reduced to the number of leftovers. No one had much of an appetite.

"What about that nice Mr. Goddard? Will we see him again?" Abby asked.

"He finally made a call to his in-laws," Sam replied. "They've invited him to Phoenix for the holidays. It's a long, overdue visit."

Jake nodded toward the clock. "Sam, you're going to be late."

"He said he would be here, right?" Jake asked. The words no sooner left his mouth than a figure emerged from the elevator. Dark suit, starched tie, short cropped hair. Jake rose as the man approached and stopped in front of the bench. FBI Agent David Brackin shook hands with Jake. "Are you sure you don't want company?" Jake asked Sam.

Sam smiled. Although she would appreciate the moral support, this was something she needed to do on her own. "It wouldn't do your career any good to be seen gloating at Murphy." She turned to Agent Brackin. "I appreciate your coming down for my hearing."

"I'm sure half the town saw the special on the news last night," Brackin said. The smile reached his eyes and Sam canceled her thoughts that he would make a great palace guard.

"Erin did a pretty good job and Murphy's repeated 'no comment' made him look even more guilty." Sam stared at the solid oak doors to the meeting room with trepidation.

"Ready?" Brackin asked.

She fingered the white envelope in her hand as Jake kissed her for luck. The decision had been easier than she had thought.

EPILOGUE

Jimmy Taggart walked out of Locombe State Prison a free man. He was flanked by Rose, Emilio, Attorney Bigalow, and fifteen members of the press. One other person he hadn't expected also waited by the curb—his father, William Taggart.

Erin Starr did get her exclusive and was the only one to interview Jimmy prior to his release.

That afternoon Anne and Howard DeMarco visited their daughter's grave. Temperatures had dropped to forty-five degrees. Anne brought a silk poinsettia plant and set it on the ground. "At least this one won't die." She sat back on her heels and studied the dead plants. "We should pull everything out and start over." She had this conversation with Howard every year and every year he reminded her that Catherine had planted and cared for these plants when she was alive. They had been her favorites.

"Maybe next spring," Howard responded, as he did every time Anne started to lose hope. "Maybe next spring they will grow."

He helped Anne to her feet and they watched for several minutes, staring at the inscription on the tombstone. It had been seventeen years, but for Anne and Howard DeMarco it might as well have been yesterday. Everyone had told them the pain would lessen but the publicity these past weeks made them realize the pain was just as strong.

Anne pressed a hankie to her face. "Mommy and Daddy love you, precious."

They were just turning to leave when something strange started to happen. It was a slight variation in color at first. Anne had to look twice to make sure her eyes weren't deceiving her. It was like watching a time-enhanced commercial. Dried leaves regained their structure and turned green—the azalea, creeping phlox, even Catherine's favorite rose bush. Then small buds took shape, grew and erupted into full bloom. White and pink phlox spread rapidly across the gravestone, as though on a mission, their flowers a brilliant display of watercolor. The air soon filled with an over-powering floral aroma.

Anne clutched Howard's arm. "Do you see? Do you see, Howard?"

"Yes." Howard choked out what sounded like both a laugh and a sob. "Yes, Anne. I see."

The earth had welcomed home the spirit of Catherine DeMarco.

End